BUY BACK

BUY BACK

BRIAN M. WIPRUD

MINOTAUR BOOKS ✦ NEW YORK

BUY BACK Copyright © 2010 by Brian M. Wiprud. All rights reserved. Printed in the United States of America. For information, address St. Martin's Press, 175 Fifth Avenue, New York, N.Y. 10010.

www.minotaurbooks.com

Library of Congress Cataloging-in-Publication Data

Wiprud, Brian M.
    Buy back / Brian Wiprud.—1st ed.
        p. cm.
    ISBN 978-0-312-60188-1
    1. Insurance investigators—Fiction.   2. Art thefts—Fiction.   3. Brooklyn (New York, N.Y.)—Fiction.   4. Organized crime—Fiction.   I. Title.
    PS3623.I73B89 2010
    813'.6—dc22

                                                                    2009046145

First Edition: June 2010

10 9 8 7 6 5 4 3 2 1

For Joanne

ACKNOWLEDGMENTS

I haven't thanked Helen Hills on an acknowledgments page since my first published book. So here on my seventh I'd like to reprise my gratitude for all the continued support and love she's provided throughout my career and throughout my life. Thanks, Mom—

XOB

Let no man be sorry he has done good, because others concerned with him have done evil! If a man has acted right, he has done well, though alone; if wrong, the sanction of all mankind will not justify him.

—Henry Fielding

I SAT ACROSS FROM HUEY LaMouche at one of those little café tables, surrounded by one of those little cafés. The French kind, with Toulouse-Lautrec posters and croissants and coffee that makes my belly hurt. It was a sunny Monday morning in Brooklyn, cold and October.

Huey says, *"Il y a un problème."*

So I says, "In English, *por favor?* You grab the goodies or not?"

Huey wore a pastry apron, checked chef pants, and nervous lips that struggled with each other. He had short white hair and long, furtive eyelashes. His veiny hand stirred a mug of coffee: *tink, tink, tink . . .*

"We arrived to the target, Tommy, *et tout va bien.* Everything was good." His eyes met mine briefly, those furtive lashes fanning. "As you said, at that hour, the entrance to the museum kitchen was open. With the duct tape, we tie the prep chefs."

"Huey?" My big hand stopped his veiny one from stirring the coffee: *tink, tink, tk-.* "Did you get the goodies or not?"

His lips fell into a frown, like I'd said his croissants were soggy. *"Absolument!"*

"Then what, Huey? You had to cut and run? Caught with your

pants down? What?" I looked up and saw his wife, Ariel, behind the pastry counter. Short graying hair and short. The look she was giving me? It could freeze ice cubes. Twice. She turned away.

"We lifted the paintings, all three." Sunlight from the shop windows sparked the blue in Huey's eyes. "But someone took them from us."

I stood, my chair falling backward.

"Someone absconded with our goodies?"

"*Abstructed?*" Huey looked confused. "No, they *took* the good stuff. By our van, they were waiting for us. Two men, with guns, in black, with ski masks. We had only the stun guns. It was necessary to hand over the good stuff."

"The word is *goodies,* not *good stuff*!" My shout turned the heads of the few patrons who sat in back. I smiled at them as best I could and leaned down close to Huey. My voice was back to a whisper. "Who?"

"Who?" he says. I was close enough to smell the Pernod on Huey's breath.

"How drunk are you, Huey? One of your guys set us up. Assuming you didn't decide to rip me off yourself, it had to be one of the other two. Who else would know we were taking those paintings last night, to be waiting for you at that van?"

Now we had a rat, and no paintings. That's no way to start the day.

I reached across and took Huey by the apron. "You think it was Frank? Or Kootie?"

"You think one of them—?"

"What do you think I'm talking about, Huey? I don't know about you, but I was counting on that money."

"Please, Tommy, my apron." I felt his hand on mine. "People are looking . . ."

I'm a big guy in every respect, and didn't quite realize I'd lifted him out of his chair. So I eased Huey back into his seat.

If ever there was a time for Delilah's tantric exercises, that was it. Delilah was my masseuse.

Breathe slowly in through the nose; close the eyes.

Breathe slowly out through the lips; stroke back my hair and beard.

Breathe slowly in through the nose; open the eyes.

Breathe slowly out through the lips; focus on that goofball Huey sitting across from me.

"So which was it?" I says, all quiet. "Frank or Kootie?"

He shrugged, as only the French can, with his palms up and the mouth down around his ankles. "How would I know?"

I straightened my tie and buttoned my topcoat. Then I whispered. "You're a pro, Huey. A pro keeps an eye on his string to make sure there's no monkey business. Does Frank or Kootie gamble? Does a woman have her hooks into one of them? Find out. You have twenty-four hours."

Huey followed me into the vestibule, which wasn't easy. There was only room for me and a sheet of paper.

"Twenty-four hours?" He was looking up at me, like some scared kid at the class bully. "Then what?"

"I like you, Huey." I put a hand on his shoulder, and not lightly. "But this is business." I patted him on the cheek.

I left him standing in the vestibule.

What *was* I planning to do in twenty-four hours? I was no mobster, no goon, no hard-ass. I was the chump with four cats at home: Snuggles, Lady Fuzz, Tigsy, and Herman. Damaging people or animals wasn't my hustle, mainly because people who hurt eventually end up hurt. Even at my size, because guns change the equation. Like Pop used to say, a pistol can turn a monster into a mouse.

I didn't much like the idea of being tortured or killed, so a long time ago I decided there was a line I wouldn't cross. Just a little rule I had.

I knew that the first thing Huey would do after I left would be to tip off Frank and Kootie. Intentionally or unintentionally. This meant I'd have to put a tail on all three of them, using an investigator kind of guy, an associate. I had already put a fix on where they all lived because I liked being careful. As soon as Frankie and Kootie realized they were suspect, they would start acting mutable. Mutable means losing your cool. People who act mutable always make mistakes.

Which is why I found my emotional center at Ariel's Patisserie Bistro and stopped being mutable.

I could either freak out or figure out.

Guess which pays?

DID I WANT FOUR CATS? No.

That bastard Snuggles spewed vomit around the apartment like a fire hose. Lady Fuzz sat in the litter box but managed to crap over the side every time. Tigsy was diabetic and needed shots twice a day. Herman wouldn't eat.

Then why did I have four cats?

I asked myself this question every day, usually as I was cleaning up barf or shit from my rugs and furniture. Then again, I asked myself a lot of questions about why I did the things I did, and the answer to my questions was invariably the same: *It seemed like the thing to do at the time.* That is to say, circumstances seemed to indicate this was the best thing I could do given a series of scenarios, a set of options, especially those that lead to possible gain. *Love or money.*

I was in corporate recovery, a CR. Some liked to joke that's shorthand for criminal. That's a little unfair, I think. I recovered stolen art, sometimes documents or antiquities or collectibles. This meant I had to find the person who took it. Only I didn't put the cops on the crooks—if I did, my entire network of information, my ways into the underworld, would have collapsed and I'd've been nothing better than the cops or Interpol at finding the things these victims lost. I brokered the goodies back to the insurance companies, for a percentage. A finder's fee. A vig.

I said these victims—museums, collectors, and institutions— "lost" pricey stuff. Well, they're stolen, sure, but the screwups by the museums, the collectors, and the corporations who own this stuff are more criminal than the actual gig.

That's my opinion.

Then look at the facts.

Look at the 1990 Gardner Museum gig. Two goofballs dressed as cops with no guns knocked on the door at 1:00 A.M. and the guards let them in. These two nabbed a bunch of Rembrandts, a Vermeer, and some other goodies.

Look at Edvard Munch's *The Scream*. In broad daylight, the crooks bopped in a second-story window of the National Gallery in Oslo, scrambled in, and snatched the painting. Hardly broke a sweat.

Look at the São Paulo Museum of Art, which more recently lost a Picasso when three men used a car jack to crawl under a security gate. In three minutes the burglars were in and out with some choice art.

Look at the famous estate in Ireland, known for its fine collection of Goyas and Vermeers, which has been robbed successfully no less than four times over the last thirty years or so. Do they not even lock the doors at night?

Look at what's called the Kingsland Hoard. A musty old eccentric named Kingsland (a.k.a. Melvyn Kohn) died on Manhattan's Upper East Side, and his apartment was loaded with three hundred individual pieces of stolen art, all of it missing from various collections. When I say "missing," I mean the museums didn't know exactly what happened to the pieces.

This is not the work of cat burglars, of slick hondos like Tom Cruise or Matt Damon tiptoeing around rooftops. There are no laser beams to dodge, usually not even motion detectors like suburbanites use to protect their patio furniture. Just some rent-a-cops and cameras to watch the goodies go bye-bye. You should see the video of the hooded thieves walking across the lawn of the Oslo museum—in broad daylight—with the Munch under their arms. I kid you not.

And this is only the stuff the public hears about. Art is stolen all the time from private collections, all under the radar. Insurance companies don't like it, and try to get their clients to improve security. Any idea how much museum guards get paid? Any idea how hard it is to plug all the holes—even obvious ones—in museum security? Any idea how expensive it is, and how the museums don't like using a lot of their operating budget on high-tech security? At this point it's all the insurers can do to contain the situation to acceptable losses.

They also want to keep the museum from calling the cops. The insurers know that as soon as the police get involved, the crooks wink out and the art is never seen again. Almost never. At least I can usually get it back and recover most of the insurer's losses. Sending a goofball to jail gets the insurance company bupkis; it doesn't service the bottom line.

Ever been to a museum and see a little sign where a famous painting used to be saying it's on loan to some other museum? Or that the masterpiece is being cleaned? Yeah, right. That sign usually means me or someone else is working on getting it back from a goofball.

Art and antiquities theft is a routine for the insurance companies, like if you own a car you have to fill it with gas. Like with the price of gas going up, you don't sell your car. You live with it.

It's part of doing business and passing along the expense. The museums pay the higher premiums because they have wealthy patrons, some that probably own the insurance company.

Everybody who pays health insurance, or runs an eye along Manhattan's skyline, knows insurance companies have big buildings and deep, deep pockets. Anywhere there are deep pockets, people will come looking to slide a hand in and ease out loot for themselves. Not every thief is up to jacking art, mainly because most crooks are stupid and can't plan much beyond holding up a liquor store or jarring the back door of a bodega after hours. This is why they became crooked to begin with, by default, because they're not bright.

If you're a little bit smart, and a little ambitious, it's no stretch to steal art. Turning it into cash, on the other hand, can be a problem.

Three things you can do with a stolen Monet: swag it, shop it, or settle it. The three S's.

Swag means you have to find a fence to sell the goodies. This is messy. The fence will try to rip you off, maybe forcibly take the art from you at the payoff. And if you don't like it, what, you'll call the cops? Even if the fence does pay you, it will only be five percent of the value. The value that the fence decides it's worth.

Shopping accounts for more than a few unsolved art thefts. A sponsor interested in growing his personal collection instructs a crook to bring him, say, a handful of specific Impressionists from the walls of a museum. It's like the thief is shopping for his boss.

Settling a Renoir would be to sell it back to the insurance company for a percentage of its value. To accomplish this, the insurers need me, a CR, to network and find the thieves and cut a deal for the return of the masterpiece. I have one foot in the corporate world, with the insurers, and one in the underworld world, with the thieves. I have to know a little about art and antiquities, too, that's helpful. Got a degree in art history from Brooklyn College.

So as I said I had four cats I didn't want, but it seemed like a good idea at the time. It was a way to get what I wanted, which was a particular woman. *For love.* Vegas showgirl. Figure like the mud flap girl. There are killer bodies, but Yvette's was death itself. She was in a financial jam, so I let her move in with her cats. In my defense, no guy with a pulse would have thought twice about this. Then one day she's gone with my checkbook. The cats were still there destroying my apartment.

Likewise, it seemed a good idea for me to both shop and settle at the same time. *For money.* I saw easy to steal, then lined up the boys to steal it, ones I knew who'd successfully boosted something else. Then the plan was to broker the goodies back to the insurance company. I was carrying some of Yvette's debt and needed to whammy major cash in a hurry. It seemed like the thing to do at the time.

How good was that?

About as good as the four-cat idea.

I WAS WALKING DOWN SMITH Street, down a canyon of cutesy brick shops and cafés, away from Huey's bistro. My thumb hovered over the speed dial for Blaise Jones, the guy who could put tails on Huey's crew.

My phone rang before I could place the call. I recognized the incoming number. It was Max, one of my best clients, from United Southern Assurance. USA for short.

I didn't have to guess what the call was about.

"Tommy. Max." The voice was nasal and taciturn, like those guys who call the horse races. Taciturn is like when someone says things without emotion. Flat.

"Max. What can I do for you?"

The taciturn voice says, "Whitbread Museum. Last night. Three guys."

"Yeah?"

"Three guys, three paintings."

"Which artists?"

"Hoffman, Le Marr, Ramirez."

At least I knew Huey wasn't lying about scoring the paintings.

"How'd it go down?"

"Duct-taped the kitchen staff. Pried open a door from the caf-eteria to a hallway."

"Museum call the cops?"

"No. They had instructions. Some they followed."

"Interview them?"

"Yeah. Their shift is 7:00 P.M."

"If I can find the goofballs who swiped them, what's your range?"

"Fifty."

"Whoa. That all? The Hoffman alone is worth—"

"Fifty, that's it."

"On it."

"Call me tonight." Max and his taciturn voice were gone.

USA had put me in charge of finding the paintings I'd had Huey steal but didn't have. You have to love irony, only it's better when it happens to someone else.

I rang Blaise Jones.

"Whatsup, Tomsy?"

"Blaise, I need tails on three local guys. Can you cover?"

"Heh." That was Blaise's little bluster, his way of saying there wasn't anything he couldn't cover. He had a lot of operatives for this kind of work, mainly teenage badasses from the projects. They could hang around on a street corner doing nothing and would look completely natural. Blaise knew that because he was from the projects himself and was only just a little older than the punks he hired. To look at Blaise and his gold teeth, you'd think he was a rapper or a drug dealer. Perhaps he was those, too. All I knew was that I could count on him to cover this kind of thing.

I gave him the addresses, all in the neighborhood, names, and descriptions.

Frank Buckley was a sous chef at Traviata and looked like a human hyena. Eyes that bugged out, black hair that grows only on one side of his head, no chin, long neck—one ugly hondo.

Kootie Roberts was a Monday chef at Caribe and bartender at Hank's. That's a dive bar on Atlantic way down near Flatbush. A lifter, Kootie isn't as big as me, but he could roll a house uphill. Huge jaw, all scalp, only wears T-shirts, rarely a jacket. His muscles generate so much heat he doesn't need a coat. I kid you not.

Then there was Huey, and we know what he was like.

"Duration?" Blaise says.

"In twenty-four I need a list of everywhere they been and the times. May need another twenty-four after that if nothing budges."

"Any special treatment?"

That was Blaise wanting to know if I wanted any of the guys rolled, their apartments searched, blinded with Liquid-Plumr, like that. I'd never asked for any of the extras, but he always asked anyway. To tell the truth, I found some comfort in the thought that I had that nasty card in my deck, that I could play really dirty if I had to. Like I said, though, I had four cats.

"Not this time. Incriminating pictures would be nice. You on it?"

"Heh."

FOUR

I HAD TO SEE JOHNNY One-Ball. Johnny is a fence. Someone tried to rip him off, shot him between the legs. So now he has only one.

He lived on Smith Street, the restaurant row in Brooklyn not far from Ariel's Bistro. It's in a brownstone neighborhood called Carroll Gardens, which is next to Cobble Hill. The only way you can tell one neighborhood from the other is by a slight difference in elevation and real estate price tags. Cobble Hill is higher in both.

The populace was basically comprised of the "neighborhood" people and the hipsters. A "neighborhood guy" was born in Brooklyn and probably went to PS 58. The older ones were once longshoremen, the younger ones in the trades, cops, or firemen. They ate pasta with red sauce that they called gravy, and only went to the traditional Italian restaurants and bakeries in the neighborhood. Many hadn't been to Manhattan—called "the City"—in years. They are proud to be called neighborhood guys.

Hipsters were the newcomers, gentrifiers, the ones who commuted to Manhattan and drove up the real estate prices. They patronized a booming business of new restaurants on Smith Street where they drank PBR and hand-rolled their cigarettes. Hipsters were easy to spot. The male versions wore porkpie hats, too-small sweaters, black plastic glasses, and old-school Chuck Taylor sneakers. The female version sported funky two-tone glasses, star tattoos, '70s ski vests, and old-school Pumas. The hipsters had cornered the market in what was hip, as the name suggests, but disliked being called hipsters.

Neighborhood guys and hipsters pretend the other group doesn't exist. Like two groups of ghosts that can't see each other.

There was a third part of the population few knew existed. Like most of the trades in New York, art theft has its neighborhoods, and this was one of them. Many professional thieves—and by that I don't mean stickup guys and sneak thieves feeling up glove boxes—keep gainful employment in the restaurant business. Like almost anybody else, they need a regular job, if nothing else to explain to curious police and the Internal Revenue where they derive their income. Waiting tables or cheffing also makes for a nice alibi. Most restaurants in New York close late. If you're a waiter or chef, you may not leave your place of employment until real late. Or you could be prying open the bathroom window at a check-cashing place. Restaurant workers cover for each other.

The neighborhood had a lot of restaurants where the tips were good and apartments rented out a little lower. Carroll Gardens was farther from most of the Manhattan places where the art or other goodies were stolen from but not too far. That the area was a haven for goofballs wasn't common knowledge, and it wasn't like every other person on the street was a goofball. Only those in the business knew.

Jo-Ball was a maître d' at Dominic's, an Italian place farther down Smith Street. It was an old-school place, not hip. Italians from all over Brooklyn would come there for their Sunday pasta and red sauce. Jo-Ball was the man with the toupee and the suit who greeted everybody, flirted with the old fat broads from Bay Ridge, and made sure the customers felt special.

His talents didn't stop there. Johnny also moved goodies, liquidated them into cash. You might say we were competitors. He brokered a thief's goods onto the art market, and I brokered a thief's goods back to the insurance companies. There was no bad blood between us, just a little spirited competition now and again. We also used each other to keep a finger on the pulse of what was what, who had done what. Shop talk, key to any business, even between competitors. Maybe whoever took my goodies was trying to broker them to him, or someone else. Would this be a way of putting the goodies into my hands? Jo-Ball and I had an understanding that we wouldn't undercut each other. If the paintings were mine first, I was pretty sure he'd hand them over, for a finder's fee.

Dominic's was still shuttered at that hour, but I knew Johnny got coffee and breakfast up on Court Street at Donut House. It's a diner. White flecked counter with matching stools on the left wall, tables along the right wall, bathrooms rearward. I found Jo-Ball in a baby blue track suit, at the far back corner table facing out. He always sat that way, facing out, in back. He only had one ball left and meant to keep it.

"Tommy!" One of his fat hairy hands waved me over to his table. "Siddown. You want something?" He gestured to Garrison, a thin black guy behind the counter. "Garry, sweetheart, can we get Tommy a cup? It's good to see you, Tommy, siddown."

Ten minutes ago I'd been at a café table across from a nervous Frenchman with eyelashes. Now I was squeezed in at a Formica diner table across from a baby blue Italian in a wig.

Jo-Ball pointed a wedge of bagel at me. "Tommy, why you wear a pinstripe suit all the time? The insurance guys make you do that? Is that scarf silk? You hear about last night?"

I loosened my scarf as Garrison poured coffee into a cup next to me. "My pop used to say, why not look your best all the time? Thanks, Garrison."

Garrison says, "You having breakfast, Tommy?"

So I says, "Nice of you to ask, but I'm good."

He nodded and went back behind the counter to serve someone else who'd just come in. I turned my attention to Jo-Ball.

I dumped four sugars in my coffee. "So what happened last night?"

Jo-Ball's eyes were laughing at me. "Maybe, Tommy, you wear the tie 'cause no matter what you done you look like you ain't done nothin'." He didn't know I was into anything more than brokering art back to the insurers. He shouldn't have, anyway. So he says, "You're serious, you telling me you didn't hear about last night?"

I shrugged, only it was small, not French.

"So you didn't hear?" His eyes were both laughing and searching. "The Whitbread Museum. Three guys. Three pips from the wall."

Now I caught myself overstirring *my* coffee—*tink, tink, tink*—so I took a sip. "No kidding?"

"Kid you not," he says. "That's why you're here, am I right? You wanna know did I pick up on it already or not."

"Did you?"

"Why should I say?"

"Nobody called me yet. If the three pips are already yours, then they're yours. I don't grudge you anything, Johnny, you know that. And if I spook the goofballs who took them, then they'll just come to you all the faster."

I saw Johnny's eyes focus beyond me, over my shoulder. Slowly, he settled his coffee cup into its saucer. His hand slid under the table. "Don't turn around, Tommy."

"Johnny, you do this every time anybody comes into the diner. You're a paranoid. Just see you don't shoot me under the table by accident." I knew he carried a little automatic in his waistband. "So, about the goodies?"

Jo-Ball still looked over my shoulder, nervous. "I got a line on it, but indirectly, you might say."

I leaned across the table, my voice lowered, and I says, "Indirectly?"

Jo-Ball nodded, his eyes finally meeting mine, the eyebrows wiggling. "A certain party came to see me here *yesterday* for breakfast."

"Sunday morning? Anybody I know?"

"Could be." He chuckled. "Wanted to know what I'd go on the three pips, in advance. So I says, 'I don't shop.' And the party looks all smug and says, 'Going to highest bidder. So you're not bidding?' I says, 'Show me the swag, then we talk. I don't shop.' I'm like worried this whole time that somehow this is a setup, that I'm eating a bagel with a cop."

"So what happened?"

" 'Fair enough,' she says, and makes for the door."

"So this is a woman?" There aren't a boatload of women in the art theft world. Some, like Gloria the locksmith, but few.

"She's not exactly new to the art world. I know her provenance. C'mon." Jo-Ball's eyes laughed at my confusion. He slid out from behind the table and gestured toward the front door. "We can't talk here. Let's walkie talkie."

I headed for the sunlit glass front of Donut House, inspecting the line of customers at the counter. Which customer was making Jo-Ball nervous? There were three of them.

Only the old man eating a soft-boiled egg was there when I came in. His chin came within an inch of his nose when he chewed: no teeth. The other two were an Arab buck in a trench coat dunking a tea bag, and a pug-nose woman in her thirties poking at her BlackBerry. She looked up at me, then Jo-Ball, then back down at her machine.

We got outside and glanced back at the diner. Nobody following. "So, the old man with the soft-boiled egg, you figure him for a shooter?"

"Hey, I'm the guy that's been shot, so don't make fun." Jo-Ball was zipping up his jacket.

His face exploded.

Yeah, I mean exploded. Like an M-80 stuffed in a watermelon. He was facing the street, so the blood and meat and bone splattered all over a town car idling at the curb, the limo driver reading a paper inside.

All that was left of Johnny One-Ball's head was the bottom jaw. The bloody tongue was wiggling around in the air like it was looking for the roof of the mouth. A second later his body collapsed forward, denting the town car's passenger door. Blood gushed from his neck into the gutter.

Inside the limo, the driver was bouncing around in a panic, Jo-Ball's bloody toupee sliding down his windshield.

I stood there like an idiot, my mouth hanging open, trying to get a grip on what just happened. Shit like that goes down so fast, and is so screwy, it takes you a couple long seconds to deal with what you've just seen, and to do something about it.

I remember my first reaction was to touch the roof of my mouth with my tongue, and be glad I felt something. That's when my brain unfroze. *There might be another bullet for me.*

Something like an angry bumblebee zipped past my cheek as I jumped back toward the diner.

The second bullet thonked into the light pole. I scrambled my way through the glass doors into Donut House. I found myself on the floor in front of the counter with the woman and the Arab, both of them cursing in different languages about the mess outside. The old man was still eating his egg at the counter, smacking his rubbery lips.

I hadn't heard any shots.

I hadn't seen any shooter.

Just the same, I knew it was a sniper's bullet that took out Jo-Ball's head.

FIVE

POP USED TO SAY THAT men are like rhinoceroses. They mostly stand alone, can't see much farther than themselves, and can be grumpy. I am, anyway. Plus they have these little birds that stand around on them that they don't know whether they should be concerned about or not.

Every guy has his appetites. Some spend their whole lives trying to shake them off; others accept and indulge them. May the little birds of bacon, brandy, and broads forever roost on my shoulders.

The way I see it, these appetites make life more than just tolerable. Hey, if you're not going to live a little, you might as well be dead, am I right?

This is all sort of a screwy way of explaining that after Jo-Ball's head exploded, and after I spent hours waiting to be interviewed by police detectives, I headed directly for Delilah. She was my masseuse, like I think I mentioned.

Delilah had an apartment in Brooklyn Heights, which is closer to Manhattan than Carroll Gardens and Cobble Hill. It's across the river from downtown, at the foot of the Brooklyn Bridge. Funny thing, though, is that a lot of the best part of Brooklyn Heights, where the buildings have a view of the bridge and Lower

Manhattan, is almost totally owned and occupied by the Watchtower Society. Jehovah's Witnesses, people with almost no appetites at all. They live and work there. In the morning, you see them come out of their apartment buildings—happy, calm, and glassy-eyed. Two by two like animals from the ark, they exit their apartment buildings in their Sunday best. They're walking a few blocks to the big-ass factory buildings where they make the religious pamphlets handed out at subway stops. At five, they file two by two out of the pamphlet factories the three blocks back into their apartments.

Is it just me, or is this creepy? Like pod people or something. Normal people in the neighborhood call them "zooks." I'm guessing that's a combination of zombie and spook, but I don't know for sure.

Delilah's apartment is in one of their buildings, right at the water on Columbia Place. How she manages this, since she is obviously not a zook, I'm not sure. Maybe one or more of the zooks let this bird rest on their shoulder.

So when I go to see my masseuse, I have to pretend I am a zook so I don't blow her cover at the front desk. When I pass a zook handing out pamphlets on the street, I always collect a recent one. It helps with the disguise. I go to the zook at the front desk of her building holding the pamphlet and smile like a brain-dead pod person. That's right, I look like a moron, but to the zooks, this is normal. They ring Delilah's apartment and let me go up.

As soon as I stepped through the door she could see I was pretty stressed out.

She says, "Tom, what's with you?"

So I says, "You wouldn't believe it if I told you. But I will. Just not this second."

So she went to work on me straight away, and after I started to relax, I blurted out most of the story. I had already told her I was shopping and settling at the same time. I did that because she's not the judgmental type.

Delilah didn't say anything, just listened and did her thing. She's not a small woman, and by that I mean she's tall like me and muscular. She doesn't have much if any fat on her. I'm one of those Budweiser horses; she's one of those horses at the track. Except she has a long brown braid and almond eyes, like she's part Oriental. Maybe she is. She was wearing a kimono. But that didn't mean anything. I was wearing one, too.

When we were finished, she poured me a glass of pinot, and we sat across from each other at the Scrabble board. We played nine-tile Scrabble whenever I came over, for an hour at most. The game had been started the week before, and we were each five words into the game. My last word had been "furtive" and I attached it on the end of her last word, "spin," to create "spine." I scored eighty points on that play because I used seven letters and got a fifty-point bingo. That's huge. During the week, she'd played "fe-cund" off of my *f* for thirty-six using the triple word space. Fe-cund means fertile, like soil, or a girl that gets pregnant real easy.

Delilah still hadn't said a word about what I'd told her, and waited for me to take my turn first, which didn't take long because I already had a number of moves figured out in advance. Though I was relaxed, I was still emotionally numb as I clicked my tiles in place.

I spelled out "deluxe" using her *d* and picked up a double word space for twenty-eight points.

Her dark eyes looked up from the Scrabble board. "So have you heard from Yvette?"

I didn't expect that question. So I says, "I didn't expect that question. No. Thank God."

"How long she been gone?"

"Four weeks."

"Miss her?"

"Good riddance."

"So what about the cats?"

My eyes met hers, and she held up her hands. "I'm just asking, Tom. But I guess the question is why someone shot Johnny. What do you think?"

So I says, "Jo-Ball had people pissed off at him all the time. No, I think the question is why the shooter took a shot at me. Was he just trying to tidy up? Or had he missed me with the first shot and hit Jo-Ball by accident?"

Delilah's eyes rolled back to her tiles as she moved them around on her tile pew searching for a word. "What you're telling me is you don't have an answer to either question."

I finished my wine. "It's early."

"Answers are sometimes more dangerous than the question, Tom."

"There's not a lot of options here, Dee." I went in search of the wine bottle, and when I got back with it, she says, "There are only as many options as you allow there to be."

I had to laugh at that. "Bullshit. Life is no different than the tiles you pick in Scrabble. Sometimes you pick all vowels. No seven-letter bingo with a pew of all vowels."

"You can at least be creative with the tiles you're dealt." She carefully laid out the word "extract" and batted those dark almond eyes at me.

"Cute trick—and that's all that is, a cute trick. My problem is this thing with Jo-Ball has put a lot of negative energy into my business. Him getting tweaked is going to make all the goofballs dive for cover, including the ones who took my goodies. I have to use all my positive energies to find out who took the paintings from me, try to recover those assets. My business was counting on that money. More important than that, other businesses are counting on that money."

Delilah fixed her eyes on me, head to one side, but I kept looking at my tiles.

She says, "Other businesses?"

I didn't look up and didn't say anything.

I share a lot with Delilah, but there are certain things a man needs to keep to himself, especially things a man isn't proud about. Or that make him feel like a sucker. The truth was that I was in for some serious money on account of Yvette. Like a moron, I bailed her out, and not just to a landlord, but to a kind of a bad Vegas dude who took over her debt to the landlord. So I had to take a short-term loan. A loan from an individual, not a bank, if you get my drift. A guy not too unlike the guy I had to pay off, but at least a Brooklyn shylock, name of Vince Scanlon.

So she finally says, "I can lend you some money, Tom, if it will keep you from getting killed."

I smiled like I was sad. Which I was, to be honest. Sad because I thought I could help Yvette, sad because Delilah thought she could help me. "If it was enough to help, Dee, it would be more than I'd be willing to hit you up for."

"You big sucker." She smiled like she was happy. "Too gallant for your own good. Come on." I turned and watched her slip into the bathroom.

"Where we going?" I stood, thinking maybe I was in for another massage.

Delilah came out with a towel, a scissors, and a razor. She waved a hand at one of the dining room chairs. "Sit."

I got all squinty. "What's this about, Dee? I don't need no haircut."

"You need a shave."

My hand covered my beard like it might slide off. "Shave?"

"We're going to shave it all off."

"Shave?" Now both my hands were protecting my beard. "What the hell are you talking about?"

"Thomas . . ." Whenever she uses my full name, I know she won't take no for an answer. "Indulge me. You need a new look, a fresh perspective, and the way to start is with a clean face."

"What the hell are you talking about?"

She guided me into a chair and draped a towel around my neck.

"You big dummy. Without a beard you'll be less recognizable." There were snipping sounds, and black and silver clumps of hair fell on the white towel. "Let's say the sniper was targeting you. Do you think he and whoever hired him had a picture, maybe a description? First part of that description will be the beard. Take that away and you at least have a little advantage. Besides, you'll be a lot more handsome without the spinach chin. You may want to lose the suits for a while, too."

The grumpy squint left my eyes. "Oh, I see what you're talking about. I ever tell you you're smart, Dee?"

So she says, "Say it with flowers, bub."

CHAPTER
SIX

THE WHITBREAD MUSEUM WAS MY next stop. I had my own reasons for the visit, of course, but Maxie was expecting me to interview the guards. They came back on duty at seven o'clock, and between losing my goodies, Jo-Ball's head exploding, the cops, and the massage, my day had already been pretty much eaten up.

You would think people who owned a museum would have good artistic sense, wouldn't you? Then why was it that the trustees at the Whitbread approved the redesign of the stately museum facade and entrance to include a flying saucer?

Of course, when I say flying saucer, it only looked like one. A grand marble stair used to soar up to huge doors. Like a bank, or on a Greek deli coffee cup. Someone had the bright idea to rip that out and shove a massive glass disc entryway at ground level. I can't tell you how stupid this disc looks smashed into a dignified building. Everybody who passes by thinks so, too, I kid you not.

The museum was closed, and a sign said so, but I knew a door in the saucer that was always open for the change of the guards. One of the day-shift guards approached me. He gnashed his dentures at me, tugging on his belt.

"Closed, pal. We closed at five."

"Freddy, it's me, Tommy Davin."

Freddy looked stuck with a pin from two directions. At least the dentures didn't pop out and land on the floor. Almost, though.

"Fucking aye, Tommy. No more spinach chin. I didn't know who you was."

"I know. Looks strange. Feels strange." I moved my naked jaw side to side and missed the comforting crunch of whiskers on my neck.

Freddy leaned in close and pointed. He smelled faintly of sour beer and Tic Tacs.

"Kirk Douglas," he says.

"Kirk Douglas?"

"Did you know you have a cliff chin? Kirk Douglas: He had a cliff chin." He pointed to his chin, and his hand trembled just a little bit. Some of the other guards called him Unsteady Freddy. There was a tightness to his eyes that along with his particular aroma tipped that he was a boozer.

"That's very insightful, Freddy." I stuck a forefinger on my chin and felt the divot, or cliff, or whatever. It was deeper than when I was younger. "I'm here about last night. For the insurance company. Interview the staff when they get in. Atkins here?"

"Ernest Borgnine. He also had a cliff chin."

"I thought you worked nights, Freddy?"

"Rotation. I go back on night shift Thursday."

"Atkins here?"

"Should be leaving soon. Might catch him. You know his office, right?"

"Right." I moved past him toward the coat check near the entrance to the administration part of the museum. On the way I saw the signs for the new Lee J. Rosenburg Wing.

Get this: A new wing doesn't always mean a new wing. It can, but for Lee J. Rosenburg, a powerhouse on the museum board of directors, it meant an existing wing named after him with some of his bragging rights on display. He had an impressive collection of Mondrian paintings. You know them when you see them. Large squares of color on white backgrounds divided by dark lines. Most of the paintings have very literal names like *Composition in Red, Yellow, and Blue,* nonrepresentational stuff from the early 1900s Mondrian called "neoplasticism."

I hadn't seen the Lee J. Rosenburg Wing yet, so I made a detour to check out the Mondrians. Pretty impressive seeing a bunch of them together like that. I know a lot of people may feel that this stuff isn't art, it's just squares of color, anybody could do it. Let them try. Then again, a Mondrian would be a boatload easier to forge than Mona Lisa's smile.

Like I said, I had a degree in art history, Brooklyn College, but I started out as an art student. I wanted to paint. As a freshman, I took my little easel around the piers in Red Hook painting industrial decay against the sky. I soon realized, though, that I didn't have an eye for capturing what I saw in my mind. That may not make a lot of sense until you try painting yourself. It's aesthetics. I didn't have much. Just the same, I wanted to spend my life around art.

Anyway, I was impressed by the Mondrians they had put together for Lee—most were his. They hadn't named a wing after him because he was such a nice guy, either. The whole flying saucer makeover of the museum was a fiasco, way over budget and behind schedule, and he was bearing down on Sheila McCracken, the museum's director, to resign. She got wind of his scheme and hatched the plan to name a wing of the museum after him to make him play nice. It worked, but she was really close to getting the axe, and as a result having panic attacks. How do I know all this? I was dating Sheila at the time.

I turned and set course for the administration area.

You can see how lax museum security can be, even when a museum had been robbed. A door after hours shouldn't be left unlocked like that even if it is convenient and you have one geeze in dentures there to make sure nobody takes a billion dollars in art. I should not have been permitted to walk the museum after hours without an escort, and the doors to the administration wing should have been locked at all times.

Atkins was the head of security. I found his office and walked in. Nothing special. Just a white office, with a desk and a lamp and a visitor chair and some inspirational posters on the wall about safety and security. His computer was on; Atkins was out. Someone with less scruples than me could have rummaged his computer for security codes, guard schedules and names, where they lived—all kinds of things that could be useful if you wanted to jack paintings.

Atkins came in the door behind me. He bounced a couple feet in the air. "Shit!"

"Atkins, calm down, it's me, Tommy."

"Tommy! I mean, shit, you about scared me to death, big guy like you hiding in my office." Atkins had a very neat mustache, with wax or some shit on it, and very pink lips for a man. It's not his fault he had pink lips, he didn't wear lipstick or anything, but still, his lips were more pink than most men would want.

"Sorry if I scared you. I'm here about last night. To interview the night shift."

"Well, for one thing, your beard is missing. You're supposed to have a beard. And mustache. All that hair on your face is gone."

"I cut it off."

"I didn't recognize you. And you have a . . ." He couldn't think of the word and pointed at his chin.

I pointed at mine.

"I have Kirk Douglas's chin. So I'm here about last night. For the insurer. To interview the night shift. Guards and kitchen staff."

"They said you were coming." Atkins circled around me and jiggled his computer mouse around until his screen went dark. "The kitchen staff is down there now, but none of the same guards are working tonight as *last* night. Except Freddy. None of them saw anything anyway. The crooks just popped out of the kitchen, grabbed the three paintings right there in the hallway, and went back out through the kitchen. The camera covering that section of the museum is multidirectional, and the camera was looking the other direction during the thirty seconds that it took to lift the art. Bad luck."

Not bad luck at all. It was the way I planned it, real cute. Atkins himself explained to me that the camera's light blinks every sixty seconds. That tells the guards that the camera is working and not malfunctioning. It also means the camera—hidden inside a tinted dome—is looking in a particular direction. Every ten seconds it looks in another direction until after five views it comes back to the original position. In this case, when the light blinked, it was looking at the room with the three paintings I wanted. So I set it up so the goofballs looked around the corner with a dental mirror and waited for the green light to blink. Ten seconds later, they had fifty seconds to lift the goodies before the camera looked that way again.

"That is bad luck, Atkins."

"What I'm telling you is none of the same guards are here tonight, and even if they were, they wouldn't be able to tell you anything. I have one of the guards set up down in the control room to show you the surveillance tape of the kitchen staff being subdued, but the thieves obstructed the kitchen camera afterward, so we don't have tape of them exiting with the paintings. Not that we need to see that—the paintings are gone."

"Freddy was here last night."

"Freddy? Oh, yes, well, he was down front, where we're letting him finish out his career. I don't know whether you noticed, but he drinks." He looked at his watch. It was one of those super watches that if it fell on your foot might bust more than one toe. "Gotta run. You know your way to the kitchen and the control room?"

"I do."

We stepped out of his office, and he locked the office door.

"Be sure to give my best to Sheila," I said. Sheila and I had a good time in the beginning of our relationship, but panic attacks aside, she had a temper that set dry grass ablaze. The staff lived in fear of her, which was why Atkins went a little pale when I mentioned her name and only nodded to indicate he would relay my message.

I went one way down the hall, and he went the other.

You'd think Atkins would have been a little agitated over what happened the night before in his museum, seeing as he's head of security. Then again, I always figured him for a clock puncher. I was right. Like I said, art theft is business as usual to these people.

Anyhow, Atkins wasn't going to be any help getting my paintings back. Neither were the guards, since they didn't see anything, which was exactly the way I planned it. I have to say, investigating my own theft kind of sucked, since someone else ended up with the paintings.

I spent the next hour questioning the kitchen help. The answers were unsurprising. Huey and the other goofballs—believe it or not—did things right down the line. They said little, just things like:

"On the floor."

"Face down."

"Spread-eagle."

"Hands behind your back.."

"Be smart, stay healthy, don't move."

The kitchen staff (the ones that spoke English) mentioned the leader seemed foreign, but none of them guessed French; mostly they said Middle Eastern or Russian. That's probably because we don't have a lot of French wandering around Brooklyn. A foreigner was a foreigner to these guys, who were just little brown food-service-prep guys from South America.

They also mentioned one guy was the muscle—Kootie. They had no description of Frank. They sure would have if he wasn't wearing a ski mask, I can tell you. None of the South Americans mentioned anything about three other crooks who took the paintings from my goons. Not that they would have, since that happened out by the van and beyond the range of the security cameras.

After the interviews, I went to the control room and reviewed security camera recordings. I'd told my goofballs where to find the kitchen camera once they'd taped up the staff, and I watched the whole thing go down exactly as it was supposed to, right up to the point where Kootie stood on the counter and put tape on the camera lens. Even if he hadn't, as Atkins said, the only thing we would have seen was them walking back through the kitchen with the paintings two minutes later.

Clockwork gig. It went down pretty much the way Huey described it. That didn't tell me much about who took the paintings, but it did tell me something, at least by way of elimination. Huey was telling me the truth. At least up to a point.

I was heading toward the museum exit when I felt drawn to the Mondrians again, so I slipped once again into the Lee J. Rosenburg wing.

There were two paintings of the bunch that sort of stood out from the rest. I stood in front of them, admiring the color and composition.

"What do you think you're doing?"

I turned, and Sheila McCracken was in the exhibit entryway. Sheila's name is Scottish, and she looks every inch of it. Dark mane of red hair, green eyes, wide jaw, slightly wider shoulders. Not a small woman. I don't mean fat, but she had hips, and a sizable rack.

"Hi, Sheila."

"You're working for Max?"

I nodded.

"You've interviewed the staff?"

Nod. "Kitchen staff."

"And Atkins?"

I nodded a third time.

"So you think you can wander around the museum after hours as you please?" Sheila smiled and winked with both eyes. That sounds friendly. It wasn't.

"The Mondrians were on my way to the exit." I gestured to the two paintings in front of me. "You afraid I might steal some?"

Her eyes went rapidly between me and the paintings. "You can't wander around the museum unescorted. I'll take you to the exit."

I cocked my head at the two Mondrians and smiled. "You did a nice job with this wing, Sheel."

"Tommy, don't call me Sheel. I don't like it." Her voice boomed around the room. Based on our history, it didn't surprise me she was getting so upset. "You're leaving. Now."

I shrugged and walked past her. "You look good, Sheila."

She didn't respond and didn't have to. The sharp clack of her shoes on the polished floors behind me spoke volumes. *"Freddy!"*

The rummy practically fell out of his chair. "Yes, Ms. McCracken."

"You know Mr. Davin?" She waved a hand at me as I stopped in front of his security dais.

"I do."

"Was he in the appointment book?"

"Appointment book?" He began fumbling with a register.

"Did he sign the appointment book?"

"I thought that since, you know, Tommy has been here before . . ." Freddy was frantically flipping pages in the book, knowing full well there was no appointment or signature.

I says, "Sheila, no need to bust Freddy's shoes. I'm partly responsible."

So she says, *"Irresponsible."*

"Freddy and I will play by the after-hour rules next time, won't we, Freddy?"

"I can only hope there isn't a next time." She smiled and did that double wink thing before making tracks for the administration wing.

I looked at Freddy. "You can stop flipping pages, Freddy, she's gone."

He slapped the book shut and gripped his forehead. "I could go for a snort."

"Take it easy, Freddy. If McCracken is conflicted or transitional, that doesn't have anything to do with you."

"She'll try to get me fired for this. I'm only still here because Atkins is a softie."

I patted him on the shoulder. "Try cutting back on the booze a little, OK, and eat healthy. Baby carrots are good."

It was ten o'clock by the time I walked out of the flying saucer. I called Maxie's number, left a message telling him I had the essentials and would get back to him.

Time to head home. I was starving, tired, and deserving a cocktail. I hailed a town car; they aren't supposed to pick up street fares, but will in Brooklyn because the yellow cabs are scarce.

I sank into the squishy leather seat, my mind spinning with everything I needed to do, with everything that had gone bad that day. It could get worse, I knew. The cats hadn't been fed. They might have become hostile about that and acted out. You know, like by shredding the kitchen cabinets to get at their Cat Chow.

CHAPTER

SEVEN

MY APARTMENT WASN'T LARGE, AND the cats didn't make it any larger. The abode was as big as it needed to be for a single guy, what they called a parlor floor in a brownstone on Degraw Street. Originally my four-story building was a single-family home, but the parlor had been walled off from the upper and lower floors. I used bookshelves to make a bedroom in front. The middle was where the couch and TV were. The back was where you found the kitchen. Pretty standard setup. In fact, you couldn't really set it up any other way and make good use of the space. The kitchen was at one end, the entrance in the middle. Couldn't move the kitchen, and wasn't cool to have visitors enter your bedroom as soon as they came in the front door. I like black and gray modern-style furniture offset by colorful abstract art prints of artists like Hoffman. Indirect lighting was key, and a no-clutter rule was in effect. My deaf landlady lived downstairs with her poodle; my upstairs neighbors worked at night. I can play my Perez Prado mambo and Xavier Cugat cha-cha CD's as loud as I want.

Like I said, I already had anxiety about what I might find the Fuzz Face Four had done to my abode.

Don't worry, I'm not one of those guys who bore people with the details of my cats. *Yvette's cats.* Mainly because when I got home the cats were beside the point.

My front door was splintered at the lock, pried open. That seemed a little more damage than even these four cats could manage.

The furry foursome were gone.

So was their food, the cat boxes, and the litter.

I guessed Yvette had come and taken the little darlings. But why had she wrecked my door? I hadn't changed the locks because I hoped that one day she'd sneak back and take the beasts.

That's when I found a paper towel on the kitchen counter by the black kitchen appliances. Scrawled on the paper towel in ballpoint was this:

SHE WANT CATS SHE COME TO GUSTAV.

There was this little skull and crossbones after the name Gustav.

Breathe slowly in through the nose; close the eyes.

Breathe slowly out through the lips; stroke back my face where the beard used to be.

Breathe slowly in through the nose; open the eyes.

Breathe slowly out through the lips; focus on the bar in the corner where the brandy was.

You can imagine the emotions that rumbled through me at that moment, especially after the day I had already had.

My first reaction was anxiety about the safety of the cats, that Gustav—whoever he was—would hurt the scratch-happy felines. I was relieved that he had taken the litter box and the rest of the cat stuff. To have taken that stuff, too, Gustav must be serious about taking care of them awhile. The idea behind the note seemed to be making Yvette contact him, to get something out of her, and that would only make sense if the cats were alive.

I took the brandy off the corner bar and poured myself a snifter. My anxiety about the cats was replaced by a slightly different feeling.

The cats were gone.

The brandy tasted pretty good at that point in time, but it wasn't clearing my head.

In times of distress like that, I found it therapeutic to go take a walk over to the scrap yard.

I poured my snifter into a travel coffee mug, rebuttoned my coat, and fit the door loosely back in place.

My neighborhood was a great place to walk because it went from commercial and residential to light industrial. I liked to walk south on Smith Street because you see it all. It started with the smart shops and hip bars and restaurants. Topping the hill at Carroll Street, the subway shot out of the ground and began to ramp up to elevated tracks on the right. On the left opposite the rising trestle, the apartments and shops gave way to open lots and vacant warehouses. The train trestle swung out and crossed over Smith before Ninth Street. This is where the serious industrial stuff started, like cement plants and fuel oil depots. In the sky ahead was an elevated portion of I-278. They call it the Gowanus Expressway. They call it that because it goes over the canal. It hummed and twinkled with traffic.

Below the Gowanus Expressway was Hamilton Avenue, and the intersection with Smith Street.

Before that intersection on the left, between Smith Street and the canal, was a concrete plant.

Before that was the scrap yard, where eighty-foot dump trucks delivered metal for recycling. One giant grabber machine put scrap from the trucks onto towering mountains of rust, and another giant grabber machine put scrap from the towering mountains of rust into a barge parked in the canal.

I liked those giant grabber machines. If you haven't seen one, picture a toothy iron dinosaur, and picture it biting piles of metal and spitting it out into a steel barge parked in the Gowanus Canal. Makes a boatload of noise. Some of the workers had painted eyes on the grabbers. At night, the metal monsters chomped scrap into the night. There are lights mounted on the grabbers, so you see the iron dinosaurs' jaws and pale eyes swinging in and out of illuminated clouds of dust.

I liked to watch the scrap, too. You could sometimes make out what different pieces were, whether an old fuel tank or a car fender or a metal trash can or a bunch of iron fencing.

It's interesting, even karmic. No, I mean it. Circles within circles, but always circles. People run around in this life making money to buy stuff they throw away, and in the end, a lot of it ends up here only to be ground up and spit out, melted down to make more stuff. I sometimes wonder when I look at my toaster whether it's made from parts of Pop's old Dodge Polaris.

I'll take that a step further. People are made of scraps, of fragmented experiences and emotions all melted together, and there's a process where we in turn dump bad energies and forge them into something new and positive. Like getting Yvette out of my life, out of my heart, and becoming whole again.

Then there's the whole death thing. No matter what, you end up being reduced to smaller pieces and being made into something else, even if it is worms.

Circles within circles.

Life is like a scrap yard. That was my emotional center as I sipped brandy and watched the grabbers devour and gyrate in the dust clouds, eating tattered metal. My mind eventually drifted back to current events: *The cats were gone.*

Like I said, I don't mind cats, I actually like them, I just don't want them in my five-hundred-square-foot abode. Cat toys were still dotted around the floors—Gustav would be sorry he forgot those. The kitties, with nothing to amuse themselves, would be extra hard on his furniture.

That gave me a chuckle. This moron who busted up my door and wanted to extort Yvette now had four cats living with him. How's that for justice?

Yeah, but who was this Gustav? Never heard of him. Then again, Yvette had a pretty haunted past there in Vegas, and maybe more so back in Eastern Europe where she was raised. The longer I knew her, the more ghosts appeared, and not just shady debtors. There were casual references to mobbed-up boyfriends, psychiatrists, probationary hearings, DUIs, and sexual harassment suits. Like I said, I fell in love with her, mostly because she was a stone cold knockout. At the same time, the longer I knew her, the more anxiety I had about her past. Delilah will tell you that certain people have conflicted chakras. What do I think? People with constant trouble are mostly those who make it. Yvette was one of these people. While she was still around, I knew this in my gut, though if you had asked I wouldn't have said so. When she bolted, there was a note saying basically that she "had trouble coming her way." I was sort of OK with the exit because I knew in my heart she would always be in trouble, and I didn't want that in my life even if she was built like a mud flap girl.

On an emotional level, I was very upset when she left, don't get me wrong. Rationally? It was good to have my closets, kitchen, bathroom, and life back.

Better if she hadn't stuck me with the cats, of course. She'd always said they were the most important thing to her, so for her to leave them tells you a lot right there. She must have fed Gustav that line, too. How many jerks would kidnap cats? Or is it catnapping?

I had been wrong. The day wasn't getting worse. It was getting better. I finished my brandy and saluted the monster grabbers. A tall kid with rosy cheeks passed by me and gave me an odd look. I guessed he had never seen anybody commune with a grabber.

Time to head home and take my abode back.

At home, I went to the stereo and put on *Havana, 3 a.m.* I'm just saying, but that's Perez Prado's masterpiece, his perfect album. The music is instrumental, from 1956, and nails the Afro-Cuban sound to the wall. To most people it would sound like Latin music, sort of like mambo, and there is some mambo on the album. Blaring brass, rolling congas, barking saxes, and guttural shouts; the music is regal, sexy, and robust. By robust I mean full of life force. I'm not Cuban or Latino or anything, but this music puts me in a really good place, makes me feel anything is possible. It makes me dance inside.

So I danced inside for the next three hours and ate baby carrots while vacuuming fuzz and litter off the rugs. Then I cleaned the floors. Then I rolled the furniture with no less than ten sticky lint rollers. The cat toys filled half a garbage bag, I kid you not. I also used my screw gun to piece the front doorjamb back together. The activity, the work, the dancing centered me. I couldn't worry about Yvette's troubles. About this screwball Gustav. About the kitties. I had my own worries. I had my inner dance.

I finished cleaning around one in the morning, drank more brandy than I should have, and watched a talk show until I conked out on the couch. I forgot to eat. Except for the baby carrots. Ate a whole bag.

When I flicked off the tube and stumbled to bed, I noticed something white on the floor by the front door. It wasn't a toy mouse but the corner of an envelope sticking under my door. On the front was the word YVETTE. I was too tired and drunk to be concerned about Yvette's privacy, so I opened it.

I had to use the bathroom's bright light to realize that it was written in something like Cyrillic script. A letter from Gustav. The guy had the balls to come back while I was cleaning. Maybe it was a more formal threat written in her native language. Not long, just one paragraph. Maybe a love letter. Cute.

I tossed the letter on the table by the door and flicked off the lights.

Even if the day ended on a positive note, the sour ones played through the night. I can't say I slept.

CHAPTER EIGHT

My Heart, Yvette:

I have finally made my way to New York only to discover you have left. Why do you continue to elude me, and elude our destiny? From the instant I saw you eternity's sea opened before me awash with waves of our love. In Las Vegas you could not see this, and I attempted to demonstrate the power of the love that could be ours. You owed money and I made that criminal pay with his life for his threats to you. That you ran from me to New York made me sad. But I realize that such great love must be earned as in history through a quest. This is why I am here and will seek you wherever you go until you too see our destiny. This is why I will vanquish any other that comes between us. Who is this oaf that cares for your lovely cats, the lovely animals I adored in Nevada? I have been following him, knowing his travels, and will spare the oaf so long as he eventually guides me to you. The cats I will care for until we are united.

With an ocean of adoration filled with fish of affection—

Gustav

NINE

NEXT MORNING I FOUND A stranger in my apartment.

When I passed the mirror on the way to the bathroom I saw a guy with a Kirk Douglas chin instead of a Tommy Davin beard. I about had a cardiac. Except for the shoulder-length hair, I looked a lot like Pop at this age.

The screwiness of that morning didn't end there. Or was it a continuation from the day before?

To get my day off on a better track I put some Cugat on the sound system. He was a character, Xavier. Wore white suits, had a pencil-thin mustache, and carried around a Chihuahua. At some point I think he married Charo, that Latin bombshell you saw on *Laugh-In* or whatever back when I was a kid. Cugat was big after the Second World War, even made it into the movies. I stuck to his instrumental music, and it's more refined than Perez Prado's stuff, more elegant, and I wanted to feel a little elegant and in control. Mostly rumbas, cha-chas, like that.

I had to get dressed, and Cugat was helping me get over not only having a naked face but having to pick out a new wardrobe, one that wasn't exactly elegant but I had to pretend it was and get over it. In clothes different from my usual suits, you know, like Delilah suggested. So I put on chinos, a white oxford shirt, and a rumpled sweater from a bottom drawer. Mom gave me the sweater for Christmas 1996. I remembered because she always gave me a stupid sweater at Christmas, but this was the last one, just before she died. That's the only reason I hadn't thrown it out like the others. This one had reindeer on it prancing across my chest with snowflakes. I had to laugh when I stood in front of the mirror. There was the stranger again, but he looked like an English teacher, or somebody from Vermont, either or both on a bad day. My collar-length hair looked funny without the suit and beard. I thought maybe I would drop in on my stylist to get a trim.

Made coffee, ate a slice of toast, and enjoyed the lack of an audience. No cats waiting to be serviced. Which reminded me about Tigsy's shots for his diabetes. I looked in the fridge.

This Gustav guy even took the insulin and the hypodermics from the crisper drawer. He really knew these cats, alright. I could only imagine how he knew so much about them. It pretty much followed that if he knew the cats real well, he knew Yvette real well. Ex-boyfriend? I had a good little laugh at his expense and returned to my coffee. It figured she'd have some poor schmuck like Gustav in her wake. Exactly the kind of guy she would have creeping around in her past, which was all the more reason to keep her out of my life for good.

Anyway, the missing insulin eased my lingering anxiety about the Fuzz Face Four. Was it up to me to try to contact Yvette somehow, tell her about the catnapping? My masseuse said I was perverse using the word "catnapping" because it means sleeping for a short time, not the abduction of cats. OK, so I'm a little perverse. I think it's funny, so shoot me. On second thought, don't.

I was determined that Yvette's problems remain completely

hers. Now that the cats were out of my place, that was more true than ever.

On the coffee bar was my notepad in a slice of sunlight. I wrote down details of projects for work in that leather-bound pad. It was compact, slid into my inside jacket pocket. I would have written down details the little brown prep chefs told me the night before if they'd told me anything I didn't already know. I slid the pen out of the side of the pad, clicked it, and began writing the day's priorities.

Ten minutes later I was done. So I picked up my cell phone and dialed the locksmith over on Atlantic Avenue. She picked up.

I says, "Gloria? It's me, Tommy."

So she says, "I don't know nothing about it, Tommy, as God is my judge."

"Relax, Gloria."

"I knew you'd call me about Sunday night's gig at the Whitbread."

Two years before, Gloria had settled a few paintings from the Whitbread through me. She and her brother took advantage of the construction scaffolding for the flying saucer by feeding a guard dog a slumburger and climbing to the museum roof.

A slumburger is hamburger meat with over-the-counter sleeping pills in it and makes guard dogs, no matter how vicious, pretty useless. Repo guys use them all the time. Inside, they lifted four small Robert Henris—little scenes of Paris in oil on small wood panels.

"Gloria, would it make you feel better if I asked you whether you did Sunday night?"

I could hear her taking a long, deep drag on a cigarette. Then she exhaled. "No, Tommy, it would not. I know you still don't trust me about the Henris."

"I trust you on that one, Gloria. You're too smart to have tried to pull something like that. The museum was somehow mistaken."

A kink in the story about her fetching the four small Robert Henri cityscapes is that the museum claimed there were seven Henris missing. This discrepancy was never resolved, and the museum and the insurer weren't happy that I was only able to recover four. Max was real unhappy and pressuring me to tell him who the goofballs were, but my sources have to be one hundred percent confidential. That's an important rule in my business. Gloria swore she wasn't holding out on me, and I can't imagine what incentive she would have had to do that. Why would she sell only four back to me? Unless she was shopping, but then why sell any back to me at all? It didn't make sense. Like I said before, about that guy who had an apartment filled with boosted art that nobody was missing? It could have been a clerical error by the museum, though they showed me spots where all seven had been hanging. I still was sort of scratching my head over that one.

"I called about a lock, Gloria. My apartment door, someone broke it. I want you to fix up this door so Godzilla and his big brother couldn't get in. Metal plates, steel reinforced doorjambs, the works. Can you do that?"

"I thought you rented?"

"I do."

"Your landlord paying for this?"

"My dime. She doesn't need to know. Today is Tuesday, the day she goes to see her son in Staten Island."

"You want this today?"

"Personal favor?"

She laughed, and then coughed, and then laughed.

"OK, baby. You were pretty white with me over the Henris."

"I have to go out. Want me to drop the keys by?"

"I make keys. I don't need them."

"Right. I'm on Degraw. Parlor floor."

"We'll fix you up and leave the new key under the mat. Ciao, baby."

It's one thing to take a man's cats when they're not his. It's another thing to bust in his door and make free use of his place. If Gustav didn't hear from Yvette, he might come back at me to get to her. I wasn't going to live with the anxiety of maybe finding him waiting for me in my own apartment one night. Having the love note translated was an option, but whatever he said in there, I didn't feel it would be instructions on exactly where he could be found.

I dialed my cell again.

"Blaise, it's Tommy."

"Heh."

"What you got for me?"

"No report from the field yet, Tomsy. Want me to e-mail it to you?"

"Got my e-mail?"

"Heh. Got it, my man. Have you down as Big Tomsy. By noon OK?"

"Good."

"Peace out."

So that was two items off my list.

I flicked off Cugat in the middle of "Besame Mucho" and made for the street.

TEN

LIKE I SAID, I NEEDED money, which is why I needed those paintings.

It was Tuesday, the day I had to make my next payment to Vince Scanlon.

Vince didn't like me being late with the payment, so I made a point of making it early in the day to keep him from getting nervous. He was up on Court Street and owned a toy store more or less across the street from Donut House. His shop was jammed with brightly colored action figures, squirt guns, Wiffle bats, the whole gamut. It was getting on toward Halloween, so there was a gamut of plastic pumpkins, costumes, and masks, too.

Strollers were parked out front of Vinny's Toyland like horses in front of a saloon. My neighborhood is known not only for art thieves but also for moms with strollers, at least during the day. They refer to these women as stroms, and by midmorning it's like an army of them have invaded the streets. It can be hard to get around on foot. They not only push around tots but pretty big kids, too, ones that can walk, I'm not sure why. Maybe it's just easier to get around with a restrained kid on wheels. That way the tykes don't wander into traffic or stick a finger in a dog poop. I waded through half a dozen preschoolers and their moms on the way to the back counter.

Vince is maybe sixty, stooped, his hair dyed red to cover up the gray. The part in his hair was always straight and white, on the left, with the hair neatly pasted down on either side. For some reason he'd chosen to give up on regular clothes and wear jumpsuits. I guess it is easier to put on one piece of clothing than two, and you don't need belts, either. That day's jumpsuit was tan. He had a pink monkey puppet on his hand and was making it dance on the counter for a drooling toddler strapped to the front of a pageboy strom.

Vince was like the Mister Rogers of shylocks. You'd expect a Brooklyn leg breaker to be a goombah sipping espresso in a dark corner of an Italian pastry store, not doing *Sesame Street*. It's been my experience, though, that people aren't always what you expect them to be, and that likewise people don't always do what you expect them to. Pop used to say people are like the moon—you only see one side but there's another in shadow you never see.

Vince sees me, and the pink monkey looks my way and says, "Wowee, it's Tommy! Hello, Tommy!" The pink monkey spoke in a high voice like you would expect. He was waving at me. The pageboy strom with the tot drifted back to her tribe.

So I says to the monkey, "Hello, Pink Monkey. I have something for Vince."

The monkey clapped his hands. "You have the money? I'd hate to see anything happen to you."

I tried looking at Vince. He was looking at the monkey, but messing with me. So I looked at the monkey. "Whoa, monkey, easy. I said I have the money."

So the monkey puts his hands together like he's praying. "Poor Johnny One-Ball got his head blown off. They're saying you were there and that the shooter took a shot at you. Vince thought you might be in some kind of jam. If you take a bullet, he doesn't get his money and bad things happen."

"I'm really touched by your concern, Pink Monkey." I slipped a white envelope from inside my overcoat and handed it to the monkey, who accepted it with open arms. Inside was thirty thousand bucks in hundreds, the last of my cash reserves except for the couple hundred spending money on me. I was tapped out.

The monkey made the envelope vanish under the counter and reappeared.

"Thank you, Tommy! I'll see Vince gets the money. It better be all there. Don't think you can get out of your obligation by dying, Tommy. Your friends and family will suffer even if they don't know why."

I don't like threats, even from a pink monkey. They give off bad energy. Still, it doesn't pay to beat up hand puppets, especially if they're attached to a shylock. So instead of yanking Vince's arm out of his torso and beating him to death with the pink monkey, I said, "You and me will be square next week, monkey."

I pushed my way through the stroms and made for the door.

Outside, I crossed Court Street and went down the block to Donut House.

I stopped in front of the place, right where Jo-Ball had the top of his head exploded, and saw it all happen again. Kind of funny that the last thing he said to me was something about getting shot in the nuts, that he had a right to be nervous about being tweaked. I don't think it's possible to have illustrated his point better than by what happened next. He couldn't have been more right, but I'd bet he wished he weren't quite that right.

My tongue swelled with a bitter taste. I could picture Johnny One-Ball's tongue waving around in the air, the top of the head missing. Then him falling against the car and the blood gushing into the gutter. Then the bloody toupee sliding down the town car windshield. Christ. There are things I wish I never saw, but that topped the list—first, second, and third. I made a mental note to pick up more brandy to make sure I went to sleep fast and hard that night.

You could see the sidewalk had been scrubbed, but dark blood splatter was still visible on the concrete. I turned. The dent was there in the light pole, the one the second bullet made.

Yeah, more brandy would be necessary.

I looked up the block toward where the bullet must have come from. I say "must" because the Jo-Ball splatter went the same direction the bullet was traveling. Unless you want to start getting into some weird whiplash theory like with the Kennedy assassination, which I don't. The shooter wouldn't have been out in the open, but the shot must have come from some distance because there was nobody standing nearby. It stood to reason that the shooter, then, had to brace the gun against something to make an accurate shot like that. There was only one stoop on that block of Court Street, and I counted thirty strides from the point of impact to the stoop. That's about a hundred and twenty feet. Some marksmanship. Like I said, I'm not into guns, a little rule I had, but it doesn't take an expert to realize that this must have been a difficult shot done with something more than a handgun. I looked from the stoop back to the point of impact, and at the light pole. I'm sure the police did the same thing. There was little doubt that the shooter was standing where I was, his rifle resting on the stoop. I was curious how he disguised the rifle so nobody passing looking that way would notice. Also why there was no gunshot. I didn't hear any. Then again, Court Street was a commercial strip with all kinds of noises, anything from trash trucks and backfires to buses and construction work. Still, I thought I would have heard a gunshot.

I walked back to Donut House and pushed through the doors. The only customer there was the old man with no teeth. Only he had a cup of coffee in front of him, and didn't seem in any hurry to finish it.

Garrison was behind the counter. Like I said, he was a thin black guy in his thirties with eyes that don't exactly look the same direction. He'd poured me a cup of coffee the morning before.

He says, "Here's a black cat!" He spat on the floor and crossed himself. "You come back here after what happened yesterday? Tom Davin, of all people?"

I sat at a stool. "You still serve coffee in your place, Garrison?"

He poured me a cup, carefully, like I was a pit bull. "You know, Jo-Ball may have just ruined my business."

"I'm sure it was nothing personal, Garrison. Look, there was a woman here Sunday morning having breakfast with Johnny. Just before he got shot he told me about it. Did you see her?"

His eyes wandered around the room a little, like each was watching a different fly buzz the room.

"You shaved, Tom. You look almost friendly."

"Know who she was?"

"I seen her, sure, with Jo-Ball."

Garrison was not part of any crew, and not a goofball, and as far as I knew had no idea that Jo-Ball was anything other than maître d' at Dominic's.

I dumped four sugars in my coffee. "How often she and Jo-Ball have a sit-down?"

Garrison shrugged. "Hell, I dunno. I only seen her that once. Say, what do you care about this gal, anyway?"

"I have a special interest in what they were talking about."

"You work for insurance companies, don't you?"

"I do."

"This for his life insurance or some shit?"

"Can you describe her?"

His eyes went looking for the flies in the room again. "I don't think so."

"Was she white or black or Hispanic or Chinese or—"

"White." It almost sounded like he was guessing an answer on a game show.

"So she was white. Tall, small, fat, thin—"

"Medium."

"Hair?"

"I think she was wearing a hat."

"Red, white, black, pink—"

"Man, I dunno."

"Eye color?"

"Man, I dunno."

"Did she say anything to you?"

"Nuh uh. I think Jo-Ball ordered for both, the way he does. Did."

"Can you at least tell me what she was like? Did she remind you of anybody?"

"Man, I dunno."

As any cop will tell you, eyewitness accounts can be insanely screwy. I remember once in high school the NYPD came in and were trying to interest seniors in joining the force. We were in the auditorium, and they staged an incident in which a student ran through and stole the policeman's cap and ran out. Then the cop called on us to describe what we saw, what the hat thief looked like. I got it a hundred percent right, and it made me think that maybe I had what it took to be a cop, except I wanted to be a painter. Anyhow, nobody else in the room could agree on what color hoodie the thief was wearing (purple) or if he was wearing a hat (he was, a white visor) or if the guy was ethnic (he was Bobby Chin from my English lit class—even with the sunglasses I recognized the lucky dragon ring on his left hand). It was kind of amazing nobody could even agree on how tall or short he was, though he did a little jump to snatch the hat off the cop. Witnesses are terrible witnesses. Garrison was worse.

So I says, "So you never seen her before anywhere, or since?"

He says, "Nope."

We stared at each other. I looked at one of his eyes, and then the other. Neither was lying. Considering his eyesight may not have been that great, I could hardly bust his shoes much more on the girl.

"OK, but if you remember anything more, there's twenty bucks in it for you."

"Tommy, I'd tell you if I remembered. All I know is she came in here and had breakfast with Jo-Ball on Sunday, over there, and then took the car service that was idling out front. There's always one there waiting for a call. They like my coffee."

I looked up at him over my coffee cup, squinting. "Twenty if you know the car service."

"Had the company card in the window. Shit." Garrison covered his face with his dish rag, thinking as hard as he could. "Blue diamond-shape card . . ."

I smiled. "Blue Diamond Car Service?"

I STEPPED OUT OF THE diner, and you know where I was headed.

For the second time in two days there was a surprise waiting for me outside Donut House.

Two police detectives approached. Same two who interviewed me the day before. This was no cause for worry. Normally.

I apologize in advance to the cops in their private lives, where I'm sure they're good people with positive energy. I hope so for their wives' sake, anyway. Maybe my profession makes cops hostile toward me in particular, and that has altered my perception of them. They don't like anyone muscling in on their business, coming between them and what they consider crime. Plus maybe they don't like my size. I'm harder to intimidate.

I'm just saying, but police are not my favorite people, and I don't think that I'm totally alone in that department.

I guessed these two were heading into Donut House to further interrogate Garrison.

One of these detectives was a heavyset Chinese, with blue eyes, freckles, and thinning hair swept back. His name was Doh. His smile was always forced and out of practice, his eyes long-suffering and probably focused on retirement. The other detective was a short, bald Italian with a bushy black unibrow. His name was Crispi, and he looked like he could get angry at a buttercup.

Doh says to me, "Just the guy we wanted to see."

Those are words you never want to hear from a cop.

So I says, like a hello, "Detectives."

Crispi folded his arms. "What're you doing here, Davin?"

"Coffee."

Doh showed me his forced smile. "We hear things about you, Davin. In the neighborhood."

"Good things, I'm sure."

Crispi refolded his arms. "We hear Scanlon has his hooks in you."

"He sells toys."

"Not all he sells." Doh leaned in like this was big news. Everybody in Carroll Gardens and Cobble Hill knew Vince Scanlon was the local shylock. Well, maybe not all the hipsters that were gentrifying the neighborhood. True locals and goofballs knew.

Doh hadn't asked a question, so I had no response. He finally continued. "If there's a connection with Johnny One-Ball's murder, we'll find it."

I glanced down at the blood spatter on the sidewalk, then pointed at the dent in the light pole where the second bullet hit. "Serve and protect. Any idea who took a shot at me, and why?"

"Police business," Crispi said, his jaw muscles rippling.

"Detectives, just so you two remember, I'm a victim of attempted murder. Part of your job is to apprehend and prosecute whoever it was that took a shot at me."

I turned and went down Court Street.

Doh calls after me, "Davin . . ."

I kept going.

Pop used to say, *Just because someone asks you a question, doesn't mean you have to answer.* That goes double for cops. The only words you need to say to a cop are "I want my lawyer present."

Blue Diamond Car Service was north on Smith near Atlantic and was sort of famous in the neighborhood. Interesting story. Back when, some screwball decided to try to extort the Transit Authority by firebombing the subway. So he was sitting there with his first bomb, a jar of gasoline I think, in a paper bag on the floor between his legs, and it went off. Yeah, while he was still sitting there. He was badly injured; likewise some people in the subway car got injured and killed. Somehow this screwball survived, though worse for wear, and escaped down a subway tunnel. He came out at the Bergen Street stop at Smith Street and walked into the Blue Diamond Car Service, which was run by Arabs. Picture this guy, burned pretty much to a crisp, and he walked into the car service looking for a car. The Arabs freaked out—they came here to escape a war-torn Middle East. First year in business, and who came in but some guy who looks like he's been torched by a car bomb. They called the cops; the ambulance took him away. I can't remember if the screwball lived, but if he did he probably wished he hadn't.

Cut to three years later. My dentist, he's on Court Street. Enter another screwball, one in a puffy down coat who came into his office and confronted the nurse with a gun, forced her and my dentist into a corner. Nobody else was there. The desperado rummaged the receptionist desk looking for cash. Apparently, this latest dummy thought dentists got paid mostly in cash as opposed to insurance claims. It was at this point that my dentist pulled a gun from his sock. To tell you the truth, I had no idea my dentist carried, but I later learned that he and a bunch of other dentists have this gun club. Because he has precious metals in his office, like gold, he was able to get a carry permit. Anyway, the burglar took a shot at my dentist. My dentist, in turn, unloaded his entire magazine of nine shots at the screwball, who dropped his gun and ran out after being hit in what my dentist thought was the hand. At first he thought he'd missed the guy, because the burglar hadn't fallen down or anything, like on TV. Then he sees the blood and figures he'd hit him in the hand. So this screwball ran all the way down to Smith Street, and where do you think he ended up?

You got it. At the Blue Diamond Car Service. He stood there with blood pouring out from under his down coat asking for a car to Bay Ridge. My dentist actually put eight slugs in the guy's chest but somehow missed the heart. (My dentist now has a bigger gun with bigger bullets.)

The Arab dispatcher behind the counter, Sammy, was once again faced with the walking wounded. Sammy yells at the screwball, "Why do you people keep coming *here*!"

Now you had Johnny One-Ball getting his head exploded onto a Blue Diamond town car parked at Donut House. It was like I should have guessed it would have been them.

Gruesome stories, but the repetition says something about life. Maybe it's that irony thing, one of life's circles.

Sammy is pretty old now, his black hair with a lot of gray in it, thinning some in back, but still thick as a rug everywhere else. I don't know what kind of Arab he is. I'd seen him and knew who he was, but he didn't know me from a lamppost.

Car services are humble establishments that are all pretty much the same. A small paneled waiting area the size of a large rug sits in front of a counter. In front of the counter are some beat-up chairs and beat-up magazines. Behind the counter is a large map of New York City, a list of rates to the airports, a CB-type radio to talk to the cars, and in this case a wary Arab.

"You Sammy?" Of course I knew it was Sammy, but it was a way to break the ice.

He looked at me like I might burst into flame, and didn't answer me, waiting for what might come next.

"My name is Tommy Davin. I'm a neighborhood guy. I was at Donut House yesterday when that thing happened. I was standing right in front of one of your cars when it happened."

Still Sammy said nothing. He didn't even blink. These were eyes, I think, that had seen it all, and were sure they would see more. Sadly.

I almost expected him to shout, *"Why do you people keep coming here!"*

"Horrible thing, what happened. I was a friend of the victim. I'll tell you why I'm here. I want to give you fifty bucks to tell me who hired one of your cars on Sunday morning, the day before this happened. One of your drivers out front of Donut House was hired by a woman."

Sammy looked down his big brown Arab nose at the Grant I had set on the counter. Then at his big logbook next to it. Finally, he says, "The TLC forbids me to release such information." TLC is the Taxi and Limousine Commission, which polices car services and taxicab companies.

"I know, Sammy. I'm asking for you to make an exception. I'm asking for you to go through your logbook, flip to day before yesterday, and see who hired the car on Sunday. It will take maybe thirty seconds. Fifty dollars for thirty seconds is, let's see . . ."

"Six thousand dollars an hour," Sammy says, like in a whisper. "Why do you want to know this thing?"

"The fifty bucks is also so I don't have to answer that question. Look, I'm not asking for the name of your driver or anything like that, and I'm not going to hurt anybody. I want to find out where the woman went in the car, the destination. What harm could come of that?"

"The TLC and police would not like it. I should call the police." The smallest of smiles pushed at the corners of his mouth, like knowing what he should do gave him the upper hand.

"You could do that. But will the police pay you six thousand dollars an hour for the trouble?"

There was nobody else in the place, no drivers, no customers.

So Sammy looks at the logbook, looks at me, and says, "I cannot help you, and am going to the bathroom. Please be gone when I return or I will call the police."

Grant went with him. As soon as I heard the bathroom door latch I spun the logbook around and flipped it open.

I was gone before he returned.

For fifty bucks I'd bought a drop-off address and the last name French. The car wasn't hired by a company, wasn't on an account. Cash.

The address was the Williamsburg Savings Bank Building, an Art Deco skyscraper that is to Brooklyn what Big Ben is to London. There's a glowing clock at the top with red hands. The building gets thinner as it goes up, in steps, until just above the clock there's this tiny dome. The dome looks kind of stupid, like a tiny yarmulke on a giant. Brooklyn has a downtown area with some big buildings, but Billy Bank is still the tallest building around, and the clock could be seen from miles in all directions, even from my neighborhood.

Ms. French may or may not really have offices at Billy Bank, and she may not really have used her real name. Doubtful on both counts. The Grant in Sammy's pocket may not have bought me much.

In one week, the following Tuesday, I needed the last payment for Vince. Fifteen grand. If I didn't come up with it, I'd owe twenty-five grand the following week, a ten-grand late fee. After that, the pink monkey would firebomb my apartment and remove the nose of my closest family member or friend. I needed those paintings, those goodies Huey lost. Max said he'd pay fifty grand for them. I was supposed to get forty percent, that's standard for the setup, netting me twenty grand, but the crew would never stand for splitting thirty grand. Huey would take his forty percent, leaving Frank and Kootie with only nine grand. That's way below scale. So if I only got thirty I'd have to lower my percentage to keep the troops happy, which would make me unhappy. I'd have to negotiate that fifty up. I was expecting Max to offer one hundred, which would put me square with Vince with plenty to spare. Of course, I could try to finesse some money out of Huey's end from that, but not another ten. This sucked.

If Billy Bank was a dead end on Ms. French, my next connection was Huey, Frank, or Kootie. If they didn't take it directly, they leaked it to someone else, because I didn't tell anybody. They were the connection I had to work on. If that didn't give me dividends, the goofballs who took the pips from my three stooges were almost certainly in the business. So somebody must know them. Before the day was over I would have to feel up the neighborhood to see if I could scare something up. That's what I did for a living, after all, what I did best. Something, even something small, should pop. Goofballs don't keep secrets very well, not inside the industry.

Not for nothing, but I was still getting pretty anxious about having to start looking from scratch.

My phone vibrated, and I had a new e-mail. I was hoping it was Blaise, that he might have some information on my goofballs that would give me a lift.

It was from Max at USA.

Lunch me. 12:00 Sushi Ole.

TWELVE

SUSHI ISN'T MY THING, AND I think Max knew it. Which I guess was OK because I hadn't been very hungry since Jo-Ball's head exploded. Ensuing events hadn't exactly kicked off any cravings, either.

Usually I can eat, like to eat, need to eat. My six-foot-six frame needs nourishment, and let's remember that I'm a man of appetites. Just not for cold rice rolled up in clammy seaweed, or dead fish that hasn't been shown some hot coals. Somehow adding wasabi is supposed to make everything OK. It doesn't. Well, more for the rest of you who like this stuff.

I'm not crazy about the atmosphere at sushi places, either. The seats and tables are designed by a smaller race of people for a smaller race of people. I'm just saying.

It didn't help that this sushi place was in downtown Manhattan. You don't want to be in or around the financial district at lunch if you can help it. All those giant buildings empty onto the street, and there's a sense of desperation as hundreds of thousands of workers hit the bricks in search of food. Delis and restaurants in the area had a hard time meeting demand, much less making ends meet what with the commercial rents down there. In a sit-down place the tables were practically on top of each other. In delis, people ate standing up. I don't like eating standing up. The neighborhood was so pressed for noon nourishment that food carts appeared at corners, creating long lunchtime lines, further snarling up the sidewalks and foot traffic.

Fortunately, I exited the subway at Fulton Street station a little early, so the lunchtime herd hadn't begun its daily stampede. I started toward J&R, a music store. Thought I might browse the Latin jazz section. I'd been thinking about adding to my Ray Santos collection.

My phone blurped. An e-mail came in. It was from Blaise, as promised.

There was no hello or anything at the beginning of the e-mail, just a name like BIG GUY or UGLY GUY followed by a list of places and times.

I could hardly see the screen, so I stepped off the sidewalk, into a hat store. They still have hat stores in New York, and this one had a lot of the classics, like the ones Sinatra and Dino used to wear. I always liked hats, but they don't look good on me. I got a big head, and a hat tends to make it look bigger.

"Can I help you, sir?" Behind the counter was a Latina woman with fancy turquoise fingernails and matching pants. The pants were tight either because they were too small or she was too big or most likely some of both. She seemed nice enough. The walls were lined with lighted display cases of hats, mostly what they call fedoras.

So I says, "What do you got that will make me look like Frank Sinatra?"

So she smiles and says, "Why do you want to look like Frank Sinatra? You way more handsome than him. The right hat will make you look even more handsome, quito."

Nice lady. Smart lady. "Can I try some hats on while I check an e-mail?"

"Summer hat or winter?"

"I guess winter. It's almost Halloween."

She looked at me with one eye and wiggled a turquoise fingernail at me. "We'll try gray and brown hats first."

She started pulling out hats, and I stood in front of the mirror and scrolled down through the e-mail.

The gray hats seemed a little too formal, but things got more interesting when she got to the brown hats. Things also got more interesting when I scrolled down past Frank and Kootie's activities to what Huey had been up to:

FRENCH GUY
1000 TO DELI CIGS
1015 SMOKE AND CELL AT BISTRO
1025 BACK INSIDE BISTRO
1300 SMOKE, CELL
1310 BACK TO BISTRO
1505 LEFT BISTRO, WALKS
1520 ARRIVES DOWNTOWN STARBUCKS, COFFEE
      WITH BIG GUY AND UGLY GUY
1550 LEAVES STARBUCKS, CAR SERVICE, BLUE
      DIAMOND
1600 BLUE DIAMOND DROP OFF CONFIRMED BILLY
      BANK
1615 SUBJECT LEAVES BILLY BANK WITH GYM
      BAG, WALKS
1625 ARRIVES STOR-RITE, 3RD AVENUE
1655 LEAVES STOR-RITE, NO BAG, MEETS RED
      APPLE CAR SERVICE OUT FRONT

1720 ARRIVES BOND STREET LOFT/APARTMENT
     GRN BLDG @ UNION
1820 LEAVES BOND STREET LOFT/APARTMENT
1830 ARRIVES RITE AID SMITH / PRESIDENT ST.
1840 LEAVES RITE AID, WALKS
1845 ARRIVES BISTRO
===END===

Reports for Kootie and Frank were boring. They got up late, ate breakfast or ran errands, went to meet Huey, and then went to the restaurants where they work.

Huey's movements, though—they had me dancing inside. My grandmother and her schnauzer could figure out what Huey was up to. What you like to see when looking into something like this is what they call commonality. Billy Bank was a commonality. Likely as not there were no "other three guys" out by the van. Huey had a deal with me but then went and found another buyer for the paintings—Ms. French, to be exact. Got paid when he visited her at Billy Bank, put the money in a storage locker. When he handed over the paintings was unknown since he didn't have anything with him when he went to Billy Bank. Usually you move the goodies in a giant portfolio, without frames, of course. These portfolios are big black flat art briefcases. Don't believe what you see in the movies—no goofball rolls stolen paintings, and if he does he only does it once and eats cold cereal for his effort. Roll an old painting, you mostly end up with a canvas tube full of pretty paint chips. You don't cut it from the frame, either. Try that when you're in a hurry and see what you get. Not exactly like slicing a cheesecake, especially with all that oil paint. Easier to skin an elephant. A pro lifts the whole frame, pops the art out later, then deep-sixes the frame even if it is gilded.

Huey ripped me off. Now I needed to squeeze him for my share of whatever money he got. I was in a much more positive place than when I got the e-mail about the sushi. I began to hum Prado's version of "Peanut Vendor," a real peppy little tune.

Now I had to decide how I would squeeze Huey. I could have told Huey either he had to cut me a big slice of the pie or I make trouble for him in the business as a fink. Or better, trouble for him in his home. With his wife.

The green loft at Bond and Union Street?

That's Bridget's place.

She goes through a lot of sheets.

Latina hat girl says, "Ooo, mister, I like this brown one on you, it goes with your eyes. For you, nothing too close in color to your hair. The eyes, ah, that's muy bueno."

So I says, "You think so?"

I adjusted the hat and looked at the clean-shaven Kirk Douglas in the brown overcoat and brown fedora in the mirror. I tried to ignore the stupid snowflake sweater I was wearing. He didn't look like what I was used to. Still, chica was right. The brown hat did look good on me, didn't make my head look like something orange ready for carving and putting on a stoop. I did need to cut my hair, though. The hat would work better with shorter hair.

I looked at her in the mirror. "Do you know Perez Prado? His music?"

A little confused, she said, "My grandfather, he listens to mambo."

"How much for the hat, chiquita?"

"A hundred and seven."

If someone was going to blow my head off with a sniper bullet, I might as well have a hat on to hold the pieces together. I was so deep in shit with the pink monkey, what did another hundred matter? Besides, I was dancing inside because I knew who'd ripped me off and that I was close to making Huey hand over whatever he'd been paid so my problem with Scanlon would go away and Yvette would be completely out of my life.

I handed the Latina hat girl my credit card and replied to Blaise's e-mail.

> great work, BJ . . . stay on FG,
> drop UG n BG . . . photos at green loft?

My new hat and me were headed to lunch with Max when I got a reply.

> MY MAN TOOK A COUPLE CUZ HE KNOWS GRN LOFT.
> XTRA $40 FOR GRN LOFT PIX.

I sent back:

> 40 aok - u r the best.

THIRTEEN

SUSHI OLÉ WAS ALL DONE in blond wood, with blond tables and chairs very close together. Max was easy to spot in a lunchtime crowd. He was as tall as I was with short black hair and a white complexion. It was like when we were kids there'd be some lad who suddenly got taller but not wider. A beanpole. Maxie was an adult beanpole. Like you saw from the way he talks, though, Max is all about precision and economy. I've never seen him dressed in anything other than dark suits and white button-down shirts.

Given how Max was, I guess sushi fit his personality. The food is neat, compact, perfectly arranged. I noticed he consumed his sashimi from left to right, back to front, at regular forty-second intervals. His eyes always stayed on me.

I'm not sure what Maxie would have done with a pork chop, peas, and mashed potatoes with gravy. I'd like to have seen that sometime.

The corner table meant I had to sit next to the wall, and had to wade through a row of people trying to enjoy their lunch to get there. I just said excuse me a thousand times, bulldozed my way in, and sat backward on the little chair, which made a loud creak like it was complaining I wasn't a little Japanese guy.

"Max."

"Tom."

"Museum?"

"Yeah, interviewed the kitchen help."

"McCracken?" He was talking about Sheila, the museum director I had dated.

"Just for a second. Atkins, too."

"Progress?"

"Some."

"Some?"

"I know who took the paintings."

"And?"

"I'm waiting for some leverage to make one flip."

"Leverage?"

"He likes girls. His wife wouldn't like it."

"When?"

"Today, probably."

"Probably?"

"Like I said, I'm waiting. For a photo."

"Photo a sure thing?"

"I haven't seen it, but I commissioned it. Anyway, I don't have to have the photo to talk to the goofball."

"So not probably."

"Today. Is fifty really all you can do?"

"Fifty."

"That's not a lot for three pips. They comp on the Web much higher than that."

I had done my homework and comped the goodies prior to arranging them to be gigged. There's an art auction Web site where you can look up auction sales, how much works by various artists have gone for at Sotheby's and other houses. Appraisers use the site. I have to pay for access, but that's an easy write-off. All together the Hoffman, Le Marr, and Ramirez would have cost a million five to replace with comparable works by the same artist. A fence would pay at most ten cents to the dollar and like I said low-ball the value. With insurers the appraisals are aboveboard and verifiable, so I expect fifteen percent to settle an item. I should have been getting a hundred fifty grand, or even a hundred at the low end. My part of that would be forty, so after I paid Scanlon's monkey I'd still be keeping my head above water.

"Fifty."

"Max, that's not a lot of incentive for the businessman with the goodies. He can maybe get that in swag without risking exposure."

"The industry is cutting fees. Looking at alternatives."

"What kind of alternatives?"

"New deterrents. New recovery methods."

"Is my part in this being phased out? I'd like to know."

"You're cozy."

"Cozy?"

"Too cozy."

"I'm a clever guy, but not always smart. I don't get what you're saying."

"The missing Henris stank."

"Max, I had hoped we were past that."

"USA is not past having to do a partial settlement. We don't pay so they can swag."

"Like I said, they only took four. Somebody at the museum must have taken the other three."

"Believe a thief?"

"I do. They're just people, Max. They're business people who are interested in making money through mutual benefit, profitable relationships, and trust."

"You succeed because you are embedded with thieves."

"Unless the collectors and museums are magically able to protect their goodies, and keep some kind of proper inventory, the art is going to be stolen. How are you going to get the goodies back if you don't find the goofballs who took them?"

"What if there were no more goofballs?"

I shrugged. "I don't follow."

"If the stealing stops, the payouts stop."

"How's that going to happen?"

"Alternatives."

I don't know if you noticed, but we'd come in a circle, which meant to me he had told me as much as he was going to.

"Well, in this case, your alternatives may be very limited by the fifty figure. This goofball already has a buyer, and the art may already have changed hands, meaning I may have to step beyond my target and go after whoever he sold it to. My costs go up with that, not down. And here you want to pay less."

"A fence?"

"Probably."

"I hear there's one less."

"One less?"

"One less fence."

I'd forgotten to look in the paper about Jo-Ball's head explosion, and was sure that they would have reported that he was the beloved maître d' of Dominic's, Brooklyn's favorite Italian eatery. Max, of course, knew better.

"That's true."

"I hear you were there."

"I was."

"Why?"

I shrugged. "Keeping my ear to the ground. That's what I do."

"So do we."

I didn't know if he was implying anything, like that they'd heard I was shopping and settling. To have asked him what he meant might tip my mitt, so I brushed aside the remark.

"I'll do my best with the fifty, but that figure is a low percentage play."

"Maybe your percentage is too high."

I wasn't going to let him have the satisfaction of imposing his negativity, even though I had a brief fantasy of folding the little Japanese table in half on his head.

"My percentage is what it is. Like yours."

His chopsticks actually paused, causing his eating interval to change from forty seconds to forty-five.

"Mine?"

"Everybody has their percentage. I earn mine, so I get mine. My fees are based on the comps and save you guys big bucks."

I couldn't believe it, but his eyes showed what I can only describe as curiosity. He's a client, and you always let your client keep the upper hand, or let them think they have it over on you. Right up until the point they start hinting they don't need you. Or that you need them. At that point you become the whipping boy.

Tommy Davin is nobody's whipping boy.

I took that opportunity to stand up over my doll chair and leave. I think what I left unsaid was clear enough. If he wouldn't pay what the price was, I'd find somebody else who would.

EXITING THE CARROLL STREET SUBWAY station back in Brooklyn, I still had reason to be hopeful that in a week I'd have the fifteen grand if not more. Hopeful that all I had to do was lean on Huey with the photo of him going into and coming out of that green loft. I'd take a healthy percentage of whatever he got from Ms. French and price Max out even if he offered more.

I checked my e-mail, but the incriminating photos hadn't come through. As soon as they did, I'd go visit the bistro and show Huey the pix on my phone, make the goofball give me the money or have his meal ticket punched. The bistro was named after his wife; Ariel owned it. Huey was her employee. For now.

You'd think I had enough to worry about, like that it was windy on Smith Street and I had to make sure my hundred-dollar hat didn't fly off.

I was still worried about the cats, though—whether Tigsy had his shot and Herman had eaten. I had hopes that Snuggles and Lady were bringing projectile vomiting and shitting to a new, unprecedented level at the expense of Gustav's wits.

Without the incriminating Bridget photo, I didn't even want to stroll by the bistro and maybe run into Huey smoking out front. I could have walked around the block to my place and checked out the progress on my new front door. Until I caught a reflection of myself in the window of the Neapolitan Barber Shop. Of the new hat. Of my hair.

I'd never walked into the Neapolitan Barber Shop but decided to give it a shot. There are faded red curtains framing the shop window, and a mural of Capri fills the back wall. The wall to the right of the mural was mirrors and giant red and chrome barber chairs. Standing next to and about as tall as one of the chairs was a golden brown man. He was in a smock, sixties, with a golden brown pompadour. It wasn't a toupee, but a work of his own art crafted from hair dye and probably six pounds of hair spray. The artist's toothy smile showed obvious pride in his creation. I'd of course seen this guy and his hair around the neighborhood, and through the shop window, but like Sammy he didn't know me from nobody.

He had an old-world Italian accent. "You a-shaved!"

I guess he did recognize me.

So I says, "That's what they keep telling me. I'm Tommy Davin."

"I know who you are. I am Guiseppe Contagliere, but my customers call me Jocko." He tilted his head at the barber chair. "Sit!"

I hesitated. To tell you the truth, in all the years I'd been in the neighborhood, I'd probably seen a customer in Jocko's place maybe five times. I felt sorry for the old guy, guessed he'd seen Carroll Gardens go from a family neighborhood in the fifties to a war zone in the seventies and now booming with gentrification. His place, like Dominic's Restaurant, and a handful of other places, was a tiny island of the past in a rising sea of hipsters and real estate speculators. Jocko probably owned the building and didn't need to cut hair except that it was what he'd always done and needed to do to get up in the morning. The barbershop would turn into a mod dress shop or brioche hut the second they were patting the dirt on Jocko's grave.

I dropped my overcoat and new hat on one chair and sat in the other.

Jocko swept a sheet over me, and fit my neck with a slip of tissue before cinching the bib tight to my Adam's apple. Years of sitting in a stylist's chair had made me forget the barber experience, the smell of the bay rum and talcum. I was suddenly eight years old again, my pop sitting by the barbershop window reading a racing form and smoking a White Owl Invincible.

I watched Jocko's polished black shoe kick a wooden box next to the chair, and he stood on it. Good thing. Without it, all he'd be trimming was my armpits.

"Tommy, you hava lotta hair. How much you want Jocko to take?" He was leaning in close, the brown shelf of his pompadour perfect above his deeply wrinkled face. Juicy Fruit was on his breath.

He held the scissors up, ready to go at it. I was now worried not just about the money and the cats, but about getting the dorky haircut I had when I was eight, the one where the hair in back always stood up. I put a hand up to my earlobe.

"Bring it up to here. But make sure the hair in back doesn't stand up, OK, Jocko? It's very important my hair in back stays long enough that it doesn't stand up."

He put a hand on my chest. "Tommy, what kinda barber would Jocko be if he make the hair in back stand up? Eh? I been in this business for fifty years." He stomped on a pedal, and the chair jerked backward to where I was half laying down. The scissors began to flash.

Well, at least I was helping this poor old guy out like I'd been thinking about doing for twenty years. My stylist could maybe fix whatever damage he did.

"OK if I make a phone call, Jocko?"

"Sure, sure . . ." He was hacking away on one side, and I dialed a number and put my phone to the other.

A deep voice that sounded sleepy but musical answered. "Walter here."

"Walter. Tom Davin."

"Tommy, honey, how are you? You back in Vegas? I have a new show at the Starlight. You and Yvette should come, I'll comp you tickets. I have some new dresses that are fantasmo, nothing but, fit me perfectly. I lost four and a half pounds."

Just so you know, Walter is a female impersonator, very talented. I thought I should mention this because you could get confused about who I was talking to. Walter and Yvette were friends. As much as anybody in Vegas showbiz are friends, anyway.

"We split, Walter. You haven't heard from her?"

There was a sob on the other end. See? That wouldn't make any sense unless you knew Walter was light in the loafers. I can't describe what he looked like while I talked to him, but you can be sure he was in some sort of silk robe.

So Walter says, "I am so sorry, Tommy."

"It's best, Walter, believe me. Look, I can't talk long. The point is I have her cats, she left them with me, but somebody took them."

He says, *"Oh my God."*

So I says, "Yeah, and there was a note saying if she wants her cats back she has to see Gustav. You know who he is?"

"Oh my God."

"So you know who he is?"

"I don't feel comfortable talking about Gustav."

I rolled my eyes, and switched the phone to the other ear to make way for Jocko. "Sweetheart, the point is, I'm a little worried about the cats. Sure, she stuck them with me when she took off, and I'm glad they're gone, but just the same, I hate to think this guy Gustav might hurt them if Yvette doesn't contact him. I don't know where she is and frankly don't want to know, but if you have some way of finding her—"

"On it, Tommy. I know a *lot* of people who know a *lot* of people."

"I appreciate it, Walter. I have no idea how she should get in touch with this catnapper, that's her problem. I don't want anything more to do with Yvette. Her cats, her problem. But that's no reason the cats should suffer."

"Catnapper? *Ha ha ha.* That's fantasmo. You are such a scream sometimes, Tommy, I swear. Look, I'll put the bloodhounds on this and let you know."

"Thanks. Hope the new show is a smash, honey. I'll come see it next time I'm in Vee."

"Ciao!"

The call was over, and I looked at my e-mail. No photo yet.

Jocko stomped on a pedal, and the chair popped upright. He now went to work on the back of my head.

I says, "Not too short, OK?"

So he says, "You know, there was a day that I cut the hair of John Gotti?"

Gotti was a famous Brooklyn mobster in the eighties.

"No shit?"

"Right in this chair."

"No shit?"

"It's true, right in this chair." Jocko was behind me snip-snipping. "If I mess up the back of Gotti's head, the hair there, which was very thin, he have me killed. I still alive. So now you think I mess up the back of *your* head? Eh? You have a lotta hair back here, Tommy. Too much. It is good you came to me. You going to Johnny's funeral tomorrow?"

"You knew One-Ball?"

"Of course. My customer for many years, the week before he died. Terrible what happened to him. You were there, so you know. Of course it will be a closed casket. Someone must have been very angry to kill him this way. Some of course think it is the Black Hand."

I guessed as the local barber, he was expected to know everything about everybody. Even so, his words gave me hope that somehow Johnny's death had nothing to do with me, that the second shot was maybe something to throw the cops off.

So I says, "Jocko, I knew Johnny for many years, like yourself. A wonderful person."

"Yes."

"A family man. Until his divorce."

"Yes."

"Beautiful kids. Except the daughter."

"Yes."

"You've been around a long time, though, Jocko. Sometimes you have a window only into certain things about a person, at a certain level, but not more."

"*Yes.*"

"See, I knew Johnny professionally, not just at the restaurant, if you know what I mean."

"Yes, yes, of course."

"Well, I didn't really figure he was that mobbed up to get taken out like that. Their style is to squeeze someone like Jo-Ball for all he's worth and next you know he's in the canal bobbing for jellyfish. A sniper just isn't their style. That's West Coast shit. And let's be honest. The wiseguys aren't around so much anymore. I don't doubt Johnny may have paid some sort of vig to the local association, but . . ."

I felt the straight razor begin to scrape the back of my neck, and I tensed. That brought back memories. Scared the hell out of me when I was a really little kid in the barber chair, I don't know why. Made me cry.

In the mirror, Jocko's brown pompadour and brown face appeared over my left shoulder, the gleaming old straight razor in his hand. "Are you asking me a question, Tommy?"

His wet old eyes locked onto mine, unblinking. I couldn't tell if he was pissed off or not. I didn't really like the way he was holding the straight razor.

"Can I tell you something, Jocko, mano a mano?"

His brown eyes sparked with interest. "I would be honored, Tommy, to have your confidence."

"You know I was there when he was shot."

"Yes."

"There was a second shot, and it just missed me."

"Ohhhh . . ."

"You see? I don't know if they were really trying to kill me or just took a shot at me as a witness or what. I would value your opinion of this matter."

Jocko touched the flat of the razor blade to his chin. Thoughtfully, his eyes turned on the shop's front windows. He stepped off his box and circled around in front of me. He pursed his lips and gestured at me with the razor.

"It used to be that a barber would be asked by the Black Hand to perform services. A customer in a barber chair is . . . unsuspecting."

There was an awkward pause that caused me a little anxiety. He was freaking me out a little with that razor, and I couldn't tell if he was doing it on purpose or I was just edgy. I mean, from what I said, why would he go at me with the razor? Because I was asking if Johnny was more mobbed up than the local deli? It sounded like Jocko himself had accommodated the mob, had set up people in the barber chair to be diced. Or worse: that on command, he'd slit customers' throats. It was possible. Some of these old-time Sicilian guys are pretty touchy about the Cosa Nostra.

I was getting mentally ready to defend myself, trying not to look at the door, or on the counter for some sort of weapon. Though in truth, I could make pretty good work of this old guinea shrimp with one swing of the fist, just below the pompadour.

I had to say something, even at the risk of inviting trouble, so I said, "I'm a clever guy, Jocko, but not always too smart. I'm not following what you're saying."

Where he was standing I could probably have kicked him in the face, too.

Then he says, "Ah, but the barber can hardly be blamed. He has to look out for his family. There are all kinds of barbers."

Now I had goose bumps.

"I still don't follow, Jocko."

He looked at the floor. "Nobody would blame you, Tommy."

"Blame me? Jocko, for Christ sake, what are you talking about?"

He made a slight shrug, the type one makes when trying to forget something unpleasant. "You were his friend. You stepped outside with him. This is all very natural."

I stared at him a moment, and then laughed. "You're joking."

His eyes had the patina of shame in them, and they met mine in the mirror. "This is what they are saying in the neighborhood."

"That it was me who set him up to get his head blown off?"

"You were his competitor."

"Friends first. Competitors second."

"He was Italian."

"Yeah, so?"

"Certain people . . . they are unhappy."

The goose bumps were back, and they were on top of other goose bumps. I leaned forward as he turned with shave cream steaming in his hand.

"Certain people?"

"Certain people."

"How can I talk to these certain people and tell them I had nothing to do with it?"

"The funeral is tomorrow at the Viscotti funeral home, on Carroll. I will be there. They will be there."

"Jocko, please tell me: Are these certain people really *really* pissed off or can this actually wait until tomorrow?"

He looked at his razor, then at me. "Wait until tomorrow."

Don't ask me why I let him finish the haircut, with the straight razor behind my head. Maybe it was because if the Mafia was going to kill me I'd rather have it done sooner than later. Save me a lot of running around trying to raise fifteen grand for the pink monkey.

FIFTEEN

I WALKED DOWN SMITH STREET feeling the back of my neck. It had been a long time since it had been exposed like that, and I felt kind of naked in the breezy fall morning. On the other hand, the feeling of having so much less hair was also kind of liberating. I was lighter, sharper. I would need to be if the Mafia was after me.

Then again, it could have been that my lighter step was just the result of not having my throat slit by Jocko.

Of course, now I had one more thing I didn't need on my plate: the local Mafia pissed off with me, thinking I killed Jo-Ball. At least I knew when and where to straighten that out.

Anyway, in a matter of moments I hoped to have things straightened out with Huey and get my due on those paintings. I was ready to confront Huey, and I could see him just up ahead in front of his wife's bistro, smoking and nervous. His white hair glowed in the yellow October sun.

I was on the southwest corner of the intersection and waiting for the traffic to clear the crosswalk. My phone buzzed. An e-mail had come in, and I stopped to read it. I shaded the screen with my hand to look at the attached photo. Yup. There was ol' Huey slipping into Bridget's green loft building. The picture was small, but I could see that white hair and hunched frame.

I looked up from the screen. Huey was eyeing me from across the intersection. He was in the midst of taking a deep suck of smoke.

I gave a little two-fingered wave, and then he seemed to recognize me. I think he was staring at me thinking I looked familiar but couldn't place me.

He flicked his smoke into the gutter, and gave me one of those little French shrugs as I approached.

"Huey, what do you have for me?" A gust of wind almost took my hat, and I grabbed it.

"Tommy, what can I say?"

"You can say what you were doing at Billy Bank yesterday, and tell me what you put in storage."

His eyes narrowed, flitted across the passing pedestrians. Some fast thinking was going on.

"Huey, it was a cute move, but I know where you've been the last twenty-four hours. All I care about is that I get my original cut, forty grand. All in all, I think that's pretty fair. If it got around about this monkey business, you might find it hard to put together a string or sell. I'd never settle any more goodies for you, that's for sure. Either that or get me those paintings back."

"I cannot."

"Cannot what?"

"I never had the paintings. It's too late anyway."

"Never too late for me to show Ariel this." I took out my phone with one hand and pointed to the screen with the other. "That's you going in to see Bridget."

Huey didn't look well all of a sudden.

"You cannot!" He began fumbling with his cigarettes and shook a smoke onto the ground before his trembling fingers shook out another one into his lips.

"Maybe you *cannot*, but I *can*—and *will*. What the hell is wrong with you anyway? Are you screwy? You think I'm just going to shrug and walk away from this money?"

A gust flipped my hat off, and I chased it about thirty feet along the sidewalk until I trapped it in the gutter at Degraw Street.

I heard a weird sound over the traffic, like a butcher's knife halving a pineapple.

I dusted off my hat and looked back at Huey.

The right side of Huey's head was gone.

He staggered, unsure of what had happened, but only his left eye and the nose remained—the other upper half was splattered on the bistro's windows.

How he was able to move or think with a big chunk of his brain gone is anybody's guess, but he was still standing exhaling smoke. Huey lifted his right hand and pawed that side of his head.

Some people approaching him on the sidewalk did a triple take, and I saw one of them try to say something to him, something stupid like "Are you alright?"

Huey's left eye actually looked at the guy. Then the eye looked worried.

This stranger actually took off his jacket and went to hold it against Huey's head, to stop the bleeding or hold the remaining brains in place. Nice guy. I'm not sure I would have done that for a stranger, much less that rat Huey, much less for a guy who was obviously a goner. Huey pulled away from the Samaritan and tried to go back into the bistro, but his hands were unable to grasp the door handle. He lost his balance and stumbled, and the Samaritan tried to break his fall.

It was then that my latest murder-induced fog lifted and I

noticed something screwy. I mean screwier than seeing my second sniper victim in two days. I noted that the blood was sprayed
on the glass bistro windows directly behind where Huey had been
standing.

I realized this meant the shot came from street level, from
across the street, from someone on the sidewalk or in a car or in a
shop within eyeshot.

Give me a golf clap for this amazing insight. What I really
should have been thinking was about that angry bumblebee. *Was
another bullet coming for me?*

Pedestrians had stopped in their tracks trying to see what had
happened and make sense of it.

That's what made the shooter stand out.

He was making tracks while everybody else was standing still,
gawking. Then he looked right at me as he was turning the corner
onto Sackett Street.

He was tall, young, and pale, with full lips and big rosy cheeks.
Or I guess his face was just flushed with emotion. His hair was
light brown and cut short so it stuck out like long fuzz on his head.
He was in a dark sweatshirt and sweat pants and white tennis
shoes. Looked like he'd just come from the gym. Except there was
a trench coat over his right arm and hand. Anyway, he looked like
a kid, not at all what I expected of a sniper.

When we made eye contact, we both knew he'd been made.

I realized this was the rosy-cheeked kid I'd seen outside the
scrap yard the night before.

I crossed the street toward him, walking fast. I didn't want to
run until the kid did, but he was out of sight. My hands were flex-
ing, jonesing to smash that punk face in and roll him up into a ball
with his trench coat and kick him down the street to the precinct.

I turned the corner and looked down Sackett toward Hoyt Street. No punk.

Hoyt Street paralleled Smith Street the way Court did but on the other side and with an inverse property value. Beyond Hoyt was Bond Street and then the Gowanus Canal. The farther down that way you went the more industrial it got, but with little pockets of residential, and maybe the stray struggling art gallery. One day it might be nice down in Gowanus. The speculators were counting on it. It hadn't happened yet.

Sackett Street in this block was lined with sycamores and brownstone building stoops, probably thirty or forty on each side of the street. The punk couldn't have made it all the way to Hoyt Street in the short time he'd been out of eyeshot. He would be hiding behind one of the stoops, or in a doorway.

I scrunched the hat back on my head until it came down to my ears, scanning the stoops. Behind me, I heard a police car bloop its siren, a local patrol car dropping in to see what all the fuss was about at the bistro. The cops would be no help to me. If I tried getting a couple patrolmen to help me search for the kid, I would only spend a half hour convincing them I knew what I was talking about. Besides, I couldn't take my eyes off the stoops for a second, and I couldn't walk down Sackett toward Hoyt without risking an ambush—and I had to guess he still had that gun.

So I waited, listening to my breath coming fast and hard. I hadn't even begun to chase the punk, but my body was getting ready for some serious exercise. If he made like a jackrabbit I would, too. I'm an older rabbit, though. He could probably distance me. Plus he had tennis shoes. I wasn't exactly in cowboy boots, but my leather street shoes weren't exactly track shoes.

Thirty seconds passed. It was long enough that I heard an

ambulance wail in the distance, and the crowds behind me thick-
ened with people murmuring about what had happened.

His head was gone.

Gone?

Part of his head just exploded.

Exploded?

Who was it?

Anybody we know?

At the bistro?

Was he shot?

The white-haired guy.

He smoked. A lot.

Then down Sackett I heard some commotion. I began to walk
toward it.

On my right, ahead, a woman was shouting.

The kid came stumbling out from behind a stoop, chased by an
old woman with bright orange hair and a broom. He'd been hiding in her doorway, and she was chasing him out. She took a swing
at him with the broom and hit the trench coat that was still over
his arm.

An ugly black gun fell from under the trench coat and clattered
onto the sidewalk. It wasn't a pistol, but it wasn't a rifle, either,
something in between. It looked like it might be a folding gun of
some kind. What I know about guns could fill a fortune cookie.
The short barrel seemed really thick.

The punk's eyes met mine.

I was about fifty feet away.

His hand reached for the gun, and all the scared drained out of
his pupils. The rosy cheeks were gone. His face was ashen, serious.
Deadly.

It was at that moment I remembered about the angry bee that had missed me the day before.

I'm going to take a second here to do my tantric exercise because just telling this part brings back the anxiety of that moment.

Breathe slowly in through the nose; close the eyes.

Breathe slowly out through the lips; stroke back my hair.

Breathe slowly in through the nose; open the eyes.

Breathe slowly out through the lips.

Crouched over, he lifted the gun in both hands and pointed the fat barrel at me.

I stopped walking. There had been no time to dodge this way or that, hide, nothing. I was too far away to charge him. I was basically screwed.

The old lady was still barking at him—she must not have seen the gun. She didn't seem to because she hauled off and clobbered the punk in the face with the broom.

An angry bee went over my head, and then I heard the chop of the gun going off. I say chop because it was the sound of the butcher knife through the pineapple. The gun had some kind of silencer on it.

The kid fell back onto his butt, dropping the gun again. That's when the old woman saw the weapon. She shrieked and vanished back into her brownstone like a witch back into her cave.

I charged.

The kid grabbed for the gun.

I was thirty feet from him.

His hand lifted the gun by the fat barrel.

Twenty feet.

He spun the gun and cocked it.

Ten feet.

He pointed the gun.

I kicked it out of his hands and jumped over him. At top speed, there was no stopping unless I tried to plow into him on the sidewalk and come face-to-face with the gun. If he'd rolled away I'd have smashed into the sidewalk.

The gun clattered into the roadway between two parked cars and vanished under one of them. I pivoted, and the kid lunged for the gun.

I got to him before he could dive under the car. Instead the punk rolled away and onto his feet. He lit out toward Hoyt, full tilt down the center of the street.

I crammed my new hat down on my head and went after him.

You know how I said I won't be anybody's whipping boy? Well, I don't like being shot at, either. It makes me really anxious, and then I want to act out. Act out like by twisting the shooter's head off and stomping on it.

The kid cut right on Hoyt's sidewalk. I was thirty feet back, my overcoat flapping behind me.

He zigged across the street; I zigged across the street.

I followed him as he went left on Union Street, down a long slope, and then right on Bond Street. Parking and boarded-up factories were on the left, crappy residential buildings on the right.

We passed Bridget's green loft building. Huey wouldn't be using any more sheets there, poor son of a bitch. I flashed on the image of him standing in front of the blood-splattered bistro not knowing part of his head was missing. That's too pathetic for words. Even if he was ripping me off, or trying to, I don't wish that indignity on anybody. Huey was a crook, and by double-crossing me he was only doing what crooks do, and you'll note that I never said anything real mean about him even though he was screwing me over. That's bad energy.

It was the punk forty feet ahead that did that to poor Huey.

I ran harder, puffing pretty good, my leather shoes slamming the pavement. Like I said, I was prepared to act out, so I had adrenaline working for me, and probably some endorphins, too. It helped that the kid wasn't as fast as I thought he would be for his age. I wondered if maybe he wasn't as young as I had thought he was. Or maybe he just wasn't athletic.

When the punk heard my footsteps come closer, he sped up, pulling away as he rounded the corner left onto Carroll Street, toward the bridge over the Gowanus Canal.

I think I mentioned somewhere that I'd been in that neighborhood for twenty years or more. In all that time, I'd never seen one of the little iron and wood drawbridges across the canal open.

Until then.

You can hardly believe these drawbridges still work, they're so old. The striped wooden gates to close the road had to be put in place by hand, and the bridge itself slid to the side, on rails like a train, pulled by cables. I kid you not, they almost have to be cranked by hand. There was a yellow Department of Transportation van parked at the other side of the bridge, with one DOT guy on each side, manning the striped gates.

I saw the kid veer away from the DOT guy on this side, who shouted something.

There was nowhere for the kid to go. The right and left sides of the street were sheet metal fences, and there was no climbing them.

An oil barge was where the bridge would have been, moving slowly, and I saw the kid speed up, even though the DOT guy was waving his arms and shouting at him.

Pretty obvious what the kid had in mind: a jump to the barge, and then maybe make it to the far side. The barge was about thirty feet wide, the canal maybe a hundred. The boat was closer to the near side.

Let me mention that the Gowanus Canal, though much better than it used to be, is still a nasty waterway. Sure, ten years before it had giant algae blooms and you couldn't even see the bottom. You could practically walk across it. Since a cleanup effort, people had seen a fish or two, and you'd see the hipsters with silly grins paddling kayaks in there, maybe imagining they were in some pristine river in the Rockies. The fact of the matter? The Gowanus Canal was not pristine. It usually smelled bad. Any time we had a serious rain, the sewers overflowed into the canal. That's when you learned how popular condoms are as birth control—and these condoms floated on the surface, in the slick of oil from leaky underground heating fuel tanks in the area.

I'm just saying, but the Gowanus Canal is *unpristine*.

So I'm hot on the punk's tail, hoping more or less he ends up in the water, because I'd always wanted to see some deserving scumbag fall in there. The punk fit the bill.

He ran around the end of the striped gate, upsetting the DOT man even more. At the edge of the bridge he took a flying leap for the barge, arms waving in the air.

I felt cheated.

He landed on his side on the barge's deck. There isn't any crew on these barges—they're pushed by tugs from behind.

I approached the edge.

You don't think for a second I'd risk falling in that water, after I just described how unpristine it was? I stopped, and watched as the kid got to his feet. Looked like he'd hurt his shoulder, as he had trouble getting up and staggering to the far edge of the barge.

Now what, I wondered. He still had fifty feet of unpristine canal between him and the far shore. I could see him trying to decide what to do. Jump in, swim for it?

The DOT guy was suddenly in my face.

He says to me, "Hey, prick, whaddaya think you're doing, huhn?"

I was in no mood for this. Of course, if I let every dickhead like that make me act out I'd've been in prison a long time ago.

At the same time, it's not good to bottle up your emotions. So I snarled.

It's hard to describe my snarl except to say that when I do it, I feel ten feet tall and ten feet wide and ready to flip cars and breathe fire. Based on people's reaction I'd say I must look the way I feel.

So I snarled, and the DOT guy went white and scampered off down the block.

I turned back to the kid.

He was still standing on the edge of the barge. The gap to his escape was getting wider as the tug steered the barge clear of the bridge and toward the pilings to dock.

I saw the punk consider getting off at the bulkhead on my side of the canal, but he looked back at me and decided against it.

He hopped off the far side of the barge into the canal, feet first.

I tried not to gag.

I couldn't see him again until he had splashed almost to the far-side bulkhead, where he grabbed onto some orange construction fencing that dangled into the water. There was a telephone company yard there, and the fence was being replaced. The orange plastic fence covered a gap between the new and old fence. He began to try to climb out. It was either climb out there or he'd have to swim a good distance up or down the canal to find another place out.

The telephone company maintenance yard had an entrance next to the Union Street bridge over the canal, two blocks north.

I began running to Union Street, but much of my wind had left me. Stopping like that had got me out of the flow, and made my muscles harden up. I reached the telephone truck yard entrance a couple minutes later.

There was a security shack at the telephone yard entrance at the corner of Nevins Street, and I jogged past it into the lot.

Someone with an accent shouted "Hey!" behind me, but I ignored it, making for the line of white telephone trucks at the bulkhead.

I found wet footprints at the bulkhead and followed them across the blacktop until they petered out at a back entrance to the maintenance building. A middle-aged Polish rent-a-cop stepped into my path. He couldn't have looked more scared if he had stood in the path of a rampaging grizzly bear. I guess I must have looked pretty ferocious, what with all the sweat and that hat pulled down to my ears, huffing and puffing. He was shaking, but he was determined to do what he was paid to do.

How did I know he was Polish? They mostly have these bushy mustaches that come all the way down to their chins. Mostly just the men.

I kid.

He says, "I need see eye-dee badge!" He seemed to be waiting for me to kill him.

You're expecting me to roar at the guy, right? For whatever reason I felt sorry for this guy, because this was probably the only time in his career as a rent-a-cop that he ever had to confront anybody, and it turned out to be a giant sweaty man in an overcoat, a stupid sweater, and a fedora squeezed on my head like a bottle cap.

"You see a guy climb out of the water?"

"Oh yes. No eye-dee. He go. Now you no eye-dee, you must go. What a day."

"Where did he go?"

"To bus."

"What bus?"

"He ask bus, I send to Third Avenue. What a day!"

I patted him on the shoulder, and he practically jumped out of his skin. "Thanks."

I went back out to Union Street and jogged to Third Avenue. This is where the neighborhood starts to get more residential again, and where until recently the biggest employer was the South Brooklyn Casket Company. That's right. Coffins.

At the corner, I could see the bus in the distance, down around Second Street. I'd never catch the bus four blocks down.

At the same time, and even taking into account that I was winded, sagging, and soggy from sweat, it seemed a shame to lose the punk when I still had him in my sights.

I waved a twenty-dollar bill at passing town cars. If you wave cash they know you're not with the Taxi and Limousine Commission, and you can hail one faster. If you were a TLC agent, getting them to stop by waving cash would be entrapment. That's what they tell me.

The second town car stopped, and I got in. The bus was pretty far gone, but we caught up to it just after Ninth Street, and I had the driver zoom around it and drop me one stop ahead of the bus.

I hailed the bus and got on. I fished out my fare card and paid.

The kid wasn't on the bus. So I went back to the driver, an older black guy with baggy eyes that told me he had seen it all several times over.

"A kid get on the bus around Union Street? He was all wet, soaking wet."

"Smelled bad, too. You a cop?"

"Something like that."

He snorted like he'd heard that response a thousand times since noon. "I kicked him out around Seventh Street. Had no fare."

While I was in the town car I had been so fixated on the bus that we may have driven right past the murdering punk and I didn't catch a glimpse of him. That sucked.

"I see. Thanks. You can let me out next stop."

"Of course."

I hailed another town car and asked him to take me home by way of Bond Street. I had a feeling Smith Street would be taped off by the police as they tried to figure out what happened to Huey's head and what happened to the guy in the fedora who chased a kid who dropped a gun on Sackett Street.

No way did I want the cops snooping into my business with Huey.

The car dropped me at Degraw and Bond. As I neared Hoyt I could see that Smith Street was blocked off by cop cars. I slid out of my damp overcoat and took off my hat, which was soaked through with sweat around the band. I kept my head down and my hat behind my back. They might be looking for a big guy in a fedora.

I walked to my place and tromped heavily up the stairs. My legs felt like they were full of sand.

In the vestibule I was reminded of the phone call I'd made first thing that morning.

My front door looked like a bank vault. That's a slight exaggeration, but the wood door frame now had brushed steel reinforcements at the hinges and locks. Yeah, that's *locks*. There were now two, the old one and a new one in a fancy brushed steel plate. That meshed with more brushed steel in the doorjamb where the dead bolt latched. So my front door, which previously was all wood and delicately Victorian, was now part Frankenstein. Let the werewolf do his worst, he wouldn't get past this monster.

However, it hadn't kept werewolf Gustav from tucking another love note under the door. He must have been there recently, after they installed the door, maybe even while I was chasing that punk. It said YVETTE on the front, just like before.

I found the key, which was also made of gleaming brushed steel and had four edges, not just one. I slid it in the lock and felt five bolts unclick and snap out of the latch. There was a clean mechanical *ka-chunk* with the turn of the key. A reassuring *ka-chunk*.

I tossed the second love letter on top of the one from the day before and closed the door behind me. The inside of the door wasn't quite as ironclad; I guess it didn't need to be. There was a bill on the bar for five hundred, even. Not sure where I'd come up with that money, but needless to say the pink monkey had dibs.

I stripped out of my clothes and took a shower, one that used up everything the hot water heater had.

Still in my towel, I fell heavily on my bed and groaned.

The squares in the tin ceiling had a complicated but repetitive pattern that was soothing to stare at, almost therapeutic. My feet hurt. I hoped I didn't get blisters.

Would have been nice to catch that punk.

SIXTEEN

My Heart, Yvette:

I do not know if this oaf has given you my first letter. It is
best if he has. Yet I know you must feel my essence no matter
where you are. Surely you know I am here, I am searching.
Will you not reveal yourself? Will you not emerge as the sun
on the ocean, a radiant blossom of beauty for which there is
no compare? It is tedious here in Brooklyn, watching, waiting, following, trying to compel this oaf to lead me to you.
He is an idiot, and his apartment smells. His small brain
cannot understand the zevasta warnings that in our country are so well known to eons of traditions. How you could
be with such a man is incomprehensible. Wherever you are,
do not delay, delicate flower of the dewy meadow.

The cats are fine, but I now understand why the oaf's apartment smells.

Cascades of petals—

Gustav

SEVENTEEN

MY EYES OPENED. IT WAS dark. I'd slept.

Someone was knocking on my new Godzilla-proof door. I kept the lights off and put my eye to the peephole.

It was Frank and Kootie. You know, Huey's boys, the ugly one and the muscle.

I was all quiet like, just looking, when Frank says, "Tommy, we're here to make peace."

I let a beat go by—basically still trying to wake up and get a handle on all that had gone down, that it wasn't some screwy dream. What the hell time was it anyway?

"OK, you boys go around the corner to the tiki bar. I'll meet you in the back room there by the fireplace in fifteen or so."

I watched them exchange a dark glance and exit the foyer to the street.

Yeah, there's a tiki bar around the corner from me on Smith Street. Back in the day, when I was a kid, my parents would take the family out to a restaurant near Times Square called Hawaii Kai. They had hula dancers, the crazy bamboo decor, wild drinks, and a doorman that was a midget. Naturally, me and my kid sister, Kate, loved the place. It was like Disneyland to us. Then suddenly in the eighties it seemed all the Polynesian restaurants became passé, which means out of fashion. Now they seemed to be coming back, because there was one right around the corner from me and it was pretty popular with the hipsters. Not so popular with me, though. The crowd was too young, the music too loud. Which suited my purposes that night. If I was going to meet Frank and Kootie, it had to be in a public place where nobody could hear our conversation but us.

I had to be careful. I didn't know exactly what they wanted. Two days, two guys, two less heads. Then again, the kid had lost his gun; it might take him a while to find another. New York isn't exactly Texas. Guns and ammo are hard to come by in the five boroughs.

A pair of jeans from ten years back, a sweatshirt, and a long raincoat was the new casual outfit. There was no rain, but I'd sweat out the sweater and the top coat. They were still damp.

The police still had Smith Street north of Degraw taped off. Bright work lights lit up the block in front of the bistro. Still searching the crime scene for the bullet maybe, I didn't know.

Frank and Kootie were in back of the tiki bar at a low table, across from two couples at the fireplace. I kid you not: a tiki bar with a fireplace. This was Brooklyn, after all, not Waikiki, and October. Frank had a glass of brown liquid I assumed to be whiskey of some kind, while Kootie sipped an ultralight beer.

They were like a pair of meatballs at an Italian wake: nervous and gloomy. I stood over them.

"What's what, fellas?"

So Frank says, "We admit we took the paintings for ourselves. That was Huey's idea, it was his gig, we played along, what were we supposed to do? But as God is my witness, Tommy, we don't have those fucking paintings, and we didn't get our cut."

Kootie flexed his jaw.

"Why you telling me this?" See, Huey wasn't supposed to tell these idiots who he was working for, or about me. Ever hear of how in California, when it's on fire, they cut down a bunch of trees so the fire won't jump place to place? In our business, you try to leave gaps in who knows what so if one person gets hooked by the fuzz the damage doesn't spread. As we've seen, though, Huey thought he could make deviled eggs in the shell.

The two goofballs exchanged a glance.

Kootie says, "We figure you tweaked Huey for the double-cross. That's the word on the street."

Then Frank says, "And maybe had Jo-Ball tweaked, I dunno. We're just saying there's no need to be crisp with us. We'll do what we can to make right, but tweaking us won't get you anything. We don't have the paintings or our cut. I wish we did." He looked kind of upset about that last part in particular.

They thought I killed Jo-Ball and Huey because I was double-crossed. These idiots didn't think that maybe it was the other buyer ripping them off. I was thinking Ms. French ordered the hits, hired Huey, and then tweaked him so she could pocket the whole take. That didn't mean I should ease Frank and Kootie's anxieties. I could use their fragile emotional state to my advantage.

Slowly, I sat down across from them. I looked at one, then the other. With a shake of my big head I sighed and said, "I wish I could believe what it is you just said, Frank."

So Frank starts in again with his Catholic guilt. "Honest to God, Tommy . . ."

Kootie kicks in. "The thing is, we'll help get the paintings if we can and give them to you. Whatever."

I looked all squinty at Kootie. I sensed he lacked sincerity, like they were mostly calling me out to apologize so I wouldn't tweak them. "You say that now. But Huey said he was going to give me the goodies, and he was obviously lying. Instead, he decided that you guys would clip me. Now here you are telling me you'll deliver the goodies, again. Why should I believe you?"

"For Christ sake, Tommy, you think we want our heads exploded, too? Had no idea you were such a hard case . . . that shit is fucked up, man . . . fuck!" Frank spilled his drink in his excitement. "I mean, I understand why you're crisp . . ."

"The thing is, Tommy, whatever." Kootie stared at his beer. "You did what you had to do, fair enough. We're just saying that we're here to help you get the money he got for the gig. And if you want to give us a little something for our trouble, you know . . . whatever."

You had to laugh. These goofballs weren't as concerned about getting killed as not getting their share.

I waved a hand at Frank. "Get yourself set up with another drink. I'll have a brandy."

Kootie and I didn't talk until Frank was back at the table. Anxious eyes were on me.

I says, "Who is the one Huey sold the paintings to?"

Frank makes a face like his gut hurts and says, "Wish we knew, Tommy. All Huey told us is the scam would double up our end."

Kootie cleared his throat. "Thing is, he didn't say much about the upper end."

"Much? What is much? He told you about me, didn't he? I was the upper end until this woman. And he doesn't mention who she was?"

"Sweet Jesus, Tommy, he told us he was protecting us, that it was better we didn't know who she was." Frank took a big gulp of his drink. "What he did say . . . Kootie, tell him, it don't make any sense, for the love of God."

I folded my arms and looked at Kootie, waiting.

He winces, and says kind of quiet, "He said it was a buy back."

I'm not sure I hear it right, so I say, "A buy back?"

The two goofballs nodded together.

"How much were you offered for the paintings?"

"Hundred," they said.

"Your internal split?"

"Me and Frank each got a thirty," Kootie said.

My deal with Huey had been for whatever I could squeeze out of Max. Had I squeezed a hundred I would have bagged forty percent, leaving Huey to split sixty. It was customary for the crew leader to take forty percent, so these two knuckleheads would get eighteen had Huey not double-crossed me. *Had* they been paid.

"You guys met Huey in a coffee shop yesterday. What did you talk about?"

"He was going to pick up our money." Kootie looked like a kid who'd dropped his lollipop.

"He was going to give us our split tonight, like, right now." Frank's lollipop was in the dirt, too. "Shit."

"What if I told you guys I know where the money is?" I was assuming that the money was in the duffel bag Huey put in the storage locker on Third Avenue.

The goofballs leaned in, and Frank knocked his drink over again. "God damn it!"

"It's in a storage locker," I said, "but before I tell you where, you have to get the key."

They nodded eagerly.

"The key to the locker was probably on Huey when he was shot."

Frank perked up. "We'll go to the hospital, put on some scrubs, see if we can find it."

I says, "Hospital?"

So Kootie says, all glum, "He's not dead yet. Whatever. I don't think he's going to make it. His brain is mostly gone."

"Get the key to the storage locker, and then we'll go get the money." I got to my feet. "I'll let you split a single twenty-five share if you pull this off. If not, well . . ."

Smiling, I walked out on them. If I put my hands on the hundred, I'd take Huey's forty percent and give the goofballs their thirty each. My money troubles with the pink monkey would be solved, and I wouldn't care who had the paintings. Maxie could go jump in a lake.

Did I really think these two goofballs could come up with the key? It was a long shot.

Still, it was a shot.

Fortunately not a shot buzzing past my head.

EIGHTEEN

OUTSIDE THE TIKI BAR THE streets were wet. I zipped up my raincoat. Looked like I was the rainmaker of Carroll Gardens. I snapped my fingers, people's heads exploded. I put on my raincoat, it rained.

The clock in the dry cleaners told me it was eight o'clock. My stomach told me I hadn't eaten anything but toast in two days. And I wondered why I was running out of energy chasing that punk who jumped in the canal full of used condoms and fuel oil. That mental picture didn't help my appetite. I did need to eat, though, whether I was hungry or not.

While doing some serious rumination about what was what.

I don't do sushi. That doesn't mean I have something against Orientals or their food. There was a new Thai place a few blocks down. That's actually sort of an ironic thing to say in Carroll Gardens, because there was always some new Thai place opening up on Smith Street. Anyway, I dropped in and ordered some Prom Grom Gam Gluk or whatever it's called, along with some spring rolls. Took the stuff home.

I approached my building carefully, from the opposite side of the street, out of the streetlight glare and in the shadow of the sycamores. If the word on the street was that I was on a rampage making people's heads explode, I might have other visitors, other than Frank and Kootie. Maybe the Mafia, maybe Doh and Crispi from the NYPD, I couldn't be too sure, which is why I really needed to lock myself in for the night and clear my head.

I made it into my apartment, and bolted the front door like I was locking myself in a cell for safekeeping. Instead of shades I have interior wood-slatted shutters on my windows, and I closed them tight before turning on the lights. The punk was still rattling around Brooklyn, and for all I knew he'd tagged himself another sniper rifle.

I dropped in a Cal Tjader CD. He leads his orchestra with a vibraphone, kind of soothing after the kind of day I'd had. I lit an aromatherapy candle on the coffee table.

With a snifter of brandy and my chopsticks, I tucked into the food. On my second snifter, I was looking at the ceiling, chewing the chopsticks instead of the Goo Glop Gam Jam.

This Ms. French had that punk kid out there killing everybody attached to this theft, but it all seemed so unnecessary. We were only talking about a hundred grand, and she already had the paintings, so what was the deal? I obviously wasn't a prime target or I would have been shot first—and probably second had the shooter really wanted to take me out; he was a crack shot to hit someone in the head like that. The mayhem was upsetting the police and the Mafia, not to mention me and the ones who got killed. Very unprofessional. I don't condone murder, but I at least expect people who kill for money to do it in a businesslike way. It didn't pay to upset the police and the mob; it worked against good business sense.

Also, to kill so publicly, by blowing people's brains out on a public street—it was like it had some other meaning, like there was a message.

I lifted some more food to my mouth, and the pile of slick red curry noodles suddenly reminded me of the stuff all over the town car in front of Donut House and on the bistro window.

With a jar of peanut butter, a container of baby carrots, and a fresh brandy I went to bed to watch TV. There wasn't a lot to watch except the news, so I thought I'd just ease my anxieties for a while and be entertained by other people's problems.

I was just mellowing out over turmoil half a planet away when the black lady anchor suddenly had a picture of a bull's-eye behind her with the word BROOKLYN in big bloody letters across it.

"Tragedy in the Carroll Gardens section of Brooklyn today. In broad daylight, a sniper shot a restaurant worker in the head. Darla Draco is on the scene. Darla, isn't this the second shooting like this in Carroll Gardens in two days?"

The TV screen split between the black anchor lady and a reporter with too much blond hair and too much makeup. I've noticed those two things sometimes go together. She was holding an umbrella, and she was standing just around the corner from where I was in bed drinking brandy and eating carrots and peanut butter. She was standing where the police had all those bright lights on Smith Street. Pretty screwy to be watching TV and see what's going on down the block from where you're watching TV.

"That's right, Lola. This is the second sniper attack in this neighborhood in two days, both in broad daylight. And the local community is not happy about this."

The screen went all to one picture of the front of Donut House earlier in the day. Darla's voice kept going.

"Yesterday, a customer of this coffee shop on Court Street was gunned down when he left after breakfast."

Garrison's face filled the screen, a yellow microphone in his face, the inside of the coffee shop behind him. His name appeared at the bottom of the screen.

Darla's voice asked Garrison questions, and I guess she was holding the mike.

"Garrison, you actually witnessed yesterday's brutal murder in front of your restaurant. What was that like?"

"It was like nothin' else. Man's head exploded outside. Don't see that every day and don't want to."

"He was shot in the head?"

"That's right, just after breakfast. Terrible."

A snapshot of Jo-Ball in shorts and a T-shirt was suddenly where Garrison had been. Johnny was kneeling next to a golden retriever. I never knew he had a dog. Darla continued to tell us more.

"This man, Johnny Culobrese, was a beloved fixture in the neighborhood, the maître d' at Brooklyn's famous Italian restaurant Dominic's. At eight forty-five yesterday morning he was shot down in cold blood."

Now they were interviewing the old guy who owns Dominic's, Louie Parella, and his name was on the screen. I knew him a little. Never liked him, though. His eyes were close together and never stood still, with dark circles under them. His hair was dyed black and slicked. Not the kind of guy I generally think of as trustworthy to look at. Still, I'd never heard anything bad about him, except that he was a son of a bitch to Johnny most of the time.

"Mr. Parella, you knew Johnny—he worked for your restaurant for many years. Tell us about him."

"I loved that man like he was my own brother. My own brother! I'm sick. I'm sick. How could this happen, in a family neighborhood? The police are down the block, I don't think they have any idea what's what. Two innocent people dead in two days! Tomorrow is another day. Who's next? One of my customers? We pay taxes, don't we? I have a business to run."

We cut back to Darla in the rain, standing next to a uniformed cop who looked like brass by all the medals or whatever on his chest. His name appeared on the screen, and under that it said NYPD SPOKESPERSON.

She put the mike to him.

"Can you tell us what the people of this besieged neighborhood should expect when the sun comes up? Is there a serial killer on the loose?"

The cop looked like he was nursing a sore tooth, but my guess was he was tired of news reporters trying to create a panic.

"Darla, the department has every available resource on this, and we are looking at a variety of motives and suspects at this time."

My door buzzer sounded. I climbed out of bed and peeked through the shutters. Doh and Crispi were on my stoop. Is that screwy or what? It was like the TV was telling me what was going to happen next.

The cop on TV kept talking as I peeked at the detectives.

"We don't believe these murders were random, and we encourage the public to come forward with any information they may have about the incidents this morning and the morning before. They should call 311 if they saw anything here that may help us."

I shut the TV off and sat in the dark listening to the front buzzer. It stopped after ten buzzes.

I saw a lot. I wasn't calling 311, though. I was pulling the covers over my head and going to sleep.

I was ready to move on to another and better day. Only I wasn't real confident that one was in my future any time soon.

NINETEEN

BROOKLYN STREETS PLAY MUSIC AT night like a symphony.

The music of human activity bops along right up until about 1:00 A.M. It's then that the music slows. You still have the burble of people going home from bars, a car zooming down the block, the stray truck rumbling slowly on night deliveries. By 3:00 A.M. things quiet down even more. Foot and car traffic tapers off, buses rarely hum down Smith Street, and there's only the occasional rhythmic clunk and rattle deep in the ground, the subway work trains collecting garbage. On a Tuesday night in October at 4:00 A.M., the music of the street is about as slow and quiet as it gets in Carroll Gardens. I think the guys in the front of the orchestra with the fiddles are about to nod off and the conductor can barely keep his baton in the air.

At 6:00 A.M. the sky is waking up over the dark brownstones even if most of the apartment windows are only just beginning to light up. It's like that moment you see on public TV when the philharmonic is about to play. The conductor suddenly taps the podium and raises his baton, ready to make some noise with the next movement. The orchestra seems to sit up straight and take a deep breath, ready to charge into the next part, something that moves and gives life. Imagine that baton-in-the-air moment being the better part of an hour, because it may last that long before the heating oil delivery trucks and trash trucks come booming down the block. Blue jays conk, crows caw, and starlings squabble. A steady flow of buses hiss down Smith Street, and the subway trains rattle the glassware. Traffic helicopters chop and chatter in the distance. This music is light but quick, letting you know that the full flush of rush hour is about to have the whole orchestra sawing and banging away at their instruments.

So I'm suddenly like a poet or something. Well, I had a lot of time that night to listen to Brooklyn's night quiet, and think about what it sounded like, and imagine it on public television as a symphony. Not bad for a guy with an art history degree and questionable scruples. I slept a little. Not much.

Believe it or not, I didn't spend the night thinking about much of anything about my predicament. I just lay there listening to Brooklyn and to myself breathe, my heart beat. The sound of me being alive. Had the punk's aim not been put out of whack by the old lady's broom, I wouldn't have heard that sound anymore. I wouldn't have been in Brooklyn, but somewhere else. On my back in a satin-lined box, a hairy-lipped woman leaning over trying to paste the pieces of my face back together.

OK, so maybe I did think a little about my predicament. I didn't want to end up standing around Smith Street with half my head missing. Seeing Huey like that was actually worse than seeing Jo-Ball's tongue wiggling in the air. Like I said, it seemed humiliating. Images like that in my head, small wonder I was a little sleepless.

I wasn't going to let the situation get the better of me. Pop taught me not to let that happen.

So by six I was up and making pancakes to Tito Puente's timbales.

Those are a kind of drum, sort of like congas, and nobody beat up timbales like Tito. The album was from the fifties, called *Night Beat,* all instrumental. Tito's drums beat out a rhythm that argued with trumpets, fought with saxophones, back and forth, with little side commentary by guitar and piano. There was something driving and urgent about this music. It was much darker than Prado and especially Cugat. Dark and urgent. That's how I felt.

I ate a pile of pancakes and drank black coffee.

I showered, shaved, and put on a brown suit, one with a vest.

By eight I was in the lobby of the Williamsburg Savings Bank pointing a twenty at the guard. I had my back to the stream of people flashing their IDs over the automatic gates so they couldn't see my motivational tool.

"I'm looking for a guy who visited the building yesterday. I want to know which office he went to."

I was faced with a black woman with a wide jaw and beaded hair. Her uniform was only half as tight as she made the corners of her eyes.

She says, "Who are you?"

So I says, "I'm one of those people who looks for people but nobody knows I was ever there. Except the one person with the extra cash."

She curled her lip at the twenty but glanced nervously to either side. "Who do you think you are?"

"Look, darling, you can either help me or I'll come back later and find someone who will. You know your fellow employees. You seriously think one of them wouldn't like to make a fast buck and flip through the images of that security camera? Either you take this or one of them will. Makes no difference to me except I have to come back. But that's what I do. Twenty bucks for five minutes is two hundred and forty bucks an hour."

We both looked over at the camera positioned on the security dais. It looked like a softball with a camera lens in the front. Visitors to the building stood in front of it holding a driver's license and told the camera who they were there to visit. Or in some places they just take the picture to print out a building pass with your photo on it. Either way, the photo of Huey would have a company name attached. As soon as I came in and saw the camera, I knew they had the information I wanted on their system. Maybe they even had as far back as Ms. French.

The woman kind of growled, but I don't think it was at me. She slid next to the computer and said, "Time?"

"How far back does it record?"

"Forty-eight hours."

Like I figured. Sunday, the day Ms. French had breakfast with Jo-Ball and then came here, was recorded over. I was kicking myself for not coming to Billy Bank before. At least Monday afternoon, when Huey came to get his money, would be on the security hard drive.

"Monday, around four in the afternoon. You can't miss him. He has short white hair, but he isn't that old."

She poked at the keyboard with long fingernails, the kind with custom paint jobs. Then she pointed one of those nails at the screen and said, "LaMouche? Huey LaMouche?"

"That's him."

She waddled back over to me, examining the rank and file behind me shoving through the turnstiles. Finally her eyes met mine again. "You must think I'm cheap."

"Sweetheart, I'll be honest. You seem like a nice person in a job that isn't so great. Your boss is a jerk."

She stares at me a moment and says, "How you know all this?"

So I says, "I can see it in your face."

Of course, all I was doing is what fortune-tellers do: tell people the story of the human condition. Almost everybody hates their boss, and fewer still ever really dreamed of becoming a security guard. Frankly, she looked like she thought she deserved better. How? Maybe it was the fingernails.

"I make closer to five hundred an hour," she says.

I held out my other hand, where only she could see it. It had another twenty in it.

I says, "See? I even knew you were smart."

Flattery is everybody's friend.

She practically smiled when she made the two twenties do a vanishing act. "He went to Dunwoody Exports, fourteenth floor."

I practically smiled back at her. "We never met."

I left Billy Bank then because I couldn't exactly dash upstairs at that time without that security guard worrying I'd make some sort of trouble. Besides, I needed to find out more about Dunwoody Exports before I went barging in there.

On the street, I found a coffee cart at the corner, and I bought a cup. The sun shone low on Flatbush Avenue, Manhattan orange and twinkling in the distance. I sipped my coffee in the shadow of the cart, wishing I could have Blaise put a man out front of the building to watch for Ms. French, but Garrison's description was too weak to make the ID.

Skip, my nephew, would be the right man for this project. OK, so "man" might be stretching it a little. He's thirteen, going on forty. I pushed some buttons on my phone.

"Hullo, Uncle Tommy."

"Skip?"

"How many people call you Uncle Tommy, Uncle Tommy?"

"You have a point. Just didn't sound like you."

"I'm eating cereal."

"Explains it."

"And they put braces on me."

"Sorry to hear that, Skip."

"And my voice is changing."

"That happens."

"Why didn't you text me?"

"I don't text. I only e-mail."

"Well, hello Mr. Caveman!"

"I can only keep up with so much technology."

"Let me guess: You need something?"

"It's not your birthday."

"That was last month, and you didn't call then, either."

"You want some work or not, Skip?"

"Sure, yeah, why not."

"Got a pen?"

"I got a brain."

This kid, my nephew, he had some kind of mouth, didn't he? I don't know if it comes across, but he was pretty sarcastic. Maybe I was a smart ass to adults when I was a kid, but I'm an adult, and this crap from a nephew can be pretty annoying. I let it go because I wasn't raising him, and I needed his help.

So I says, "Dunwoody Exports. They have offices in the Williamsburg Savings Bank, in Brooklyn."

"Oh, is that where the Williamsburg Savings Bank is?"

You want to smack kids sometimes, don't you? But it's best not to act out with the youngsters, so they tell me.

"Get me everything you can on these guys, this afternoon if you can."

"Want me to tell Mom I need to skip class so I can make your deadline?"

"Skip, take it from me. Sarcasm is bad karma. If you want forty, make it this afternoon. Thirty if it's tomorrow."

I killed the call before he could make another smart remark.

Kid was a jerk. Made sense, though. His dad, Ralphie, who sold cars out in Bay Ridge, he was a jerk, too. Felt a little sorry for my sis, Kate, but she's the one who married Ralphie, her choice, her problem.

TWENTY

THERE ARE A LOT OF things screwy about funerals. For me, it's having all those people from different parts of your life together in one room, next to each other. Friends, relatives, acquaintances all bunched up together. In Brooklyn, even more. The guy who slices your ham real thin at the deli, who you know only as Bobby, he will show up to your funeral. In Brooklyn, people go to funerals of friends' parents or uncles who they may have never met. My accountant goes to the funerals of his client's relatives. So you get the picture. A Brooklyn funeral can get crowded, and with faces that are so out of place that you don't recognize the person. It's a little embarrassing. I arrived on time, 10:30 A.M.

My neighborhood is known in certain circles for art thieves, and others for Italian pastry, and in still others for the many fine funeral homes. How this came to be, I don't know, but we have something like eight in a ten-block radius. All Italian. Back in the day, a mobster got shot up, there were big traffic jams around here. The B75 bus had to be temporarily rerouted, and there would be a line of cars over to Green-Wood Cemetery, which is a mile away or more in Sunset Park. The hearse would be passing through the cemetery's stone archway just as the last flower wagon was leaving Viscotti's.

You should see Viscotti's. It's on the corner, sort of a brownstone mansion four lots wide surrounded by an ornate black iron fence. There's a big garden out front with a fountain and a pond and a boatload of ivy. At night it all lights up with little white lights. It's pretty, but in a dark and kind of spooky way, even during the day. I guess it wouldn't make sense for a funeral home to look like an Easter parade.

I know that in other parts of the country it may be customary to have funerals at a church. We do that sometimes. Brooklyn was going on three million citizens, and on its own was bigger than all but three other U.S. cities. I kid you not. With weddings and baptisms and Saint This Day and Saint That Day, the churches had a lot on their plate with fried salami on the side.

There was a line to get into Viscotti's that wound out the gate and down the sidewalk. I guess mourners started lining up early to get a good seat. The people in front and in back of me—I didn't know them. There was a side entrance for the family, people on the VIP list. The chapel at Viscotti's was pretty big, though I guessed at a certain point they turned people away when the place got full.

The line inched forward, and I had time to check out what was what.

Down the block across Court Street at the deli I could see one of those unmarked police cars. Sitting inside was Doh, his arm hanging out the driver's window, a cigarette dangling from his fingers. In the passenger seat was the silhouette of Crispi with binoculars. I guessed they could see me, so I waved. Doh pointed his cigarette at me and then went back to puffing on it. It was like he was saying *We'll see you afterward*.

I could only imagine the questions they wanted to ask me. Unless they had me dead to rights on chasing that kid, I wasn't going to tip. One school of thought might be to tell the detectives everything I knew about the kid so they'd catch him and I wouldn't have to. It might save my life, right, I mean if the kid was gunning for me?

Picture this. The fuzz put their hooks into the punk. He starts talking, maybe to try to save his toast from being burned on death row. He'll tip on who hired him, and why he exploded these guys' heads. To do that would be to probably explain to the police all he knew about the art theft world in the neighborhood.

That would include explaining my part in it.

Strictly speaking, my profession is a hundred percent legal. OK, sure, my recent activity pushed things, but that was temporary, to raise the money to pay back the loan on the mud flap girl, Yvette. Just the same, if the cops threw out a net over all the goofballs around Carroll Gardens, I could see how I might have a lot of explaining to do. To be honest, it would also ruin my career. I had a vested interest in a healthy art theft industry. That may sound selfish at the expense of fine art, or the museums, or whatever. Trust me: If they grabbed all the goofballs in South Brooklyn, it wouldn't matter. Within a year there'd be another neighborhood full of goofballs. Maybe in Sunset Park or Windsor Terrace. So what's the difference?

The difference is I got to stay in the game. At least until I could pay off the pink monkey.

The line had moved me to the front gate of Viscotti's when my phone buzzed. It was Blaise.

So I says, "What's up?"

He says, "Heh. A lot is up. I see one of the dudes we followed went belly up. Is there exposure, Tomsy? Give it to me straight."

He wanted me to tell him if there was any connection between me and Huey's head exploding.

"No direct exposure."

"Talk to me, Tomsy." That sounded a little like a warning.

"I didn't tweak him. Something I'm working on may have something to do with it, though."

"You about to get hooked? Don't want your phone falling prey, coming to me."

"Am I a kid, Blaise?"

"Happened to many a man."

"I'll throw it in the canal before I'd let them get my phone, and besides I know my rights."

"Good to know. I got a right to be careful."

"I look out for my friends, you know that. Life is all about keeping friends and avoiding enemies."

"Like I said, I got a right to be careful."

"OK, I understand. You're smart."

"Heh."

"I'll probably need more help with this over the next couple days. Still open for business?"

"I'll take your calls, Tomsy. Look, I didn't call just to razz you. Blaise may have something that could help. Lost and found—but there's a heavy price."

"Explain."

"I think somebody lost something yesterday in all the excitement."

"Explain."

"It's black and dangerous."

"I'm a clever man, Blaise—"

"Heh. I know, but not too smart sometimes. This missing item was found under a car. On Sackett. One of my peeps bought it from a ragman."

The punk's gun. A ragman is someone who picks bottles out of the trash. One of them must have found it and tried to sell it down at the projects.

"Damn, Blaise. That's an important missing item."

"That's why I'm calling you. The man don't pay, and it's too hot for the street. Nothing like it around here. German."

"I've seen it. How much?"

"Heh. I have to think about that, Tomsy, see if the value goes up. Sorry, my man, but this is business."

To be honest, I wasn't sure I wanted to have that gun near me. Burning hot piece of evidence connecting me to the exploding heads. Might implicate me. Then again, it could still have latents on it from the kid, even DNA from his sweat.

"Just as well, Blaise. You deserve your due. I'm busted at the moment, and I think it's better with you right now than me." At that point I was two people from the chapel entrance. "I'll be in touch. And I appreciate the call."

"Peace out."

I put the phone away as a bent old Italian lady in a black dress handed me a funeral program.

The chapel looked like a cross between an airport on Thanksgiving and a flower show. I was seated only a few pews from the back. Viscotti's would have to close the doors soon or answer to the fire marshal.

There were a lot of older women in my pew, and in many of the pews. I didn't recognize most of them. The Vietnamese lady I recognized from the cleaners. I wondered how many of the other Italian broads were ones Jo-Ball charmed while he was maître d' at Dominic's.

Jocko was sitting with a bunch of older Italian men in the third pew in the front. The first pews were what looked like Jo-Ball's family and kids, including the ugly daughter. Between Jocko and the family, in the second pew, was Louie Parella. Next to a couple guys in sharp suits.

Sharp suits or tracksuits. They're always in suits, aren't they?

The sharp suits had big hair and starched collars, no doubt Louie's silent partners or his purveyors at Dominic's. Like I think I said earlier, the wiseguys weren't common like back in the day. Now the sharp suits looked and acted more like businessmen. They moved legitimate merchandise. But if Louie wanted to buy his produce or meat or pasta from someone other than the sharp suits? Louie's nice Mercedes might mysteriously catch fire. Dominic's might have a grease fire and the extinguishers mysteriously wouldn't work. Accidents happen every day. Sometimes mysteriously.

Those would be the guys I needed to talk to.

Jocko turned his head and whispered to someone across the aisle. He caught sight of me and gave a nod, looked toward the suits, then me again, then toward the front. I hoped I could count on Jocko to help me with this. I mean, what if the old barber was cracked and these suits had no idea what I was talking about? What then? I didn't want to go kissing their rings and make a fool out of myself. It had always been my policy to steer clear of those guys and not let them even know I existed. Just a little rule I had.

I won't bore you with the service. It bored me; they're all the same. I understand everybody is sad, I get it, and grieving is a process. For me, though, funerals seem kind of phony, all staged so people can get up and act like the dead guy's best friend, and even more so the wife can act like she's not kind of happy the mope who farts all night next to her in bed is finally gone. I'm just saying, but Louie gave a little speech about what a great man we'd lost, and I know he wasn't Johnny's friend at all. That crap is hard to sit through.

It didn't help that I was also getting claustrophobic. For big guys like me, a lot of spaces seem smaller than they do to everybody else. If you've never been claustrophobic, it's like everybody around you is breathing your air and you're running out. You start breathing harder, but in short breaths. Hyperventilation begins, making it worse because you feel light-headed and start to breathe harder, making it worse. So once I made it out to the sidewalk, I leaned against a lamppost by some of the black limos and did some tantric breathing exercises to calm my phobia and stop hyperventilating.

My eyes were closed when I felt hands on me, pushing me backward.

I didn't have much time to react, and it wouldn't have helped much anyway because I had no balance, and was off my feet and in the back of one of the limos. Two guys with broken noses and about my size were outside, and they slammed the door.

The street-side door opened, and Louie slid in next to me. His black hair looked slick and hard like the back of a cockroach. The sharp suits were right behind him, and they sat across from me.

It was suddenly very hushed in the back of that limo, and the mix of aftershave from the three men was like diced onions.

"You don't like me," Louie said. I think he suffered from low self-esteem.

I gave a little shrug, trying to relax into the situation and figure out how I was supposed to act, because I wasn't sure what they knew. Or thought they knew.

I tried my shrug again. "So?"

OK, that's one word. Well, you know me by now. When I'm stressed, I keep the words to a minimum. Never good to yak.

"Johnny told me you don't like me."

"I don't really know you, Louie. How can I not like you?"

One of the suits spoke. He had very smooth skin, almost like he'd been a burn victim or something, only he hadn't. Just very smooth flat features and a very small nose.

He says, "Forget him. We want to know what's going on." Flat Face's little blue eyes were fixed on mine.

So I says, "Fair enough. So do I."

Flat Face thought about that a second as the limo began to move. Then he says, "It's obvious you're involved. You know something."

So I says, "Jocko tells me you guys think I tweaked Johnny and Huey."

"That's one theory."

I shook my head slowly. "Five-pound salami, four-pound bag. Johnny was my friend. Which is why I was standing next to Johnny when it happened. How could I shoot him from a distance and be standing next to him at the same time?"

"Done all the time." Flat Face attempted a smile, but it was a little scary. "You set Johnny up for the shooter."

"That could be. But why? Why not just have the shooter tweak Johnny while I'm in Vegas with an alibi?"

"Money, that's why!" Louie waved an accusing finger under my nose. "You're into Vinny Scanlon for fifteen large by next Tuesday."

I tried to look bored. "I owe Vince. Me and half the businesses in this area have been into Vince at one time or the other. Doesn't mean I go killing Johnny and Huey."

"Word is Huey double-crossed you on a deal. Johnny was in on it. Now you can't make the payment to Scanlon by next Tuesday."

Louie was right. I didn't like him, and now I had a reason. I turned to Flat Face.

"Look, I'm a business person. You're a business person. Business people find common interests. That's how they stay in business. It wasn't in either of our common interest that Johnny died. But it is in our common interest to know who made that happen."

Flat Face's little blue eyes seemed amused. "We know what business you're in. Our end has always come out of that business through Johnny. Now where are we going to collect our end, Tommy?"

I could see that they really were businessmen. Johnny wasn't their friend. He was their hand in the till of the Carroll Gardens theft industry.

"I see. Never good when a revenue stream dries up. What are you proposing?"

Always dangerous to ask a question when you think the answer is something you don't want to hear. I did it anyway. I did it to keep things on the up and up with these guys.

So Flat Face leans forward, his elbows on his perfectly creased pant leg.

"Right now your business is settling the goodies to the insurance companies. For a vig. There's nothing much in that for us. If there were, we would have been in business together a long time ago. Johnny's end of your business was more rewarding. The goofballs got the slice, he got the pie. That was good business for us. We don't want to let that go."

Louie interrupted, his finger in my face again, those deep-set ratlike eyes burning. "He knows what's going on and he's not telling. That's disrespect."

Flat Face reached out his hand and gave Louie a hard poke on the forehead. "I'm still talking."

Louie shrank back into his seat, looking wounded.

Flat Face reclined, his eyes back on me. "So. Like Louie says, I'm sure there is a lot you know that we don't about this. Like you say, we're businessmen. My only interest is in the bottom line. We've lost a revenue stream. We want it back. You could take Johnny's place."

I squinted at him. "Even if you took my entire percentage, it wouldn't come close—"

"You misunderstand me." He wagged a finger. "We're offering you a position with our firm. Swagging the goodies instead of settling them."

I nodded slowly. I looked calm on the outside. You know things are going seriously south when the Mafia offers you a job.

I heard myself say, "I'm flattered. That's very generous. I'd like to say yes right now."

Flat Face's eyes dulled. He seemed ready not to like where I was going next. It was important not to seem like I was dancing.

So I says, "Louie is right, though. At the moment, my company is in debt to Scanlon. I don't deny that. Also, this thing with Johnny, and Huey: It's put the police on me for a while. I think I need to clear all this up before accepting an offer like this. I would be a liability to your firm. Neither of us wants that. Fact of the matter is I think the entire market in goodies has taken a downturn at the moment, at least in this sector. Nobody is doing anything while the police are snooping around and people are getting shot. The goofballs are keeping their heads down and waiting tables. Can we reconvene this meeting in a couple weeks?"

Flat Face reached a hand back and knocked on the glass partition, the one behind the limo driver's head. The limo pulled to the curb. "Best if we don't arrive at the cemetery together. I like to keep my business private."

I glanced at Louie, who had shrunk into the corner, his eyes looking outside through the tinted glass. I figured I must be a breath of fresh air to guys like Flat Face who have to deal with hotheads like Louie every day.

I reached out a hand. "Thanks for the meeting. I'll be in touch."

Flat Face shook my hand. The skin was cool, and I could feel a lot of rings on his fingers.

"*We'll* be in touch."

"Either way." I shrugged, opened the door, and stepped out of the limo. The long black car zoomed up Twenty-fifth Street.

I was at the corner of Fourth Avenue, and when I looked downhill on Twenty-fifth Street I could see a long line of cars with their headlights on. When I looked uphill on Twenty-fifth Street I could see the red taillights of cars and limos stretching up to Fifth Avenue and the gate to the cemetery.

Fourth Avenue is a busy commercial road. Auto part stores, fast food, what have you. Three moving lanes in each direction, a median, and a subway below. Trucks, cars, and buses roared past me as I stood on the corner looking uphill toward the cemetery.

The sky had turned overcast, and a warm wind was kicking up from the west. Looked like rain.

You don't have to be the Dalai Lama to know that being mobbed up is definitely bad karma. Working for Flat Face would be crossing the line permanently into the illegal side of things. It was there that people got hurt. People like me. Remember? I had a rule about that.

First I was settling. Then I was shopping. Now they wanted me to swag. For the Mafia.

On top of everything else I had to say no to the Mafia.

I felt the subway rumble under my feet, and figured I'd find the nearest station and train back close to home and walk the rest of the way. I didn't have the stomach to attend the burial.

I turned to start walking.

Doh and Crispi were standing behind me.

TWENTY-ONE

"WE NEED TO TALK," DOH says, wincing like he wished we didn't have to talk. Crispi and his unibrow looked like they couldn't wait to rubber-hose me.

I says, "I'm kind of busy at the moment."

So he says, "I can see that. But we have some questions we'd like to ask you."

Doh looked up Twenty-fifth Street toward where the limo had gone. I guessed they'd been watching the procession of cars. Then they saw me dropped off by Flat Face and made a move.

I nodded. "I can see that."

Crispi jerked a thumb south. "The precinct is just over there."

I nodded. "I've seen that, too."

Doh cocked his head. "You're not going to stonewall us, are you, Tommy?"

I smiled. "Look, Detective, I know you have a job to do. I respect that. But I'm not a kid. I have standing orders with my lawyer to only talk to the police with her in the room at my side. I'm a businessman and have liability issues. So I refer you to her, Carol Doonan, she's downtown on Montague. Call her and we'll set something up. Otherwise, unless I'm under arrest, I can't expose myself or my business to unnecessary risk. That's how I keep my insurance rates low."

Doh had his hands on his hips by that point, and it looked like he was sizing me up. Crispi was all dusky around the eyes, hoping Doh would pull something.

Pull something? By that I mean try to goad me into taking a swing at him, giving him an excuse to arrest me. My size was giving him second thoughts, though.

So I says, "Let's not play any games. You're not going to get me to act out in a way that you can bust me. Like I said, I'm not a kid. I'm an adult. Let's do this like adults, in a businesslike fashion. I'll help you any way that I reasonably can to help you find who killed those guys."

Doh took out his cell phone. "What's Doonan's phone number?"

I looked through my phone's directory and gave it to him. He dialed.

"This is Detective Doh, for Carol Doonan. Tell her I'm about to arrest one of her clients, Tommy Davin. . . . Page her, then. If I don't hear from her within the hour her client is headed to Rikers." He left his number and hung up. "I'm not arresting you, Davin. That was just to get her to call. But you're up to your neck in this thing, whether you know it or not. Sooner you come in and talk, the better. We know things you don't." He stabbed a finger at me, turned, and went back to his car.

Crispi followed like a kid cheated out of his lunch money.

They roared past me toward the precinct.

I left the hum and rumble of traffic by way of the stairwell to the R train, which I took to Union Street and then walked back across the Gowanus Canal, across the drawbridge. I could see the Carroll Street bridge where the punk had jumped on the barge,

and the seawall where he'd climbed up into the telephone maintenance yard.

I was curious about what the cops knew. Assuming Doh wasn't
bullshitting me. Did they have a lead on the kid? Couldn't be that
strong if they needed to ask me questions. Then again, I did have
information that could help them. I knew where the gun was. I
was pretty sure Ms. French was involved. I knew what Huey had
been up to before his head exploded.

That reminded me of someplace I needed to go. The green loft
on Bond.

When I say green loft, I mean it's a factory space that's had one
end of the second floor renovated into an apartment. Probably the
apartment isn't legal, but then what went on in the loft wasn't
legal, either. The outside of the building is painted grass green.

There was an unmarked button next to the door. I pushed it,
heard a distant but angry buzz.

I waited.

I rang again.

I looked up.

A camera pointed down from a second-floor window. So I looked
up at the lens and waved, then put my hands together like I was
praying. Kind of stupid, I know, but at least I might look like a
harmless giant. I was sure a girl like Bridget had to be careful. She
was an independent, and she'd never met me before. I'd seen her
shopping at the Met Food on Smith Street. I'd run into Blaise
there, and he pointed her out. Cute enough, short brown hair, but
nothing too special about her figure, and lots of moles on the parts
of her body I could see.

I waited some and rang the buzzer again, and the door popped
open. A heavy chain was across the open space, and a girl with
shoulder-length brown hair and moles was looking up at me from

under it. She was in cutoff jeans, clogs, and a white T-shirt that said LIFE IS AN ONION. IT'S BETTER FRIED. I could smell cigarette smoke.

"My name is Tommy. I'm not with the cops or anything, but I was wondering if I could buy some of your time to ask about Huey."

"Got the wrong place, pal."

"The French guy who was here yesterday. He was killed."

Her brow wrinkled and then unwrinkled. "And?"

"He was here that same morning. I'm wondering if he said anything to you about anything that might give an idea who shot him."

"And?"

I thought that was kind of strange, so I says, "Look, I'm a business person, so I understand you have to look out after your business and your customers. There's the bottom line and nothing else. But it's possible other people may find out he came here. If that happens, or is about to happen, you may want to know, because the cops could come by. No business person likes the cops to come by. Always bad for business."

Her eyes widened. "Well, now I know, so why should I talk to you?"

"Because I'm a nice guy, that's why."

"Nice guys finish last."

"Maybe so, but they have good karma."

That made her think a moment, and she stuck out her bottom lip. "You do yoga?"

"I have this pretty cool tantric thing to relieve anxiety, keep me from acting out. I can show you."

Bridget set her jaw. "You're a big guy. I only take referrals."

"You know Blaise Jones?" She didn't say anything, but I could tell from the way she blinked that she did. Almost anybody involved in shady business in that neighborhood knew Blaise. "My name is Tommy Davin. Call him. I'll wait."

The door slammed shut, and I heard a big latch chunk into place.

The warm wind from the southwest was picking up. Moist air from the south hitting the Canadian air sitting over Brooklyn would mean rain, maybe a lot of it. For October it had been dry and sunny almost every day. The days were getting a lot shorter, so the mornings were cold. Real nice fall weather. I was thinking that I should go to the Botanic Gardens sometime soon to check out the maples for fall foliage when there was a *ka-chunk,* a chain rattled, and the door opened.

Bridget stood to one side, a freshly lit cigarette in her fingers. "Come on in, Tommy."

She locked the door and I followed her up the dark, steep stairs to the second floor. She did have a nice ass, I'll give her that, but she must have had thirty moles on the backs of her legs and upper arms. The clomp of her clogs on the steps practically had me holding my ears.

The loft was like you would expect—large, open, and drafty. Dark blue drapes made slits of the eight-foot-high windows along the left, and more drapes from the ceiling made a wall fifty feet in. Large Oriental rugs, fakes, were on the rough wooden floor, with a leopard print couch and Mission coffee table. To the right of the door was an improvised kitchen. In the far right corner, in the darkest part of the room, was the king-sized bed in leopard print. There must have been fifty candles in the place, scented ones, vanilla or something, but only a few on the coffee table were lit.

"Coffee?" She slid into the kitchen. The coffeemaker looked like it had made a fresh pot. Her cigarette went into the sink with a sizzle.

"That would be nice, thanks."

"Milk and sugar?"

"That works."

I went over and made myself at home on the couch. The place was pretty much the way I imagined it might be, and so was the girl. I'm sure Bridget was a different person when a customer came over. Sexy, coy, and made-up. Now she was just a girl lounging around drinking coffee, smoking, and reading the *Economist*. A copy was next to me on the couch.

Bridget handed me a large black mug.

"Thanks. I do insurance investigation work. Should I call you Bridget?"

She nodded, but sort of rolled her eyes at the same time. I got the idea that wasn't her real name, but it would do for now. Tossing the magazine on the floor, the girl curled up with her coffee in a corner of the couch.

"I appreciate you talking with me about Huey, unannounced and all."

She just drank her coffee and looked at me, almost like I hadn't said anything. Well, she was streetwise, I'll say that. If you're in an illegal trade, blabbing to strangers isn't healthy.

"So I won't take up more of your time than necessary. Huey swung by here yesterday, and he was shot and killed by a sniper soon after. He was up to something that got him tweaked, and I want to find out what that something was. I don't know if he was much of a talker. I'd guess some of your clients do a lot of talking about their lives while others say nothing at all. If he said anything about what was going on in his life, it could be really useful to me."

"Wives," she said. "Clients all talk about their wives, if they have one, if they talk at all."

"So what did Huey say about Ariel?"

"Same thing they all say. She's a ball buster." She smiled a little. "In a bad way."

I smiled a little myself. "Lot of that going around."

"She was pushing him about some sort of business deal, that he wasn't making enough money, bloop bloop bloop."

I put my coffee cup down among the candles. "Did he say anything about what kind of deal?"

She made a small shake of her head and sipped more coffee. "He didn't seem happy about being pushed around, but he works for her at the bistro on Smith. What do you expect?"

"Nothing more about the deal?"

"No details. Just that she had pushed him to make more money, that he was weak and had been taken advantage of, that she knew better, bloop bloop bloop, but of course he was going to show her she was wrong."

Remember what I said at the beginning? For love or money? Maybe Huey had done something really dumb for a woman, Ariel, to try to get his balls back in that relationship.

"So you didn't get any idea Ariel knew about the deal, that he was going to use it to impress her, to show her he wasn't a chump?"

She shrugged and rolled her eyes. It kind of figured that a man would lay that part of it out for a side squeeze like Bridget if he was going to mess up the sheets. He had to assert his male dominance to maintain his alpha sexuality.

I stood. "Thanks. How much I owe you for your time?"

Bridget waved a hand. "I don't even have makeup on."

"How about that tantric exercise?"

Her eyes widened for the first time. "Sure."

So I showed her. She did it, but too fast, so I guided her hands and helped her breathe in slowly.

Bridget showed me a smile. "Thanks, Tommy. I feel more re-laxed."

"Good. Call me if anything comes up on Huey, OK? Like you remember anything he said."

She squinted at me. "How did you know he came here? Did he tell you?"

"Professional secret." I winked.

They say a woman has to have her secrets, but a man has to *make* his secrets.

I made that up. Not bad.

TWENTY-TWO

I STEPPED BACK ONTO BOND Street and saw I had two messages on my phone.

One was from Walter.

That could wait.

The other was from Carol Doonan.

That couldn't. I listened to the message.

"Tommy, Carol Doonan. We have an appointment ten tomorrow morning at my offices with Detectives Doh and Crispi. You be here at nine to review. Call my sec to confirm. Had to move some things around for this. Not because I like you, you gorgeous hunk of man, but my other cases at the moment bore me. Yours tend to be interesting. Later, gator."

It was afternoon, the Billy Bank guard from earlier would be off duty, so I figured I might as well check on Dunwoody Exports. I walked back to Third Avenue and caught a bus. I was at Billy Bank a half hour later, and upstairs ten minutes after that.

The double wooden doors that said DUNWOODY EXPORTS LLC were locked, and nobody answered the bell.

I peeked in the door crack, and it was dark inside.

I took the elevator to the basement and walked around until I

found the super's office. It didn't say SUPERINTENDENT, but the
guy in blue work clothes leaning in a soiled executive chair at a
desk missing the legs looked the part. He was Hispanic, with a
bushy mustache and an eye cocked in my direction. The desk was
cluttered with light switches, wire, toilet floats, bus fuses, faucet
handles, receipts, and pornography. The ceiling was all pipes, the
walls all cheesecake calendars from the last ten years. An old cassette deck played a cha-cha.

I says, "Tito Rodríguez."

So he smiles real big, jerks a thumb at the cassette player, and
says, "You like?"

"He's not my favorite, but he's good."

"Who you like?"

"I have to say that when it comes to mambo, Prado is hard to
beat."

He melted with pleasure at the thought of Prado. "Yes, Prado,
of course. Can I help you?"

"I'm trying to find Dunwoody Exports."

"Fourteenth floor."

"I mean the people who work there. The place is locked up."

"Nobody goes in there much since last year. Some kind of trouble.
They still rent. You a process server?"

I leaned on the doorjamb and smiled. "I'm a Perez Prado fan
who wants to get inside their office and have a look around. I
won't touch anything. I just want to look."

His eyes darkened. "I would need permission."

I flashed a fifty. "This cut any red tape?"

"I am sorry." He smiled sadly. "I am a family man. My job is
worth more than you could pay. If I can tell you anything . . .
there's nothing that says I cannot tell you what I know about
them."

Well, I couldn't exactly expect everybody to be willing to bend, could I?

I put out my hand. "I'm Tommy Davin. Insurance investigator."

"Enrique Conzo." He shook my hand.

"You got any information worth paying for on Dunwoody?"

He smiled and shook his head. "I won't take any money. You seem like a nice guy, anyways. Like I said, they don't come around much anymore. Monday I was up on fourteen replacing fire extinguishers. Seen a man with white hair go into the office. Then I seen him come out with a bag."

"Was he carrying anything when he went in?"

He stuck out a bottom lip and shook his head. I was hoping that maybe Blaise's guys had it wrong, that he'd gone there with a portfolio, that maybe the paintings were in there. If so it would be worth risking having Gloria pick me a way in.

"Ever see a woman go in there?"

"Once. A while back. I remember because she asked me to come into her office and change a bulb. I was sort of hoping she would want me to fuck her. She seemed like the type."

That caught me off guard. I guessed he spent a lot of time down in the basement with his hardware and porno.

"The type?"

His eyes turned sly. "You know. *The type.*"

"And?"

He stuck out a bottom lip and shook his head. "Just the lightbulb."

"What was in the offices?"

"Desk, files, you know, nothing special. A lot of paintings, but they were stacked against the wall and not hanging. Hey, I did see one other man go that direction down the hall, same day as the one with white hair. He had two other men with him. Flashy suits. Hard to be sure, but they looked mobbed up."

"Did the lead suit have a flat face, very smooth face?"

"Sounds like the one."

I flipped him a card. "Thanks, Enrique. Can you do me a favor?"

He looked at the card and tossed it on the desk with all the junk. "Not if it will get me in trouble."

"Would it get you in trouble if you called me if anybody goes in that office?"

"I'll call. Just don't pay me anything."

"If I happen to find some Perez Prado tapes, would you take them off my hands?"

He answered with a laugh and a wave of his hand.

I took the stairs back to the lobby, and from the lobby I went to the street and grabbed a car home. The lack of a decent night's sleep was beginning to drag me down. When I entered the foyer back at Degraw Street, I found a note on my monsterproof door:

YOU IS WARN. SEND TO YVETTE.

There was the little skull and crossbones drawn at the bottom, like before. Also, of course, another love letter, which I added to my collection. I wondered again about having them translated— maybe Gustav would mention a meeting place and I could go over there and straighten him out—but I had a lot on my plate. First things first.

I rang Walter, only I got his machine. It wasn't noon yet in Vegas, so he was probably still in bed.

That was about all the fun and games I could take for one day. I made an appointment with Delilah later, and for a nap before.

TWENTY-THREE

My Heart, Yvette:

Enduring the test is worth it for a single chaste kiss from your butterfly lips. But the oaf must die. I will follow him and either trap him near his apartment or one of the other places I have seen him go. There was a confrontation and he has become an obstacle. And I lack confidence that my letters have felt the hands of my goddess. I will persevere. We will find eternity together. I must invest in a lint brush.

Ten thousand embraces, and a feather for a heart—

Gustav

TWENTY-FOUR

I SLEPT MOST OF THE afternoon, then showered, shaved, and dressed nice, like my old self. The punk shooter knew me now without the beard and suit, so why dress like I shopped at Goodwill? Just the same I went without the tie. Now that the beard was gone, my neck bunched up unless I went open-collar.

Rain was coming down outside in buckets, so I called a car service. Then another. Then another. When it rains, the car services can't keep up with demand.

So I took my umbrella and I walked the ten thousand blocks to Zookville clutching a soggy religious pamphlet. I kid you not, it's about a mile and a half away from my place, and as any city dweller knows, umbrellas keep you dry for a limited number of blocks.

Delilah opened the door. She says, "You look low on positive energy."

So I says . . . well, I think I just growled. I'm not sure if I really said anything.

My suit hanging up to dry and my shoes by the door, Delilah had to work me over pretty good to get me to loosen up a little. Finally she realized only wine and talk would complete the job.

I sat in a kimono on her couch with a forest fire of aromatherapy candles burning and ran down what was what. When I was done, I shrugged and looked into those dark almond eyes gazing across at me from the wing chair.

"So we've got the police and the mob who want a piece of me, and we've got this kid sniper on the loose, and my paintings are already gone, and I've got two goofballs on my side trying to steal a key to recover the money, and I have to come up with fifteen grand in six days or Vince Scanlon is going to start gouging, for money at first and then for real."

"What if you tell the police everything?"

I almost laughed. "I don't know how I leave out the part about me and the goodies, the part that could send me to prison."

"Could you tell them about chasing the shooter? That's not connected to anything else."

"Somehow I think it is, and so will Detective Doh. Ms. French is the common connection to these two, the one who tried to deal with Jo-Ball and tipped Huey. She hired the punk to start killing people connected to the theft of the Hoffman, Le Marr, and Ramirez. Frank and Kootie are probably next. And me. The police catch the punk shooter, they're going to find out all about this theft, and when they do I'm toast."

Delilah pushed out of her chair, her long braid swinging as she paced. She turned, arms folded.

"You *think,* Tommy. You don't *know.* Maybe you should look at your assumptions more closely. Open yourself to the power of possibilities."

"Like?"

"The shooter, for one. Maybe he was after Jo-Ball and Huey for another reason, not connected to the paintings."

I tried not to roll my eyes. "The stolen Hoffman, Ramirez, and Le Marr are a commonality."

"Just because a pigeon shares a branch with two other birds doesn't mean all three are pigeons."

"Birds of a feather, Dee. That's low percentage. OK, what else?"

She drifted off to the kitchen and came back with the wine, which was soon refilling my glass. Her other hand stroked my hair.

"You look great with the new haircut, Tommy. So glad the beard is gone."

"Thanks. Do I look like Kirk Douglas?"

"No."

"Sure?"

"Positive."

"Actually, I saw myself in the mirror, the first morning after you cut my beard? I was spooked. I looked like Pop."

"Tommy, you are not your father, we've been over that."

"I am like my father. Doesn't mean I am him, or am following his path."

"What was it those two said, the ugly one and—"

"Frank and Kootie?"

"Right. What was it they said?"

"They said they were going to go steal the key for the storage locker, from Huey at the hospital."

"Not that."

I shrugged. She leaned down and whispered in my ear. *"Buy back."*

"So?"

"What's it mean?"

"How the hell do I know? Huey is dead. Mostly. Let's just say he's not going to wake up and be able to tell us what it means."

Delilah sat next to me and took my hand. "Open yourself, Tommy. You know what a buy back is."

I did. A buy back is a local institution. When you go to a bar in

Brooklyn, and a lot of places throughout the city, a bartender will buy every third or fourth drink if you tip him the cost of that drink. That's good for the customer because he only pays for his drinks and not for a tip on top of that. It's good for the bartender because it inflates his tips. It's even good for the bar owner. He pays his bartender minimum wage and allows him to give away free drinks that cost the owner a quarter so the customer will tip the bartender six dollars. The owner has bought six dollars in wages for his employee from the customer for a quarter.

So the bartender and the bar owner only seem to give the drink away.

"OK, so I know what a buy back is."

"In a buy back there's the bar owner, the bartender, and the customer. Huey saw himself in this arrangement somewhere."

"He'd have to be the bartender. He took the paintings from one person and gave it to another, the same way a bartender takes a drink from the bar owner and gives it to a customer."

"So that would make the museum the bar owner, and Ms. French the customer."

My wineglass was suddenly empty again, and I set it on the table so I could rub my face. I was having a hard time putting one scheme in with the other.

"You're closing up, Tommy." Delilah was standing behind me, working my shoulder muscles. "Stay open to possibilities. You're almost there, I can feel it."

My hands were still over my eyes. "So . . . the museum *lets* Huey steal the paintings so that Ms. French will pay Huey. How does that service the museum's bottom line? Why would they steal their own paintings? Doesn't make sense."

"Tommy, you know deep down that there's an alternate perspective. At the very least I would say you need to look more closely at those involved."

I was still rubbing my face.

"I know, Dee. I can't find French to bear down on her. I guess I need to twist Frank and Kootie some more."

"Who are the other players?"

"Just the museum."

"What about Max?"

I looked up at her. She continued.

"They hired you to find the paintings. They're the bar owner."

"I could see Max involved in something shady." Delilah circled behind me, and her hands slipped around my neck. "I can see Max putting a pillow over his own mother's face. He was talking some serious trash last time I saw him. About cutting me out as a middleman."

"Sounds like something worth looking into." Delilah began squeezing my shoulders.

"Dee?"

"Hm?"

"You believe in karma, right?"

"You know I do."

"Does that mean good things happen to good people?"

The massage of my shoulders paused. "Not necessarily in a single life. Your spirituality endures."

"I know it's sort of a naive question. Bad things don't always happen to bad people. I'm just saying. It would be nice if karma worked that way. It would be nice if the circles folded back on themselves in a single incarnation."

"They do."

I shrugged. "Usually that's just irony."

"Irony is karma at work."

I looked her in the eye. "I wish I could believe that."

"I made my move."

"Move?"

"Scrabble."

"Yeah?"

She led me by the hand over to the board.

The word was "bounce."

TWENTY-FIVE

MY LAWYER, CAROL DOONAN, IS what you'd call a tough old broad. If you said it to her face, she might punch yours. Or she might buy you a drink. Her blue eyes were so pale they were almost silver, like her short hair, both of which stood out against her deeply tanned skin. Carol had her charms for her age, which if you tried to guess you might get punched out a second time. Tough but flirty, that was Carol. She liked men, and she liked gambling. If you can distinguish between the two.

I sat in front of her giant metal desk in a metal chair. Both had been in her dad's law office in the Stone Age. There were black-and-white photos on the wall of him with various New York celebrities, and color photos of Carol with Brooklyn politicians. He was dead a while.

The walls were lined with stacks of legal documents.

I was there alone for thirty minutes before she burst in and gave me a kiss on the cheek from behind. A second later she was at her desk poking at her computer.

"Talk to me, handsome man. Nice shave—and a haircut, too. A woman must have done this to Tommy Wommy, hmmm? What do we got? We have a half hour before the fuzz gets here."

"You might say a woman was involved."

"The one from Vegas? I was there, what, three weeks ago. Long weekend, busted up the tables at the Bellagio, man oh man. Met this gorgeous hunk of a man at the bar. A pilot."

"The Vegas girl is on waivers."

"Did she move in?"

"In and then out."

"Easy come easy go. No more cat hair."

"She left the cats. Four."

"Ack! What did you do with them?"

"Took care of them, what else was there to do?"

Carol's eyes left the computer screen and focused on me. "You dear, dear man. Want me to find her, sue her?"

"No money there. Except mine."

"Ouch!" Her eyes went back to the computer. "Tommy Wommy, what the hell were you thinking? Ah, but you weren't, were you?"

"How much time do we have now?"

"Twenty-two minutes, to be exact. What kind of jam are you in? Be only as specific as you need to be, bubby."

So I told her the story this way: Three paintings were stolen from the Whitbread Museum Sunday night. Monday morning, I heard about it from an acquaintance, even though it was not reported to the police. A client of mine—Max of USA—insures the Whitbread, and even before they called—which they did—I started looking into it. My first stop was Huey, because I heard he had something to do with it, but he denied it. So then I went to Johnny One-Ball, who is a local fence. He tells me he knows something about it but isn't comfortable discussing it in the diner, so we step outside. A bullet exploded his head, and another just missed mine. I was debriefed by the police, and I went to my masseuse for a workover and then to the museum to debrief the guards who were at the robbery. I went home and to sleep. Tuesday, I got a haircut, short to go with the new clean shave, and the barber told me the local mobbed-up guys think maybe I killed Jo-Ball and are not happy with me. I left there, made my way back to the pastry shop because I thought I might be able to make Huey flip. Jo-Ball getting killed might have made Huey nervous if he was sitting on the paintings. Just after I arrive, Huey's head explodes. Only this time I saw the shooter across the street, a punk kid. I chased him up Sackett, the old lady attacked him, he dropped the gun, I chased, he jumped in the canal, and I lost him on the Third Avenue bus. I went home. Wednesday, yesterday, I went to Jo-Ball's funeral. After the funeral, I took a ride with Flat Face to the cemetery, and instead of being upset, they want me to take Jo-Ball's place as a fence for local stolen art. I told them I'd think about it because I didn't want to get killed just yet. That's when I ran into Doh and Crispi, who were following the funeral and spotted me getting out of the mob car. They wanted me to come to the station and talk to them. Instead I provided them with the contact information for my lawyer, said I'd be glad to talk with them if she was there and said it was OK.

Carol stopped typing. "That it?"

"Pretty much. Oh, and I owe money to a shylock, fifteen large by next Tuesday."

"Cops know you were at the second hit?"

"Could be."

"They know you chased the kid?"

"Could be, but I was wearing a trench coat and hat. I don't think they have an ID that can stick. The old lady was busy hitting the kid with the broom, and only the one DOT worker got close enough to see my face. Oh yeah, and the Polish watchman at the phone yard. Like I said, I had a hat on, pulled down low to keep it from blowing off."

"They know about the shylock?"

"Yeah."

"They know the connected guys are hooking you?"

"They saw me getting out of Flat Face's limo. I'm guessing they know who he is, but I don't. Anyway, not sure what Doh and Crispi think of that."

"I was right." Carol's eyes flashed. "You do have interesting problems. Did the right thing to have them call me, Tommy."

"I'm pretty good doing the right thing. Whether it pays off or not is another matter."

"Especially when it comes to women."

I felt my face get hot, and I guess I turned red, because Carol looked suddenly all droopy.

"Tommy, I'm sorry I said that. I was just kidding with you. You know I love you, I wouldn't hurt you intentionally. Say you forgive me."

"I don't feel any hostility toward you, Carol. No need to forgive. You are right about the women, and I'm a little ashamed, to be honest."

"The Vegas show girl—she's the one who put you on the hook with the shylock?"

I took a deep breath. I let it out and said, "Yeah."

"You poor kid!" Carol jogged around the desk and pulled my head into her bosom like she was my mom or something. "Let's take care of the police, and then we'll look into doing something about the shylock. Which one?"

From inside her tits I said, "Scanlon."

"Scanlon? Jesus. OK, well, could be worse. I can talk to him for you."

Carol stepped back just in time for me to come up for air. "Thanks, Carol. I'll let you know if that's necessary. I think I may be able to be square with him by next week. If I can sort out these missing paintings I should be in clover."

Carol's desk phone bleeped. She went around to answer it.

When she put the receiver back down she said, "Only talk if I tell you to, Tommy. You know the drill. If I ask you to answer, there is only one answer."

I just nodded, keeping my mouth shut already.

The door opened, and the two detectives slid into the room. Doh looked comfortable enough when he sat down, but Crispi looked like he had better things to do. I remember thinking that Crispi must have been a very unhappy person to be so anxious all the time. It seemed like the only way he knew how to express himself was through hostility. Poor guy. Life's too short for that.

Doh waved at me. "He fill you in?"

Carol was back answering e-mails or something. "My client told me you wish to talk to him again. Is this about the Johnny Culobrese murder? Or about the attempt on my client's life?"

Doh shot me a glance. "There have been two murders."

"I'll answer the questions for my client unless I instruct him otherwise." Carol's eye met Doh's. "First question."

"We have eyewitness reports that a man fitting Davin's description in a brown fedora was seen chasing a young man in the vicinity of the last shooting. A young man who jumped into the canal. DOT workers were there with the drawbridge up. One of them said Davin pushed him."

I was guessing the old lady clammed up and didn't call the cops. Figures. Brooklyn natives aren't what you'd call quick to call the cops and get involved if they can avoid it. They're kind of jaded when it comes to cops and robbers. I think they believe the cops and the crooks are all connected somehow and that it'll come back to bite them in the ass if they drop a dime.

Carol smiled. "You mean someone fitting the description of someone who looks like Tommy?"

"Was it him?" Doh's thumb was in my direction.

Carol looked at me. "Tommy, did you shove or otherwise physically affect any employee of the Department of Transportation yesterday?"

"Not that I recall."

Doh looked at me. "Did you chase that kid?"

I looked at Carol, and she said to me, "You can answer."

I made a mental note to make my new fedora vanish as soon as I went home. Best hundred bucks I ever spent.

I looked at Doh. "Not that I can recall."

The detective took his finger and tapped his chin. "Funny, because the DOT guy says it was a big guy with a cleft chin. So did Smychynsky, the guard at the telephone maintenance yard. Do you own one of those hats, Tommy?"

Carol cleared her throat. "Detective, is my client accused of a crime?"

Crispi couldn't hold it in any longer. "Your client is a material witness, who for some reason is withholding eyewitness information from the NYPD. He knows something about this sniper, and by not telling us is protecting him. Which means that your client is going to be facing felony charges when this whole thing comes out."

Carol looked at me. "Tommy, do you know who killed Johnny Culobrese and Huey LaMouche?"

I looked Doh in the eye so he'd understand I was leveling with him. "No."

"My client denies the accusation that he knows who the killer is that you're looking for. Any other questions, Detectives?"

Doh slid a photo out of the inside of his jacket and handed it to me. "Know her?"

My vision swam when I saw it, and I felt a little dizzy. Mechanically I tossed it on the desk in front of Carol. She cocked her head at the photo, looked at Doh, then looked at me. "Tommy, is this Yvette?"

"Yes."

It was a mug shot. Yvette's big blond hair was messed up, and her dark eyes focused above the camera somewhere, like she was remembering something. Those eyes. They were so dark you almost couldn't see where the pupils were.

Those eyes. They could look innocent. They could look mysterious. What they were, were black windows of deceit that overlooked worlds of opportunity.

Her olive face looked a little shiny in the flash of the camera. I could see she was wearing a cocktail dress, the dark red one. Dangling from the silver chain around her neck was the pendant I'd given her. An onyx cat with little red ruby eyes.

Seeing the pendant I gave her, and that she was still wearing it, made me feel spiritually misaligned. Assuming it had been taken recently and that she hadn't been arrested anytime while she was with me and I didn't know it. The info on the bottom of the photo, about where and when it was taken, had been blacked out. I wanted to pick it up and study it some more, but Carol handed it back to the detectives.

"Any more questions for my client?"

Doh bit his lip. "I thought your client might have some questions for us?"

Carol's eyes tightened as they locked onto mine. I know she wanted me to keep my cool. I did.

"I have no questions."

That was about as true as anything I'd told them that day.

I didn't want to know where the picture was taken, or how they knew I knew her, or anything. Yvette was trouble personified, and I wanted nothing to do with it. I was hurt that she would still wear that pendant.

Doh held the photo up to me.

"Did you ever think, Tommy, that maybe this bitch has something to do with what's going on?"

"That's enough, Detective." Carol was on her feet, her arm outstretched toward the door. "The interview is over. If you have any other questions, we'd be happy to meet again with you at another time."

The smug bastards stood and left.

I just sat there trying to breathe normally until they were out of the room. As soon as they were gone . . .

Breathe slowly in through the nose; close the eyes.

Breathe slowly out through the lips; stroke back my hair and face.

Breathe slowly in through the nose; open the eyes.

Breathe slowly out through the lips.

I managed to focus on Carol sitting in the chair where Doh had sat, her silver eyes sad.

"I'm sorry, Tommy. I wish there had been some way to protect you from that. Rat bastards are trying to rattle you. Do you have any idea how they know who she is? How they would make a connection between what's going on now and this woman?"

"Her name is Yvette, Vegas show girl. I have no idea what kind of trouble she's in now. I'm out of the business of dealing with her problems."

"At least once you pay the fifteen to Scanlon next week."

"Here's something I didn't mention because it's got nothing to do with this. The cats were catnapped the other day. I came home, the apartment was broken into, and the cats were gone."

"There was a note?"

"Yeah, telling me basically that Yvette better get in touch with Gustav or else the cats might be in a bad way. He left envelopes with what looked like love letters, too. They're written in a foreign language, looks like Russian or something."

Carol slumped back in her chair. "Cripes. Tommy, even for you this is out there. I mean, out there, you know what I mean?"

I was leaning forward, forearms on my knees, looking at the corner of the desk.

"Once I pay that fifteen, she is out of my life completely. Once I've paid the fifteen, I've done my bit. I've paid my full penalty for trusting and loving and trying to help her." I stood up and felt like it took a second for my stomach to stand up with me. "I'm going to get that fifteen. I'm going to have her out of my life."

Carol eased out of her chair and reached up to hold my face. "Tommy, if she's somehow connected to the art theft or murders, she may have one last kick in the gut for you, you know that, right?"

I tried a smile, but I think it came out as a grimace. "The guts have all been kicked out of me, sweetheart."

"Be smart about this, Tommy. Keep your head, stay smart. Call me if there's anything I can do. Anything."

My feet brought me to her office door. I opened it and walked through. The elevator arrived about an hour later, and I counted exactly eight million footsteps back to my apartment and the brandy.

Only when I picked up the bottle of negativity I put it back down.

Just like grieving is not about the dead but for those afraid of dying, heartbreak is not for love lost but for the fear of loneliness.

I didn't have time to die or be afraid.

TWENTY-SIX

SO A LITTLE AFTER ELEVEN I was walking toward the flying saucer that crashed into the Greek temple. I had an appointment to see Sheila McCracken.

Unsteady Freddy wasn't on duty that day, so I just nodded at the guard and made my way toward reception. With a building pass, I waded through the art lovers and headed upstairs to the museum offices.

On my way to Sheila's office, I ran into Atkins. He turned a corner and ran right into my chest.

He bounced a couple feet in the air. Not from the impact, but the surprise. "Shit!"

"Steady, Atkins."

"Damn, Tommy, what are you always doing hiding around the corners here?" There was some pink in his face to match his lips. The mustache wiggled nervously.

"Not hiding. Walking."

He says, "Well, you take up the entire width of the hallway."

So I says, "I can't help that. I'm on my way to see Sheila."

"Sheila? Going to see Sheila? About the other night?"

"As a matter of fact."

"What about?"

"Steady, Atkins. Nothing about you."

"I have a right to know if it concerns museum security. I should be in on this meeting."

"I guess if Sheila wanted you there, you would have been invited."

"You don't have to put it like that. I know she doesn't like me."

"Atkins, you're getting anxious. Try some deep breathing, like this."

So I started my tantric breathing exercise, but he threw up his hands. "I have no time for huffing and puffing. Just remember, don't fuck me over with her. You and I are friends."

Off he went down the hall, his feet making fast clicking steps like a terrier.

Odd duck, Atkins. I couldn't help thinking he'd get a lot out of yoga.

I waited in the reception area to be called into Sheila's office and tried not to think about that picture Doh showed me. Could Yvette be tied into this? She left me a month back, before I hatched the scheme to raise cash by shopping and settling. She couldn't have known any of the participants, except maybe have seen Huey at the bistro. Could that have been it? Huey obviously had a wandering eye, but how would they have slipped into a conversation about art theft and come up with an idea to rip me off? And Yvette and Ms. French as a dynamic evil duo? That was a stretch like a ham on a rubber band.

Of course, what Doh was talking about wasn't the art gig but the killings. I didn't think they knew about that connection. Otherwise he would have mentioned it. Why wouldn't he? It was a motive, the one he was probably looking to hang me on.

I was glad I pushed through my panic attack and didn't grab

the bottle earlier. For a number of reasons. Mainly because it would have kept me from moving forward. When screwy stuff like this mess happens, you won't get to the end of it unless you keep pushing. I didn't have many answers. Yet. I sure as hell wouldn't find them at the bottom of a bottle of transformative emotions. I had to stay out here talking to people. The truth is like a cat. If you want it to sit in your lap, you just have to stay long enough in the same room. I was encouraged just knowing that I would know all the answers in a couple days, if not before. I previsualized myself a couple days from then, looking back at me sitting in Sheila's reception area wondering what was what, thinking about all the things I could have done, might have done, to figure this out sooner. In a couple days I would know, so all I had to do was stay in the room with the cat for another couple days and it would sit in my lap.

Then again, maybe the cat would blow my brains out, too. Which would suck.

I got the tap from the secretary and went into Sheila's office. She wasn't there yet. Nice office. Big window facing the park, a bouquet of flowers on a side table, a plate glass desk an inch thick on top of Corinthian pedestals, a pair of stylish sling-back chairs for the visitor. The whole place was off-white. Even the flowers. Mums.

This was pretty much the way I remembered her office; it hadn't changed that much. Except the walls. There were four Postimpressionist paintings in the room that provided the only real color. I took a tour of them, but my attention was drawn to an appointment book open on her desk. A date with the Whitbread board for their fall meeting Friday, reception and dinner, at the museum.

The door opened. I didn't try to hide what I was doing.

"Checking my schedule?" Sheila's frame was packed into a pantsuit that was off-white like the room.

"Is your schedule secret? If so, better to keep it in a safe place. Somewhere outside of this museum."

She strode past me and settled in her chair. "What is it now?"

"Mind if I sit?"

She waved a hand at the sling-back chairs, and I slung into one of them. The tubular metal frame creaked from my size. Would have been kind of funny if it had collapsed. These designer chairs aren't made for people like me. I think they're made for designers.

"So, Tommy, you finally lost the beard and cut the eighties hair. New look?"

"You like it?"

"It's new."

"What would you think if I told you the missing goodies may be an inside job?"

Sheila pushed back her hair and sank into her own chair, one of those plush jobs with a high back she could rest her head on. "Atkins?"

I laughed, just a little. "I doubt it. As much as you might want that, I don't think he has the stomach for all the excitement that comes with being a thief."

"One of his guards?"

You could see she was looking for an excuse to kick his ass out the door. Something told me she'd find one, eventually. Just not from me.

"I'm thinking higher up, Sheel."

Her eyes went dull. "Don't call me Sheel, Tom."

"Oops, sorry, forgot. Is there anybody higher up here than the guards who may have been involved?"

"Have you even checked out the kitchen staff? The ones who were overcome?"

"I didn't have to. I already know who stole the paintings. What

I'm looking for is who commissioned it. Something tells me it wasn't Unsteady Freddy."

"If you know who the thief is, why not ask him who he sold them to?"

"He's dead."

She reacted to this news by not reacting. "So the paintings were shopped?"

I looked at the ceiling and then back at her. "Something like that."

"You are a pain in the ass, Tom, anybody ever tell you that?"

"You told me I was a pain in the ass the night you threw me out of your apartment in my shorts. It was definitely a pain in the ass to stand downstairs and catch my clothes as you threw them out the window. I never did find my lucky rabbit's foot."

That night was the one where she'd had to go before the museum directors, the night she was up against it with the museum board president, Lee J. Rosenburg, for the expanding cost of the flying saucer. That was the night she cut a deal with him to name a wing after him, the one with the Mondrians, those blocks of color. I couldn't figure out why she was so wigged out that night. I guessed that she'd had to humble herself and was going to try to humble me. She took out her hostility toward Rosenburg and the frustration over her predicament on me. I was the whipping boy. Like I said, I had a little rule about being a whipping boy.

Sheila closed her eyes, resting her head on the chair back. I don't know whether she was savoring the memory of throwing me out or trying to force it from her mind.

With her eyes still closed, she says, "Can we stay on topic?"

So I says, "Who in your organization might flip?"

"Flip?"

"Where's a weak spot, other than security, other than the kitchen? How about the conservators?"

She opened one eye. "The conservators?"

"Some of them work here, right? They don't make a lot of money. They may want to make more."

"If you want the records of the conservators, you should have bothered Atkins."

"What I want is your help. It could be a conservator, but I have reason to believe it is someone higher than that. Someone in administration."

Sheila squinted at me. "Are you here to suggest someone on my staff helped steal those paintings?"

"That's kind of where I'm going with this."

There was an outside chance Ms. French actually worked at the museum, though I didn't necessarily think so. If I pressured Sheila and her staff, it was possible I might squeeze out some indication of who was involved. Possibly even Sheila herself. That fit a buy-back scenario. So I was basically rocking the soda machine to see what dropped down.

"May I ask what evidence you have?"

"The investigation and all information pertaining to it is the sole property of my client, United Southern Assurance. They pay for the information. They can provide that for you if you wish."

"So you're saying I need to call Max to get you to tell me?" She growled and closed her eyes again.

"Sheila, I'm not trying to be a pain in the ass, really."

Her eyes looked at me sideways, what I think they call askance, which means those green irises didn't trust me, and may have resented me.

I continued. "If I told you what I know, it might taint the investigation."

"Taint? Is that one of your Scrabble words?"

I shook my head. "It's only five points, and even on a triple word play, that's only fifteen points, and there's no *s* or anything to tag it on another word. You know how I play. Most of my moves are at least twenty points."

"What do you want from me, Tommy? I have a small staff, and everybody on that staff I trust implicitly."

"Who do you got?"

"I've got an administrative assistant, a quality assurance administrator, two project administrators, a special events coordinator, publicity people, publications . . . about fifteen in all. You want their names and résumés, is that it?" She looked at her watch. A Cartier.

"Sure. Can I come get them tomorrow?"

"No. The less I have to deal with you or see you or have the chance of running into you the better. Call my assistant, and we'll send a messenger."

"I may need to question your staff. That OK?"

Her fingers drummed on the desk edge. "I'd rather you ran a short list by me first. We're a team here at the Whitbread, and I don't want rampant suspicions going around. We have jobs to do, a museum to run."

"That's a deal. Well, thanks." I climbed out of my sling chair, and at the door I turned. Her back was to me, and she was flipping through a date book in front of the window. I took out my phone like I was checking a message. "Sheila?"

"Hmm?" She turned.

"How much would you say those paintings are worth?"

"We estimate the replacement value at a million three. If we don't get them back, Max will try to shortchange us, probably give us point eight." She turned, her eyes squinty. "Didn't Max give you a figure for their recovery?"

"He did. By the way, I like the Postimpressionists on the walls in here. Nobody has a problem with you hanging them on your walls?"

I could almost hear her jaw tighten.

"The office and its walls belong to the museum. That art is from museum storage. Makes no difference if they're stored on my walls. It's all the museum."

I smiled. "Well, looks nice, Sheila. I'll be in touch."

I walked out the door, and made sure to take the turns in the hallway wide to avoid spooking Atkins.

Back outside I buttoned my overcoat. The wind was up chasing leaves off the trees and making things colder than they should have been.

At the subway entrance I made a call.

"Max."

"Tommy."

"I just got through with McCracken."

"McCracken? Why?"

"Because. I think she's involved."

"How?"

"I'm not sure yet."

"Sounds slim, Tommy."

"We'll see. But if she trips and I flip her, who knows who may drop out of the setup."

"You know who took them?"

"I do."

"Who?"

"My job is to recover the goodies."

"Who?"

"Doesn't matter, they don't have it anymore."

"Who?"

"McCracken says the paintings are worth a million three, and that she hoped to get at least point eight from USA. A recovery fee of fifty is thin spaghetti. You'll have to do better."

I hung up on him. Was that reckless? Maybe a little, but I was getting a head of steam up. I needed to push everybody connected to this to make sure I could pay the pink monkey and not get killed. If nothing else, Max was an asshole at the sushi place, and deserved a shove.

I dialed Blaise.

"Yo, Tomsy. You want that hardware?"

"Not yet. What I need is another follow. Whitbread Museum, woman in a white pantsuit works there, red hair, green eyes. I took a picture of her with my phone, I'll e-mail it to you. Has a set of hips and tits on her. Museum director, name is Sheila Mc-Cracken. Need a twenty-four report on her starting as soon as you can. She's at the museum now, probably leave the building at five."

"We can cover. You want photos this time, in advance, if anything interesting happens?"

"Yes. That was good work last time."

"We take pride in our work. Peace out."

I trotted down the steps into the subway, which was still warm from summer. It takes a long time for the concrete bunkers down there to cool off. August is not only hot, but the train air conditioners ramp up the ovenlike effect.

I stared down the dark tunnel, and before long I could see a white light flickering in the distance.

The light at the end of the tunnel.

The headlight of an approaching train.

TWENTY-SEVEN

FROM THE SUBWAY EXIT AT Carroll Street I circled away from Smith Street so I could approach my place from an unexpected angle, not from the usual way a guy would come from the subway. I didn't see anything screwy outside my place, so I went up the steps to my building and carefully entered the foyer. Through the glass I could see another note on my door. No, it wasn't another note from the catnapper. It was from Frank and Kootie. It said:

MEET AGAIN @ TIKI BAR @ 5.

My phone told me I had an hour to make that appointment.

From my closet I dug out a garment bag. I put another two suits into the bag, plus socks, underwear, and toiletries.

I needed to steer clear of my place for a few days. Too dangerous. That punk shooter had a knack for finding me around the neighborhood at will. Had to mix it up.

My phone buzzed, and I saw it was Walter, from Vegas.

"Hi, Walter."

"She's been arrested."

"I seen the mug shot. Where?"

"Miami. She was staying with friends there. If you want to call them friends. Seems they were growing pot in their basement. Like a whole forest of it, under all these lamps."

"She make bail?"

"Don't know, sweetie. Didn't call me. She knows I wouldn't lend her any more money anyway."

"Glad she had sense not to call me. Can you get word to her to call this asshole Gustav? He keeps leaving notes on my front door saying he's going to kill the cats if she doesn't call him."

"That is outrageous. The part about the cats, I mean, and about calling Gustav. He's insane, as you can see."

"What's his deal?"

"He loves her. What else."

"He rich?"

"He's connected. Russian or from Kazakhstan or some ungodly place. Was new here in town but knew her when she was a kid. Went after Yvette like a bird dog. Real wiseguys only use show girls as playthings. This one wanted to play house. A romantic streak as wide as the strip and twice as long. Figures he'd go after the cats. Used to send her cases of food for them, drop by with toys. Well, it was obvious he thought the way to her heart was through the cats, you know."

"Lovesick, huh? Poor guy doesn't know what he's in for with Yvette. I almost feel sorry for him. Except the notes I find every day disrupt my flow of positive energy. I have a lot on my plate here at the moment and can't have this dope poking around making trouble."

He sighed. "I'll see what I can do about letting her know about the catnapping, Tommy."

"Thanks, Walter. Keep me informed, will you? How's the show going? You making all the Vegas boys lovesick?"

Walter chuckled. "I still turn a few heads, if not all. Ciao, Big Tommy."

Nice guy, Walter. I made a note in my head to send him some flowers. He'd appreciate a gesture like that.

I dialed a car service. Yeah, I know the tiki bar is around the corner, but I needed rolling shelter to jump into when I left my place. Blue Diamond—why not? Maybe I'd luck out and get Ms. French's driver. I'd have him drive me up to the Slope and back down. That would give me a chance to see if I was being followed.

Then I put on my trench coat and picked up my hat. It was kind of white around the band from my sweat, from chasing the punk shooter. Then I noticed a spot on the crown. I held it up to the light. The light shone through. It wasn't a spot. It was a bullet hole. The kid's wild shot just went through the hat, missing my brain by an inch.

Standing over the open toilet, I cut the hat into little pieces with shears and flushed each piece. When I was done destroying my new hat, my cell rang. The car was out front.

With my bag, I made a straight line from the front door to the town car without getting shot. Moving targets make the worst ones. I slumped down, and the driver drove off.

"Driver?"

"Yes?"

"Did you work Sunday?"

"Sunday?"

"Yes. On Sunday did you happen to pick a woman up on Court Street, at Donut House?"

There was a chilly silence. "I no work Sunday. Or Monday. Thank God."

My cell rang. It was Skip, my nephew. I'd almost forgotten I had asked him to look up Dunwoody Exports.

"What do you have for me, Skip?"

"The question is, Uncle Tommy, when will I get the thirty bucks?"

"I can't exactly hand it to you over the phone, can I?"

"PayPal."

"I don't have PayPal."

There was a snort on the other end.

"Skip, where are you now?"

"Headed to the subway."

"Yeah? Where?"

"Polytech."

"Wait for me at the corner of Jay at Tillary. I'll be right there."

I hung up and told the driver about the change of course.

In ten minutes I saw Skip on the corner. There was no missing him. Two things you can count on kids to do: have bad hair and worse clothes. His hair stuck out like he'd touched the third rail, and he and his drab clothes drooped under it. I waved him over to the car, and he got in back with me.

"You headed home, kid?" I handed him the thirty dollars.

He tucked the cash in his black jeans. "I get a drive home?"

"Most of the way." I gave the driver new orders. "Don't want your folks getting wise."

"Wise?" Skip snorted. "They're stupid."

Like I said, I was probably once a smart-mouth kid. As an adult, though, you get sad watching a kid like this try so hard to be cool. There's desperation in a jaded thirteen-year-old. Like Pop used to say, cool is as cool does, not how cool looks or acts.

"Let's have the information."

"I'll e-mail it." He started fooling with his phone.

"While you do, give me the highlights."

"Dunwoody Exports is, like, a corporation licensed and bonded in New York to ship bulk artwork overseas. Know the big bargain-basement art sales you see, like, advertised on cable?"

"You mean like 'Starving Artist Sale' at the Rumsey Quality Inn?"

"Yeah. They buy bulk paintings from little galleries clearing their inventory of crap like Mom paints in the backyard and thinks she's going to make, like, a million dollars."

I knew what he was talking about. There were a lot of little amateur painters like his mom, my sister, Katie, out there. Discount galleries took their art on commission. When they couldn't move the art, they would pay the artist five bucks and take five times that for themselves by dumping the paintings to outfits like Dunwoody. A huge amount of mostly crappy paintings found its way to the starving artist sales, including the one in Rumsey you see on TV. After those sales, companies like Dunwoody take what's left and ship them overseas, mostly to Asia. Believe it or not, sometimes the better stuff will end up being copied over and over in oil paint by an Asian getting a buck an hour and shipped back here. You see these oil paintings in some of the giant wholesale outlets and odd lots. So one day Katie may see a forgery of one of her paintings in Statewide Wholesalers out at the mall. I kid you not.

"Is Dunwoody still in operation?"

"That's, like, where this story gets interesting. There was, like, a legal action against them by some galleries who, like, hadn't been paid, and the district attorney found out the company was actually owned by a construction company in Staten Island. The company was kind of bogus, connected to the mob and maybe shipping stolen art out of the country hidden among all the crappy art."

I sat forward. "When did all this happen?"

"Like, a year ago?"

"Is that a question?"

"What?"

"When you said 'Like, a year ago?' it sounded like a question."

"You must be high, Uncle Tommy?"

"Now is *that* a question? Because you said it exactly the same way as the other thing that you said."

I was busting his shoes. I knew it wasn't a question. Just sometimes the screwy way kids speak by ending every sentence like a question, coming up in tone at the end, rubs me the wrong way.

Skip rolled his eyes and snorted. "What*ever.* Yes, it was about a year ago. It's all in the e-mail."

"So what happened?"

My nephew shrugged. "It was, like, they couldn't totally prove anything, so the grand jury didn't hand down an indictment. Dunwoody stopped their art auctions, and Molly Lee vanished."

I opened my phone and checked the e-mail he sent me to see if there were any interesting details. The front name on the company, who ran the day to day, was someone named Molly Lee. Not familiar. The alleged mobster: Jimmy Robay. Not familiar.

Where did an art clearinghouse fit in with this? Sure, Dunwoody could have helped Jo-Ball move paintings overseas and internationally. Just mix the goodies in with junk and what customs official would know?

"Next job, nephew. Find me everything you can on Molly Lee."

"Oh, yes, master! How can I *serve* you?"

"You want more money or not?" I held out forty. He took it without a smart remark. "I'm paying for the next information in advance because I don't want you directing latent hostility at me. I have enough problems."

"Like my life is problem-free? Do you have any idea what it's like being thirteen?"

"Gee, I guess not. I went directly from twelve to fourteen."

I gave serious thought to acting out. Strangling him with his own arms seemed like it would be a nice emotional release for me. I closed my eyes and imagined it instead.

He says, "What are you, like, smiling about?"

So I says, "You really want to know, Skip?"

He felt the negative energy I was giving off and shrank back into his seat.

I dropped Skip in Windsor Terrace a block from his house and headed back to the tiki bar. I could only imagine what Frank and Kootie were up to.

TWENTY-EIGHT

"WE GOT THE KEYS." FRANK'S eyes were sparkling with triumph, with the fireplace, and with a little too much of whatever brown stuff he was drinking.

Kootie was next to him with a glass of water, biting a nail. "It wasn't easy."

"Let's go get the money, Tommy, what do you say?"

I stood over them, making a point of looking able to crush them.

"Sure, but I have to make sure you guys don't try to rip me off. Kootie and I will go. We're too much of a match for each other to try anything. I'll have to pat you down, though, Kootie."

"Hold it hold it hold it." Frank waved his hands in the air. "How do I know Kootie will bring me my cash?"

Kootie pushed his water away and gave Frank a look that could have bruised fruit. "You want to explain that commentary?"

"Kootie, I'm just saying. Sweet Jesus, I trust you as much as I'd trust anybody. It's just there's a lot of money. People act different when they have a big pile of cash, you know that."

Eyes on mine, Kootie says, "Well, I'll tell you one thing. Frank isn't going with you alone. Look, Tommy, we're on the up-and-up."

So I says, "If it's two of you going, I need someone to watch my back."

Frank's glass swerved away from his lips. "Who?"

BLAISE JONES SAT BETWEEN FRANK and Kootie. His gold chains, metallic teeth, sequined Yankees hat, and sunglasses twinkled in the passing streetlamps. Blaise could sense the discomfort of his seatmates and seemed to be enjoying it.

We'd agreed to give Mr. Jones a small percentage off the top to referee.

I was in the seat ahead of them. We were in a minivan I'd ordered from Blue Diamond, headed toward the storage facility.

"Driver? Can I ask you a question?"

"Yes, of course, of course."

"Did you drive Sunday for Blue Diamond?"

"This last Sunday? Sunday?"

"Yes. This last Sunday did you maybe pick a woman up on Court Street, at Donut House, and deliver her to the Williamsburg Savings Bank?"

There was a chilly silence. "I work Sunday. Airport. Not Donut House."

"Thanks. If you happen to find another driver who did, and he'll tell me about the woman, I'll pay him for his time and give you forty bucks. Here's my card."

The driver took the card, looked at me, and then looked back at the road without another word.

"Heh. So, Tomsy, I appreciate you calling me in on this, I really do. It's like a part-tay, right, boys?"

I flashed him a smile. Blaise cracked me up. "Turn right here, driver."

Minutes later we were standing in front of the storage facility. Blaise had the bling, but he didn't have height. He was shorter than Frank, but probably a lot nastier in a fight. So I figured they were a matched set.

"OK, so Kootie and I will go in, you two watch each other out here."

"Wait a minute wait a minute wait a minute." Frank was waving his ugly hands around. "Why don't we all go in? Kind of brisk out here?"

"Yo, be steady, Eddie, be cool." Blaise stirred the air with his fingers. "Two on the outside, two on the inside, that's jake."

Kootie inflated his chest. "Let's do it his way and get out of here, get the money."

"Keys?" I put out my hand to Frank, and he handed them to Kootie. Cute.

Kootie and I were back out in five minutes. The duffel bag was under my arm.

Frank pointed at it. "Got it? Jesus, did we get it?"

I put the bag in his arms. "All yours. C'mon, Blaise. I owe you a drink."

OVER BY THE HOUSING PROJECTS where Blaise lives is a bar called PJ's. It's not anything like the bars up on Smith Street. It's where the homeboys hang. You might think I'd be uncomfortable hanging around all the gangsta types. Most white guys are intimidated by it. I think they're supposed to be; I think that's part of the point. I never asked Blaise about it, and he never offered, but I always took it for granted there was some humor built into the whole scene, and a touch of self-deprecation, like they were goofing on themselves a little. Maybe I was wrong. Anyways, it didn't bother me any, and at least I could be pretty sure I was safe in that crowd from any snipers.

There wasn't any music in the bar itself, but there was a car out front that was more or less a giant speaker with about eight homeys leaning on it drinking cans of malt liquor.

I think Blaise enjoyed making an entrance at PJ's with a giant white guy carrying a suit bag. There were some looks, and some comments that I couldn't make out. For Mr. Jones, it showed his reach went beyond Hoyt Street and Third Avenue. It kept them guessing. The walls of PJ's were scrawled with graffiti. So was the ceiling, and the tables, and the mirror behind the bar. It was like a bombed subway car from the seventies. We sat at a table in the back so we could talk. The bartender automatically brought us a forty-ounce bottle of malt liquor and two glasses.

I put a hand on the bartender's arm. "I want mine on the rocks. Please."

He looked at me, then at Blaise. He came back with a glass of ice and put it next to me.

"Thanks."

Blaise was chuckling. "Why you always have to do that, Tomsy? Damn."

I smiled. "It amuses me, Blaise. It's from a movie."

He was nodding, his bloodshot eyes looking at me over the sunglasses. "You told me. *Brother from Another Planet.*"

I nodded along with him. "And right now I'd go a mile for a chuckle."

"What kind of game you playing?"

I sighed and sipped. You know, malt liquor actually is good on the rocks. Next time I'd ask for a twist just to mess with Blaise. "Usual game. Missing paintings. Only I'm looking for the money that was paid for the paintings. The artwork is long gone."

"So your man, the bistro dude who lost his hat, he made a sign on you." In Blaise's world, a guy who loses his hat gets shot in the head. Making a sign on me meant pulling a fast one on me.

"Huey was probably worried that the people who paid him off were following him to the storage place. That they might try to take the cash back after they had the paintings. Or he didn't trust Frank and Kootie not to tag him. So in the car on the way to the storage locker he must have switched out the money, and sent the money on in the car to someone else. His wife, Ariel, probably. Which means I'll never get that money."

"I see but I don't see. Why folks losing their hats in your hood? Heh. I even hear you did it."

His eyes had false laughter in them.

"Is that what you want to know?"

He shrugged and drained his glass. "I wouldn't dis you if you did cap the mofos who diced you. That's law around here."

I looked over at the bar, and some of the homeys turned away. Blaise filled his glass and mine.

"Well, Blaise, what can I say. I have a little rule about killing people. I don't. It's bad karma, just for starters. Bad energy just gets you more bad energy."

Blaise laughed, his gold teeth flashing. "You bust me, Tomsy, you really do. If that's your creed, it's cool. You know, I think that's why I like you, Tomsy. You got creed. Not my creed, I got my own. But I like a man with a creed."

"Yeah, I'm loaded with creed."

We clinked glasses and drank.

"Can I ask you something, Blaise?"

He wrinkled his brow. "Maybe."

"You think good things happen to good people?"

"Say what?"

"Do you think good things happen to good people, to people with creed, say?"

"Hell no!"

"Never?"

"Look, my man, creed only means you have a code, a method to your mad-ass capers."

"Survivors don't tend to get too cute and double-cross their friends. If they do, eventually it comes back to bite them in the ass, right?"

Blaise leaned forward. "Why you asking me about this, Tomsy? I mean, this is Blaise you're talking to. I've messed people up."

"Just the same, but you're a good person."

"You crack me up, Tomsy. I'm only a good person where it pays to be a good person. I'd sell you out in a second if your sorry ass were worth anything."

"It pay to be having a drink with me?"

"I consider it an investment."

I grinned at him. "I consider your friendship an investment, too."

Blaise wrinkled his nose, nostrils flaring, eyes bulging. "Friendship?"

Now I laughed. "Mad-dog me like you mean it, Blaise!"

That got him. He broke into a smile that lit half the room. "Damn, Tommy, I do like your creed."

We clinked glasses again, and he said, "So how we going to keep you from getting iced?"

"Wish I knew. Whoever is doing these killings, it seems they have it out for anybody connected with these paintings."

"Must be stacks of jacks out there on this."

I shook my head. "It's only a hundred thousand."

Blaise put his elbows on the table. "Come again?"

"Kid you not."

"Sounds like the sausage people. They kill if you step on their shoelace."

I shook my head again. "But do they do it in broad daylight? No. The person goes missing, or takes a canal bath, or falls off a building. This is not the mob's style at all."

"What about the Russian flicks? They mean."

"The Russians are way out in Coney. Not their turf."

"How come the shooter ain't capped your hat yet?"

"He took a wild shot at me when I was standing next to Jo-Ball, but I don't think he was really trying. He tried again when I chased him after Huey lost his hat. Missed both times."

"Maybe they trying to scare you."

"Doing a good job. But scare me for what reason? I don't have the money or the paintings."

My phone jumped around in my pocket. I didn't recognize the number, but maybe, somehow, it was good news. "Excuse me, Blaise. Yes?"

"It's Bridget."

"OK."

"Can we meet?"

"Now?"

"You said to call."

"You remember something?"

"Maybe. Can we meet at Bar Great Harry on Smith?"

"Now?"

"Yeah, nowish. You know . . ."

"Meet me at Canal Bar on Third." Whenever someone you don't entirely trust calls and wants to meet one place, always suggest another. A little rule I had. "Twenty minutes?" Always get there first. Another little rule.

"Um, OK."

I hung up. "Got a date with an angel."

Blaise waited for more.

"A fallen angel."

"Bridget buzzed me yesterday about you. Heh!"

"What's her deal, Blaise?"

He shook his head and shrugged. "Just made the scene in February. Indies like her come and go around here. They make a stake and they gone. Can't hustle too long in one spot. Cops hang with her, but they stay too long and something bad happens."

"Like what?"

"Some john'll give her both fists. Indies, they got to keep moving to new pastures."

"Dangerous work."

"They all get the fist some time. Just the way it goes."

"Huey stopped by to visit her before he got popped, after dropping off the bag at the storage locker. His way of celebrating."

"How much she know about the paintings?"

"Nothing. Huey just went there for a screw and to complain."

"About his wife. Heh. Always. They tell me some *just* go to complain."

"I've heard that." I stood and drained my glass.

"Be cool, Tomsy." Blaise put out a fist. "I like having you around."

I bumped his little fist with my big one and hefted my suit bag.

"Let me know if you hear anything useful, OK? Be nice if I got that report on McCracken as soon as it comes in."

"Peace out."

THIRTY-ONE

CANAL BAR. IT WAS TRYING to be a dive, but it didn't
have to try hard. Just the same, they didn't have malt liquor on the
rocks, or any other way, so I had to settle for brandy. My suit bag
was on the bar stool to my right next to the wall. There was an open
stool on my left, and then some stools filled with low-rent patrons
beyond that. No homeboys, just grungy would-be starving artists
and the stray slumming hipster or local. The place was lit with
neon and bar signs. The bartender had enough sideburns for two.

The girl with the brown hair and moles saddled up on the bar
stool next to me. There was a long red fuzzy scarf wrapped around
her neck a hundred times, and there was a red beret on her head.
The lipstick matched both.

I have to say that I'm always a little surprised by off-duty professional girls. By professional I mean the entire sex industry, to
include strippers and all that. Up near Times Square there's a
"gentlemen's club," and if you pass by at certain times of day you
see the second shift arriving. These girls stand out front and smoke
before heading in to their jobs. Outside in street clothes they don't
turn a head. Inside with their hair pumped up, eyes spiked, nipples
mentholed, and body dusted in sparkles, they look like every man's

dream come true. It's not just the coats of paint and costume (or lack of it), but that the sex light is turned on inside them.

Bridget's sex light was off. I was trying to imagine what it would look like turned on and couldn't.

"How's the tantric exercise working out?"

She ordered a vodka, one from the top shelf. "It's awesome. Thanks."

"So, what's what?"

Bridget squirmed and then looked into my eyes. I knew the look. *Can I trust him?*

I says, "Bridget, you can trust me about as well as you can trust anybody. I'm a straight shooter, you know that much about me, and I have good energy flow between my head and my heart."

So she says, "Tommy, I'm scared. Every time I open the door or step outside, I think someone will be waiting. Because of Huey. They'll think I know something. Or whatever."

"Or whatever?"

From her coat pocket came a folded piece of paper, blue with lines on it. She held it out. I took it. I had to figure Bridget was as good at faking interest with her clients as looking blank much of the rest of the time. Maybe she had to save that part of her for business.

I held up the paper before opening it. "How'd you get this?"

"Under the door."

I unfolded the blue paper and my eyes went down to the bottom to see who it was from. It was signed HIS WIFE.

I can't really tell you what it said, verbatim. Now there's a good Scrabble word for you. The *v, m,* and *b* in the same word, which alone equal ten points. To spell it out it's likely you'd need to use all seven tiles and score fifty bonus points. Get that across a triple space and we're talking mega pointage.

Anyway, the letter was profane and, if I do say so, a little long for what it had to say, which was really just hostility directed at Bridget. The name Huey jumped out at me. It seemed Ariel had discovered her late husband's dalliance and felt that this was somehow Bridget's failing. There were threats, too. Threats to expose her, which I thought kind of laughable. Every male for blocks around knows when there's a professional girl working the neighborhood, and it's not like the cops didn't know. A low-profile indie like this isn't worth their time. On duty.

Another threat in there was physical. It had to do with a hammer, that's all I'll say.

I looked up. "Not a nice thing."

Her eyes were tearing up. "It was a very mean thing to do. Like him coming to me was my idea, like I was stealing her man. You know, Tommy . . ." She paused to wipe away a tear. You'd think a girl like Bridget would be hard as nails, but it goes to show you everybody has an emotional center. "You know, Tommy, I probably save more marriages than I screw up, doing what I do. The men, if they didn't come to me, would get a girlfriend who would take them away from their wives. It's true. Girlfriends start out OK with the guy being married, then they want more, bloop bloop bloop."

"I never thought of it that way." I patted her arm. "It sucks when people project their negativity at you, especially so unfairly. I'm sorry. You worried about the threats?"

Bridget nodded, pressing a bar napkin into the corners of her eyes.

I laughed as softly as I could. "Babe, Ariel is just venting her emotions the only way she knows how. I wouldn't worry. If she came to your door and confronted you, that would be something else. This is like e-mail or whatever online. People act out in ways they can't in real life."

"Still . . . what should I do?"

"Don't do anything."

"Should I go talk to her?"

I took her hand. "No. You hear me, no, do not under any circumstances go to the bistro and talk to her about this. It will only make things worse. If you get another letter, then I'll maybe see if there's something I can do, but for now, just let it go. You know, Bridget, that you're a good person, and probably a better person than Ariel. So stay that way. Hold on to your good energy. The bad energy is Ariel's, and you got to remember that part of the emotions that come with losing a husband is anger. This isn't so much directed at you as at him."

Her eyes looked hopeful. "You think so?"

"I know so. Very common for a wife to be angry at a husband for dying, and to look for reasons to be angry at him, too."

She seemed to notice my luggage for the first time, and pointed. "Is that yours?"

"Yeah."

"Going on a trip?"

"Sleeping somewhere away from home. The motel near the Battery Tunnel, I guess."

"Why?"

"The guy who's doing the shooting may have a bullet for me, so until the police find him—"

"Yuk. You can't be serious."

"I am serious. This guy may be—"

"I mean about the motel."

I shrugged as an answer.

"Tommy, that place is foul. It's a bump-and-thump." Bump-and-thump is what they call a Motel No-tell in Brooklyn.

"Hopefully it's just for one night. With two dead, it's too dangerous to go back to my place."

"Come home with me."

I rubbed my jaw. "That doesn't seem like a good idea."

"Why not?" Her feelings looked a little hurt, like she thought it was because of her business.

"If you ask me, people have the right to not wear seat belts, but I'm not crazy about sleeping in a place with cigarette smoke."

"I don't smoke at home, Tommy." She registered the confusion on my face and added, "I don't run my business out of my home. I live downstairs. I don't smoke there, only at work. Comes with the territory."

"I wouldn't want to put you out or anything."

"You'd be doing me a favor, Tommy. I'm worried someone is going to come around about Huey. I have a futon for you."

I had to think about that a moment, and did so as I sipped my brandy. Was I setting myself up for more trouble with a woman? There was no way I was going to be romantically involved with Bridget, if that's what you're thinking. I'm pretty dumb that way, but not that dumb. The mole situation on her skin was a turnoff for me, just for starters. Just that here was a woman with a potential problem and I was about to allow myself to get mixed up with it. Then again, if someone did come after her, like the punk shooter, putting my hands on that person would go a long way to figuring out exactly what was going on and maybe how I could squeeze my fifteen grand out of this situation.

Staying in a bump-and-thump can be dangerous, too, and I wasn't looking forward to staying there. Jealous boyfriends and husbands crashed in there about once a week, waking everybody up. Or at least waking the few people actually asleep. Also a bedbug scare was on in Brooklyn. Bugs crawling into my bed and sucking my blood in the night freaks me out.

So I said OK, and we walked with my bag back to the green loft. I kept my eyes open when we came close to her building, but there was just a couple people walking their dogs on Bond Street.

There was more than one door into the green loft, and this time we used one around the side. It had no bell buzzer at all, and no mail slot. I guess she liked her privacy and used a post office box for her mail.

Her apartment was completely different from the one upstairs at the other entrance. It was all Ethan Allen, with cream wall-to-wall carpet and English school oil paintings on the Sheetrock walls.

"Spare room is in back, and you can hang your stuff on the back of the bathroom door in there." She hung up her red beret and long fuzzy scarf on an antique coatrack. "My bathroom is off that way, and the master bedroom."

I walked the carpet back and found a very nice guest room, though it didn't look finished. The white walls were freshly painted, and the futon bed looked temporary. It didn't go with anything else in the apartment. The bathroom was basic and white.

Bridget appeared in the doorway. "Sorry, this part of the place isn't really finished yet. I'm working on it."

I took off my coat and draped it over the back of a rocking chair, the only other piece of furniture in the guest room. "Very nice place, Bridget. You've done a real nice job with it. Your landlord know about all this?"

"I own."

I paused. "The whole factory?" Her apartment occupied only a small part of the building's square footage, which had a footprint of maybe two hundred by one hundred feet and two floors.

"Uh huhn, through a holding company." She smiled to herself.

"I'm a speculator. When they finally rezone this area, I can sell and quit my job."

Speculators had been buying up vacant industrial properties around the Gowanus and pushing for a zoning change to develop the area along the canal. True, the canal was kind of nasty, but it was waterfront property. There could be a marina if they cleaned it up a little. Only the scrap yard downstream was any kind of functioning business on the canal. All the other businesses—except I guess the telephone company yard—were defunct as far as I could tell.

"I know what you're thinking, Tommy. The usual hooker story, right? Sits on a nest egg waiting to cash in and get out of the business."

"Hold the phone, Bridget. If you and I are going to be friends, our chakras have to be in harmony. I wasn't thinking anything like that. I was thinking you're a smart businesswoman. That's it. I try not to judge people."

Her sarcasm melted into something that looked like a mixture of sadness and nostalgia. Well, I guess nostalgia is always a little sad somehow, which is why I try never to be nostalgic. I try to keep looking forward, where there's no chance of tripping over regret.

"You got a nightcap around, Bridget?"

"I'll dig up the Napoleon."

"No need to get fancy."

"C'mon, Tommy." She disappeared from the doorway. "Life's too short not to get fancy once in a while."

I followed her into the living room and saw her open a mahogany sideboard loaded with liquor. While she made the drinks, I studied the paintings. They were textured copies, nice ones, many that showed ships or landscapes with wild skies.

"I like the Turners, Bridget. Though I have to admit I'm not a huge fan of Constable."

"I like Turner best. Romantic and yet . . ."

"Impressionist."

"You know something about art." She handed me a snifter. Looked like she had a glass of port.

"I have a degree in art history from Brooklyn College."

"Really?"

"Can you imagine me lying about that?"

She laughed, and looked much prettier. "I think artists put a lot of themselves, a lot of positive energy, into their work, and just having them around is healthy. Goya? Not so much."

"I never thought of it that way. Sure, some artists have positive energy in their work."

"Turner really does it for me. All the rich colors, soft light, stormy skies, ships, bloop bloop bloop."

"You're right. They give off a good energy here."

Bridget smiled. "Thanks."

An orange tabby was at my feet, rubbing my leg. "Who do we have here?"

"That's Turner."

"I guess you should have let me guess his name." I scooped up the cat, a male. "Friendly."

"Not to everybody. He hates the plumber. Sprayed him."

Turner was sniffing my face and neck, so I put him on my shoulder. There's plenty of room there. Tigsy used to like to stand on my shoulder.

Bridget says, "You have cats?"

So I says, "One would be nice."

She laughed. "I'm a speculator in a lot of things, but Turner Cat isn't for sale. You should get one. They obviously take to you."

Turner purred and smashed his whiskers against my ear.

"Cats and me have a similar chakra, I think. I'll try to be out of here tomorrow, but I can't guarantee my place will be safe by then."

"Stay as long as it takes to make this threat go away. You won't see me too much over the next couple days unless you turn in late. Most of my business is afternoons and nights, sometimes late. Then I sleep late. Today was my day off. Here's the key."

A large, multiedged key was in her hand, like the new one I had for my apartment. She dropped it from her little hand into my big one. I lifted Turner and plopped him on the floor.

"Just the same, I'll be a good houseguest, and I appreciate your friendship." I headed for my room. "Most of my work is during the day, so I'll be out of your hair. Just shout if there's trouble. You have my number."

She smirked, the cat now in her arms. "You know, Tommy, I actually believe you."

"Believe me?" I had almost closed the door but stuck my head back out. "How's that?"

"Rest well."

I smiled back at her. "Don't let the bedbugs bite."

I drifted into sleep worrying about whether Tigsy was getting his shots.

THIRTY-TWO

MY BRAIN SOMETIMES WAKES ME like a cat that wants to be fed. That particular morning my brain cat was working over my situation trying to find a focal point. It was anxious to see the report on McCracken's travels overnight.

At the same time, as I rolled over and tried to go back to sleep, my brain was flipping through the people involved, and it kept sorting out the weak ones. It kept coming back to Frank Buckley and Kootie Roberts.

Then my brain came around to Atkins. I hadn't given him much thought in this whole thing, but my brain was telling me he was a good inside source at the museum, that if McCracken were up to something and he knew about it, he might tell the right person. She was out to get him, he had to know that, and if he had information that could get her in trouble, it would be in his interest to use it.

Even weaker than Atkins was Unsteady Freddy. He was there Sunday night when the gig went down. He'd said he was rotating to last night's shift. The guards who worked the night shift often went to a rooster bar on Vanderbilt, off of Grand Army Plaza.

Rolled over and picked up my phone. The clock read:

6:15

The night shift ended at six.

I was dressed and out Bridget's door and in a car service half an hour later. It was a real nice morning, too. The sky was all kinds of blue and orange, the sun struggling to climb over Manhattan and warm all the cold brownstones of Brooklyn.

"Driver?"

"Hm?"

"Did you drive Sunday?"

"This last Sunday?"

"If you drove Sunday, did you happen to pick a woman up on Court Street, at Donut House?"

"I work Sunday."

"Did you pick up a woman at Donut House on Sunday?"

"What kind woman?"

I sat forward. "Any kind of woman."

"Yes, I pick up woman."

"From Donut House? On Court Street?"

"Yes, I pick up woman, but not from Donut House."

"So you didn't pick up a woman from Donut House?"

"No. I pick up woman on Sunday. Not from Donut House."

I sat back. I don't know what country he came from, but it must have had inside-out lightbulbs and chairs on the ceiling.

As we drove, I witnessed kids bundled up for school being guided out the door by their parents onto stoops cluttered with pumpkins, dried cornstalks, and plastic skeletons.

Rooster bars don't conform to the Liquor Control Board's rules on when taverns have to close, which is at four. That's when these places open. Sometimes they serve people who started their revels at midnight, the club kids, the social vampires. Mostly they serve the night shift. These poor guys have been up all night and need to sleep while it's light out. Not many people find that an easy thing to do. It helps to knock you out if you have a couple pops. If you needed an excuse to drink, this was as good as any. Except I don't think Freddy needed much excuse.

Comanche was the name of the place, and like most of the roosters, it was in a basement to help insulate it from discovery by the uninitiated. The cops know about these places, unofficially, because they're some of the best customers of the roosters. The NYPD never sleeps.

There was no sign for Comanche; you just had to know it was the basement stairwell around the corner from the shuttered fried chicken place. At the bottom of the stairs I rang the bell, and a red light came on overhead. There was a lens next to the door. I was being scoped out. Not that they could tell I was from the Liquor Control Board just to look at me, but I guess they figured they could at least refuse entry to falling down drunks. The door buzzed. I went in.

You'd certainly have never known it was seven in the morning. More like seven in the evening. The bar was on the right with about a dozen padded bar stools and ten patrons. Six tables were on the left, almost all full. A jukebox was playing Billy Joel.

Low ceilings, red lights, and cheap Remington prints were the decor. Remington is the one who was famous for his Native American portraits. Otherwise the place was just a basement tavern devoid of any natural light and smelling a little musty, a little smoky, a little yeasty. Even though smoking is against the law in bars and restaurants in New York, it wouldn't make sense for roosters. Can't exactly have people standing outside a rooster smoking or it would be obvious there was an after-hours pub there. They were running illegally anyway.

Only the sanitation workers had uniforms on, green from head to toe. You couldn't tell what the others did, whether they were night maintenance men, postal workers, or security guards. There were only three or so women.

I got the once-over as I moved down the bar looking for Freddy. I didn't exactly fit the profile in my suit and topcoat. The final seat at the bar was open, but there was a glass of beer with a coaster on top. Next to it was an empty shot glass.

I don't know about other places, but in Brooklyn, a coaster on a glass means the patron stepped out and will be back.

A large Hispanic bartender with shaggy hair and sharp side-burns was suddenly across from me. He had a dark smile and a thick neck. "You LCB?"

They ask this of me at rooster bars. They ask anybody who doesn't fit the profile. It's done because a Liquor Control Board agent has to identify himself if asked. If not, anything that happens afterward is entrapment. That's what I'm told, anyway.

"I'm not LCB. Just the same, I'm not ending my day, I'm just starting it. So I can't really have a drink and do my job, hope you understand. Got any coffee?"

He cocked his head. "It'll cost you the same as a drink."

"That's fair enough. You're in the business of selling liquor, not coffee. My name is Tommy. I was hoping to run into someone here."

"I'm Hector, and I don't want no trouble." His neck muscles flexed, and the large hands dropped out of sight. As they did so, the bar went quiet. Except for Billy Joel.

"Like I said, Hector, I'm not LCB, so I'm not trouble."

"You're looking for somebody, which means you're some sort of cop or bounty hunter."

"I guess from your experience that someone who looks like me and says he's looking for a friend has been trouble in the past. OK, I can understand why you're anxious. I'm not a bounty hunter or private detective or some ball buster. I'm not trouble, Hector, so you can relax. So can your customers." I held my coat open and turned all the way around so he could see I had no gun or other weapon. "I was hoping to run into Freddy."

The front door opened.

"Fucking aye . . ." It was Freddy registering that something in the bar was wrong. It took a few seconds for him to see me as the center of attention and realize who I was. "Tommy?"

The whole room seemed to exhale.

Hector put out a hand, and I shook it. "Sorry. I have to be careful."

"No sweat, Hector."

"Coffee is on me. I just made a pot."

"Nice of you, thanks."

Freddy's arms were waving uncertainly at me as he approached. "Tommy, what're you doing here? I still say you look like Kirk Douglas with the cliff chin."

"You told me you were working the night shift. I was in the neighborhood with a little time to kill, figured I might find you here, buy you a drink."

He slid in front of the beer and knocked the coaster off the top. "That's white of you, Tommy, thanks. But even a drunk like me knows you want information. Am I right?"

"I wouldn't try to snow you, Freddy. Of course that's why I'm here, but you're your own man. You can tell me nothing. We can talk about the Giants." I almost mentioned the Mets, but in October that can be a sore subject; better to not mention it at all. "I'll still buy you the drinks, because I like you and consider you a friend."

Freddy looked surprised, and touched. His denture glowed in the neon light. "Jeese, Tommy, that's nice of you to say. I don't got a lot of friends. Other booze hounds don't count."

Hector put the coffee down in front of me along with a container of sugar packets. "Cream?"

I shook my head. "Thanks anyway. Get Freddy whatever he's having."

Freddy ordered another beer and a shot of B&B, then turned to me. "I feel funny drinking booze when you drink coffee."

"Sorry, Freddy, but I'm just starting my day. When you're on day shift I'd be happy to drink brandy, but if I get in the bag right now I won't be able to do my job."

Freddy elbowed me. "Lightweight."

"What can I say. Some people can do it and others can't. I don't have the constitution to drink except after hours."

"C'mon, you're a big guy! You can handle it." He was elbowing me again.

"No can do. It's coffee for me."

He looked a little miffed that I couldn't be convinced.

"Freddy, you're the only one that mentioned the Kirk Douglas thing." I pointed at my chin.

He brightened. "No!"

"I kid you not."

"That surprises me." He finished his beer as the new round arrived. A trembling hand made the B&B shot vanish. "So did you really wanna talk about the Giants?"

"We can if you want, but I want to ask you about Sunday night."

"I was working then." He slurped down half his beer and began looking for Hector for another shot. Poor Freddy really was a rummy, and I felt a little guilty for enabling him. Then again, I had no doubt he'd drink just as much with me there as without, except he'd have more pocket money for food this way. Well, it was nice to think he'd spend it on food, something like a salad, and not Tic Tacs.

"What do you know about the gig Sunday night?"

I could see Freddy's eyes begin to glaze over. He was approaching a tipping point, or perhaps I should say the tipsy point. I was probably a little too late to have him talk to me sensibly. Home and bed were in his near future. That's the problem using booze to get people to talk, especially with drunks. They have surprisingly little staying power and tend to get smashed.

"I thought we were going to talk about the Giants?"

"We can if you want."

"I'm a Jets fan, anyway."

"I'm sorry to hear that, Freddy, you have my sympathies. I used to be a Browns fan. My Dad was from Cleveland."

"Tommy, do you really like me or are you just saying that?"

See what I mean? When they start to get smashed they start to get maudlin.

"Don't we always have a chat when we see each other at the museum?"

He stared at the beer that had just arrived. "I sometimes wonder about things, about how people see me."

"How do you want them to see you, Freddy?"

"I'm a pretty good guy, you know. I have a daughter, I ever tell you that?"

"You showed me her picture once."

He was fumbling with his wallet and almost dropped it, twice. "See?"

The wallet and the faded image of a little brunette girl on the lap of a department store Santa swayed in front of me. "She's in Colorado. Works in the hospitality thing. She has a degree and everything from an institute."

"You must be proud of her."

"She spends Christmas with her mother in Reno." Now he didn't seem proud or fond but a little angry. I exchanged a glance with Hector down the bar. His eyes were telling me I should be thinking about getting Freddy home. Just as well. Both Freddy and I knew I was humoring him. Saddest part was he didn't seem to mind.

"Freddy, you look a little sleepy. Been a long night. Let me drive you home."

"I got a car."

That was a scary thought.

He added, "It's at home, though, Tommy."

"Where do you live?"

"I take the bus home."

Hector stepped over and handed me a slip of paper with an address in Kensington on it in ballpoint pen. "Car is on the way." His eyes told me he kept slips of paper like this around for when he needed to pour Freddy into a car service.

"Thanks, Hector. Freddy and I will go together."

"Funny, though." Freddy pointed a trembling finger at me. "The kitchen staff was the only ones."

"Only ones?"

"That's the ticket."

Freddy began to stir the dollar bills he had on the bar, trying to figure the tip.

"So you say the kitchen staff were the only ones. The museum kitchen staff?"

He was counting on his fingers, working on the tip.

"Freddy, let me get the tip." I threw a ten on the bar. Hector nodded his appreciation from across the room. I stood. "Your ride home is coming. Let's get some fresh air."

He steadied himself on the bar and turned toward the exit. My hand was an inch from his shoulder to make sure he didn't fall. On the steps up to the street, I had my hand an inch from his back.

On Vanderbilt, we waited for the car to arrive as a new sunny Friday was under way in Brooklyn, bustling citizens looking at their watches, iPods, and phones as they headed for Grand Army Plaza and the subway. They probably had one foot in the weekend, thinking about Halloween parties or maybe a drive to Westchester to look at the fall foliage.

Freddy groaned boozily as he sat himself on a car hood.

Friday. I had the weekend to come up with that missing cash or default on my payment to the pink monkey. At that moment, standing there with a drunk at eight in the morning, up to my eyeballs in debt and a killer trying to tweak me, going back into Comanche and putting both feet in the bag seemed like a possible option. Then I would go home to my own bed and put my head under the pillow and hope that when I woke up this would all be some kind of stress dream, that I was actually someone with a normal job and a normal life full of pumpkin carving, candy corn, and football games.

"So what was that you were saying about the kitchen staff at the museum? Was this Sunday night you were talking about?"

"That's the ticket. Only ones."

"Only ones? What does that mean?"

"They're the only ones who saw the robbers. They just got in and got out. In and out." Freddy chuckled to himself. "And this all happened with Snoopy right there."

"Snoopy."

"Ol' Snoopy was there that night."

I knew the answer but wanted to hear it anyway. "Atkins?"

"Snoopy. We call him that because of the way he walks, with little steps."

The town car rolled up to the curb. "Freddy, is it unusual for Atkins to be there at three in the morning?"

Freddy stood and reached unsteadily for the car door. "He does these spot inspections. Comes snooping around. That's why we call him Snoopy."

"So where were all the guards when the paintings were stolen?"

"Snoopy had a roll call to make sure everybody was there." He climbed into the backseat. "In the locker room."

I stuck my head in after him and handed the driver twenty dollars and the address. "Make sure he gets to the door."

The Arab driver rolled his eyes. It wasn't a Blue Diamond car, so I didn't quiz the driver about Sunday.

"Take care, Freddy."

"That's the ticket."

The car zoomed off toward the plaza. I was glad that was over.

It was still too early to find Snoopy at the museum, but not too early for Ariel's Patisserie Bistro. It had been three days since Huey had been shot. Maybe Ariel had reopened. I at least had to go see, no matter how much I didn't want to. I didn't know if Ariel might somehow have the impression I had something to do with Huey getting tweaked. According to Jocko, that did seem to be the word on the street. After getting an alcoholic drunk, I might as well top that off by upsetting a pending widow.

I flagged down a town car with a twenty. No way was I walking around Carroll Gardens exposed for any length of time, not with the punk sniper out there.

The bistro was open even though it was before nine, and the French African girl at the counter purred that I could find Ariel at Viscotti's.

During the night, Huey had finally died.

THIRTY-THREE

I STOPPED TO VISIT JOCKO before heading to Viscotti's. I had run out of Bridget's so fast that morning I hadn't shaved. Besides, I wanted to procrastinate before visiting the widow. Either that or maybe he would slit my throat so I wouldn't have to visit Ariel at all.

He seemed happy to see me, like maybe he was worried Flat Face and his crew had taken me out of the game.

"Sit! Sit! Sit!" He waved the sheet, tempting the bull to charge.

I sat. "What's what, Jocko?"

The crinkly paper was tucked around my neck, and I swore I could smell a White Owl cigar.

"Good," he said. "It was a beautiful funeral."

I wasn't sure I'd ever been to a beautiful funeral. They were all pretty grim as far as I was concerned. So I said something polite. "I'm sure the family's stress over his death was depersonalized. A lot of flowers."

Jocko looked confused a moment, then flashed the straight razor. "Jocko give you a shave, yes?"

I tensed, wondering what I was thinking, coming back to his chair. I tried to relax—he had no reason to kill me. Flat Face had no reason to kill me. Yet. "Just be careful around my jugular vein, OK?"

"I never cut anybody that didn't move. Almost." He laughed to himself while he lathered my chin with hot shave cream, the smell of his Juicy Fruit fighting with the smell of the soap. "So you talk to the big boss?"

"Yeah."

"A nice talk?"

"Businessman to businessman."

"Good, *good*."

I was staring at the ceiling, listening to the long scrape of the razor on my neck.

"Let me ask you, Jocko. That guy with the flat face—was he Jimmy Robay?"

"Of course."

"He seems reasonable."

"I know him since he was a little boy. Used to sit in this chair when his family would come to Dominic's on Sundays."

I heard the front doorbell tinkle, and Jocko said, "I'll be right with you, sir, please have a seat."

Jocko spun my seat toward the mirror and cleared his throat. My eyes slid down from the ceiling to Jocko's reflection in the mirror. His eyes were dark and seemed to have drifted way back into his skull. You know Death, who wears the hood and carries the giant garden tool or whatever? It was like that, only Jocko was holding up the straight razor. Death with a straight razor and Juicy Fruit.

Like an idiot, I thought, *He really is going to kill me.*

Like I said, though, I didn't have time to die that week if I could help it.

I launched forward out of the chair.

There was that chopping sound, the one I'd come to know as the sound of a silencer. The wall mirror shattered as I stumbled and fell to the floor.

Jocko and the person who just came in were in a struggle. I was on the checked floor wrapped in the sheet, and the barber chair blocked my view. I yanked my arms, and the sheet snapped in two.

There were two more shouts behind me—one Jocko, who said "*Malocchio!*" and the other something I couldn't make out. I scrambled to my feet.

A mirror behind me shattered, and I saw Jocko staggering backward, knocking all the combs and the jar of blue liquid crashing to the floor. His white tunic was splashed red with blood.

The punk stood across the room, a red razor gash from his left ear in an S-curve down over his chin. Below the gash was a curtain of blood. Next to this curtain of blood was the punk's bloody hand, and he was looking at it with surprise. He was still pointing his pistol at Jocko, smoke curling from the silencer. It wasn't just any pistol. Exotic like the gun before.

The punk's blue eyes raised to mine.

My hand was on the counter behind me. I grabbed an electric razor and threw it at the punk, the cord trailing behind, but it missed his head.

There was so much blood on his hand, his fingers were slipping as he tried to cock the gun. I should have charged him when I had the chance.

I ducked behind the chair in front of me and heard the gun ratchet.

Like a sumo wrestler, I put my two hundred and seventy pounds behind the chair and shoved for all I was worth.

I'm happy to report the chair wasn't bolted to the floor. If it had been I would have probably thrown my back out or ripped my arms out of my sockets, and while I lay there in agony, the punk would have put me out of my misery. I would have joined Jo-Ball and Huey in the Exploding Head Club.

That chair didn't slide across the floor; it jumped in the air and hit the punk in the chest. The chair fell on its side on the floor. The punk was an object in motion, and his back slammed the wall of mirrors, cracks splintering out around him.

I had fallen to all fours when I shoved the chair and was looking up at him. He still had the gun, but his eyes were crossed, and it was like he was stuck to the wall. He looked like a bug in a spiderweb, what with the glass shattered behind him.

Like I said, the gun was still in his hands. I've got a rule about running toward someone holding a gun, even if he was injured and had a sheet of red down one side from a straight-razor cut.

I glanced over to see where Jocko was. He wasn't, so I guessed he'd gone out the back or into the back room. Well, whatever, he was on his own.

I hesitated. The punk's eyes uncrossed and tried to focus on me, the gun hand beginning to move.

I lit out the front door, making tracks on Smith. I rounded the first corner to get out of sight of the barbershop.

I made it to Bond Street and hailed a town car.

"Where to?"

"Downtown, Joralemon Street and Court or Henry, I don't care."

"You OK?"

"Yeah, I just went for a little jog. I guess I'm out of shape."

"You should be careful."

I closed my eyes and listened to my heart boxing with my lungs. "Yeah."

THIRTY-FOUR

THIS TIME, CAROL AND I went to the police instead of them coming to us.

Doh saw us standing on the other side of the police tape at the Neapolitan Barber Shop. It was maybe an hour after it all went down. He seemed surprised, but relieved, too. Crispi wasn't with him for a change.

"I hope your client can give us some serious cooperation, Doonan. Otherwise I'm going to arrest his ass for obstruction of justice."

"We wouldn't be here if we didn't want to give our full cooperation."

"Full?"

"Full. He was here when it went down, and barely escaped getting killed. He came straight to me."

"Why not the police?"

"I think a grand jury would find it reasonable that my client would run from a killer and return after a safe interval with his counsel, especially if he had been the target of two previous attempts on his life from which the police were unable to protect him. You want Mr. Davin's help or don't you?"

"That would be divine." Doh lifted the yellow tape, and we walked with him into the barbershop. There was blood all over the floor where the punk had been, and leading away into the back room where Jocko had gone to die.

We went through what happened, and where, trying to stay out of the way of photographers. Doh listened but took no notes. When we were done he led us to the back room. There was a hot plate and a small refrigerator next to a small table with a radio. You could see Jocko would have a quiet moment to himself back there. Eat his lunch and listen to the news or a ball game. Doh pointed to a large pool of blood next to the back door. He didn't say anything, he just pointed. Then he waved us to follow him back through the front of the barbershop and around the corner. Carol and I sat in the back of his unmarked car; he sat in front, arm over the seat.

"I got a lot of questions, Davin, but my first is, how do you sleep at night?"

Carol cleared her throat. "Detective—"

"I don't think he told you all he knows, Doonan." He was pointing at me but looking at her.

She and I exchanged a glance.

I said, "I have told Ms. Doonan everything I know."

Doh sighed, pinching the bridge of his nose.

"Here's how it went down, people. After the first killing, we dug around a bit about Mr. Davin. We found that he owed money. We found that his girlfriend left him. Both of these little items were well known in the neighborhood. Both of these little items interested us. Can you tell me why, Doonan? I'll tell you why. Love or money. That's why people kill. Those are the only two reasons. In Davin we maybe had both. We spoke with Huey's wife, Ariel, and she told us the ex-girlfriend used to come into the shop to buy pastry, and that she was a bombshell. This interested us. Why?"

Carol folded her arms, so I didn't say anything either.

"Because most of the time when the cause of death is love there's a bombshell. The prettier, the more trouble they are, the more men are likely to kill for them. It's the way of the world. All the men in the neighborhood stopped what they were doing to watch her go by. All the women stopped what they were doing to hate the bombshell. She had a pattern. She would go to the bistro and buy a single pastry, and then go to a mailbox at the shipping store a block down. We went there, to the shipping store. The people there knew her, she stood out, so we got her full name and ran it. Sure enough, this woman Yvette was walking trouble ever since she got to this country and especially in Vegas. You knew this, Davin, am I right?"

Carol put a hand on my arm to keep me quiet. "We're here to help, Detective, with your murder case in any way we can, but I don't see how it's helpful for Tommy to openly speculate on the character of his ex-girlfriend."

Doh rolled his eyes and continued. "She was never charged with anything too serious, but was hauled into LVPD whenever she was at the center of some sort of altercation. Was there some sort of connection between Yvette and Jonathon 'One-Ball' Culobrese? Between Yvette and Huey LaMouche?"

He cocked an eye at me.

I said, "I hope not."

So he nodded sadly. "Knowing her, you couldn't be sure, could you? Even now."

My heart felt like it was in a block of concrete. I was feeling dizzy.

"Well, rest easy, Davin. There was no connection. Except you.

You weren't killing these people, so we figured this was a dead end. Until Crispi noticed something. In one of her altercations just before she left Vegas to come here with you. You know this man?"

He held out a photo from Immigration.

It was the punk.

I looked at Carol, she nodded, and I said, "That's the guy who shot Jocko."

"Is it the guy you chased? The one who shot Huey?"

"I didn't chase anybody."

Carol leaned forward. "Detective, who is this man?"

"His name is Gustav Urushka."

My vision swam, and I had to close my eyes. Delilah was right, I hadn't been open enough to the possibilities.

I heard Carol say, "Why is Gustav Urushka trying to kill my client? And the other people around him?"

"It's the way his people do things when they want something, his people from back in the old country, Eastern Europe. They want something from someone, they have rules, a way of doing things. First you kidnap someone's kids or parents or whatever, then you start killing people around their target. Doesn't do any good to kill the person who has something you want. They call it *zevasta*. This man Gustav was in a paramilitary outfit over there, as an assassin that killed political opponents, union leaders. A prodigy with a gun—our friend Gustav can shoot people from the hip, behind the back, over his shoulder. Over there, where he came from, they all have guns because they never know when a war might break out again. His father started him shooting melons with hollow points when he was only five. He could have killed you outside Donut House, and at the bistro, but he killed Johnny and Huey instead, *zevasta,* to scare you into finding Yvette for him. Seems he got impatient and decided to take you out at Jocko's, or maybe torture you into telling. Only he didn't expect the old man to be so handy with a razor."

Breathe slowly in through the nose; close the eyes.

Breathe slowly out through the lips; stroke back my hair.

Breathe slowly in through the nose; open the eyes.

Doh says, "What's Davin doing?"

So Carol says, "Tommy does tantric exercises when he's anxious."

"Tantric?"

"Like yoga."

I exhaled. "He kidnapped the cats."

"Cats?" Doh leaned in close.

"Yvette left me with four cats. I took care of them for a month. Then on Monday night I found my place had been broken into and my cats . . . Yvette's cats had been stolen and there was a note signed 'Gustav.' And some letters. Look like love letters."

"You didn't think to call the police?"

"I considered it a domestic matter. I had no idea a guy who would steal cats and leave love letters would also go on a killing spree."

Carol put a hand on my knee telling me to shut up.

"Detective, let's keep this on the here and now, focus on progress, not recriminations. There's a killer. My client is a target of this killer, has been from the first murder at Donut House. What are you going to do to ensure his safety?"

"First, he can hand over those love letters. That would be nice." Doh flashed a reluctant grin. "Then we could put Davin on ice somewhere until we cuff Gustav. Of course, then Tommy might miss his next payment to Vince Scanlon. You know as well as I do that your client is crawling around for a finder's fee on some stolen paintings. We put him in a safe house, he isn't going to be too safe from Scanlon when he gets out."

"You wouldn't protect my client from Scanlon?"

Doh's eyes narrowed to nothing. His freckles got redder. "He's a material witness who has been withholding evidence in this case. We found the lady on Sackett Street. The one who hit Gustav before Davin chased him into the canal. She described someone Davin's size and general description, and she also said the killer's gun fell on the ground. I have to assume the killer never recovered that gun; otherwise it would have been a short chase. If we had found that gun back then, it might have told us things that would have Gustav in Rikers right now and Jocko still trimming sideburns and telling Gotti stories. So it's hard to feel sorry for your client's predicament when he seems to have an utter disregard for the safety of others." He took a deep breath, and added with no little contempt, "But if he wants protection, we'll put him up in a safe house."

"Tommy?" Carol was looking at me, and I was staring at my hands.

Doh had done a pretty good job of trying to tear me down, I'll grant him that. It was my turn.

"Detective, I respect the fact that you're anxious to find this killer, but whatever you believe about me being a material witness, the only information I've had that would help you is that this guy has four cats held captive. They're hostages. I had no idea the killer and the catnapper were one and the same."

Doh started the car and began driving. I continued.

"I doubt seriously that the love letters would lead you to where he is now, but now that I know they are important to you, we can go to my place and I'll give them to you. I had tried to reach Yvette through connections in Vegas to let her know about the cats. If she hadn't been arrested in Miami, maybe she would have called him. That was out of my hands, and I had no idea he was the killer. I don't have Gustav's gun, but if he dropped it and it was picked up on the street by local hoodlums, I suggest you check your sources nearby to see if they have it for sale. I'll pass on the babysitting, and that's a vote of confidence on my part that the PD will quickly find some guy with a major slash across his face. Jocko slit him from here all the way like this. Look for someone who has recently bought ten boxes of Band-Aids."

I almost added something else, but once again decided to keep something to myself. At that particular moment, I was feeling hostile toward Doh, and with only my own life in the balance, I didn't feel much like helping Doh solve the case. I might as well try to find Gustav myself.

Doh had brought the car around to my building. "The letters?"

I retrieved them and stood next to Carol at the curb. She handed them to Doh through the open window. "If Mr. Davin can help, tell us how. You have my number."

Doh grinned. "Believe me, Davin will be real helpful, whether he likes it or not. Gustav isn't going to give up. We know now that all we have to do is stick with Tommy and the jealous lover Gustav will show up. Only this time he's not after anybody but Tommy. So we're not real worried. Tommy is a big boy and can take care of himself. Aren't you, Tommy?"

Doh zoomed off.

Carol and I hailed an actual yellow cab on Smith, the kind you get in Manhattan. A few moments later we were rolling down Henry Street, back toward Carol's office.

"Tommy, I think you need to get out of town. I'll lend you the money, you just fly out of here. Only promise me you won't go to Vegas."

I kept staring out at the brownstones and sycamores blurring past the window.

"I hear what you're saying, Carol, and there's a logic to it. It's like Doh said, though, I have to raise that money to get this woman out of my life. If I have to tangle with this Gustav character, too, well, bring it on. I don't bend much, and I don't break. I'll get through this my way."

"But Tommy, really . . ."

"I made this situation in my own way. I brought Yvette and the four cats into my life. The only way for me to have any self-respect is to get them out of it."

"Well, you can't go home. Come stay with me."

"I already have alternate accommodations."

"Not the bump-and-thump?"

"No. A friend's."

"You realize you could be putting this friend in jeopardy, don't you?"

"This friend is in jeopardy already, Carol, which is why she asked me to stay with her."

"Ah . . . that kind of friend."

I took my eyes off the scenery and met Carol's. "No, not that kind of friend. It's complicated. A friend friend."

"Tommy, darling, lovers and friends can be interchangeable."

"Not this one."

"Famous last words?"

I shook my head at the blur of October Brooklyn. "Not this one. Can I ask you a question, Carol?"

"Shoot."

"You think good things happen to good people?"

Carol felt my forehead. "No fever. So what's that question supposed to mean?"

"I know you're a lawyer and all and see a lot of people who do bad stuff get off, and a lot of good people get left holding the bag. I guess what I'm asking is if you think it's worth being the good guy. Is it a low percentage play?"

"You talking about yourself?"

"I'm not that good. Better than most, I suppose. I just got to thinking about this because I saw myself in the mirror the other day, without the beard, and I looked like my dad. Then being shot at, knowing I might die. It scared me a little."

"Look at me, Tommy. The only thing that matters is whether it's worth it to you. If you want to know whether I think there's some sort of outside force where good things happen to good people, that there's karma . . . for me, all of that is perception of patterns, wish fulfillment. Nothing wrong with that. It's a matter of faith."

"Patterns like Blue Diamond?"

"Blue diamond?"

"Blue Diamond Car Service. The bomber, then the dentist, remember? They had a car parked out in front of Donut House when Jo-Ball got his head blown off. I mean, what are the chances that one car service would keep having these gory episodes? Maybe there's a reason for it."

Carol laughed softly. "Could just be the roll of the dice, like in Vegas. It sometimes comes up sixes three times in a row. Is that karma at work?"

"Thanks for your perspective, Carol."

"Sweetie." She patted me on the cheek. "Keep being the good guy, Tommy. We like you that way."

I looked away, out the window.

Like Pop once said, *Expectations are holes in gratification's hull.*

IT WASN'T EVEN NOON YET and I'd gotten an alcoholic drunk and a barber killed. TGIF. There was still a lot to do before the weekend, when it would be difficult to locate people because they don't go to work. You have to chase them down at their kid's soccer game or interrupt them carving pumpkins.

I had Carol drop me at Atlantic Avenue. Time to go to visit Pet Food Pete.

My phone buzzed when I was a block away. It was Skip.

"What do you have for me?"

"Dude. Like, do you ever say 'hello' or 'how are you'?"

Part of me wanted to reach through the phone and crush his skull between my thumb and forefinger. Another part of me wanted the information more.

"What do you have for me?"

"Did you even hear what I said, Uncle Tommy?"

"I heard what you said, but I don't care. If you're calling me it must be because you have the information I paid you for. What do you have for me?"

"Excuse *me* for bothering to—"

"Believe it or not, Skip, life is too short for all this bullshit. Tell me about Molly Lee."

"This chick Molly Lee is quite the, how shall I say, character. Real shady lady. Before the art export scheme and forgery—"

"Forgery?"

"Didn't you read all the stuff I e-mailed?"

"Not all. Humor me."

"Well, Dunwoody Exports was backed by Jimmy Robay, the mobster."

"Got that part."

"So while they were ripping off galleries and shipping bulk paintings overseas, some to copy, it seems a few masterpieces, like, got in the mix, and some forgeries were hitting the market here, at the auction houses. Nobody could connect them directly with Dunwoody, but because of the materials? Like, they were positive the forgeries were done in China, but, dude, nobody ever made the case against Dunwoody. Molly Lee pretty much vanishes."

"You were saying before, about Molly Lee?"

"She ran a chain of massage parlors, only they didn't do a lot of massage. You see what I'm saying."

I wanted to laugh at that. I didn't. "I get it, Skip. This woman Molly Lee ran a string of whorehouses."

"In a bunch of little cities, too, under the radar, so she thought. Baltimore, Richmond, Scranton, Staten Island, like that. The operation folded like a deck of cards when a newspaper got wind of it. Molly Lee pretended she didn't know what some of the girls were up to, and there was no proving it, either. Pretty slick. Gets out of a sex scam and then slides right out of a forgery scam. Awesome."

"There any pictures of Molly Lee?" I stopped in front of a storefront with a large brown sign reading FIDO FEED, where for the last couple months I'd been getting cat food deliveries from the owner, Pete.

"Sure. You know, like, that big, in newsprint. Sunglasses, scarf, coming out of court. Could be my mom. Ha! My mom, yeah, right. Ha! She never did anything cool like this in her life."

Poor Katie. Did she really deserve this?

"So any clue where Molly Lee got to?"

"Dropped out of the news. I'm just guessing, Uncle Tommy, but her name? You don't suppose that's an alias, do you? Get real. Like, what kind of name is that? Actually, it's kind of a cool name for a band, I must admit."

Kid was right, of course. "Molly" probably felt she'd squeezed all the traction she could out of that name after those two run-ins. These types of entrepreneurs usually went back and forth between a couple enterprises. Maybe into porn, always money there. Or bootleg movies or handbags. When they made themselves lost they stayed lost.

Only this time I had to guess she'd resurfaced as Ms. French and was muscling in on my business. Not too much of a stretch. She met with Jo-Ball, then went to Billy Bank, where Dunwoody's offices are, which is where Huey went to get the money. And you have to bet my limo ride with Jimmy Robay was somehow still connected to Molly Lee aka Ms. French.

It simplified things knowing that the killings were being done by lovesick Gustav. It meant Ms. French wasn't directing the elimination of people involved with the theft. Which was probably why they thought I was killing people who double-crossed me. Which was probably why Jimmy Robay jumped in to make me an offer to get me to stop before I found Molly. Robay probably knew what was going on, but I wasn't about to embrace a kamikaze mission and try to press him for details.

Still didn't answer the question of how Molly Lee knew my guys were going to lift the paintings for me in the first place. How could she have known? I had to press Frank and Kootie. One at a time for a change. Frank first; he was the more nervous.

On the back end was the museum. Assuming there was actually a buy back in play, there was more to squeeze out of the Whitbread about all this. McCracken was a tough customer, and her staff wouldn't be much better. The guards were still the soft spot. Freddy. Atkins, too. Like Frank, Atkins was the nervous type, and according to Freddy, Atkins was actually at the museum when the Hoffman, Ramirez, and Le Marr were boosted. Funny he didn't mention that.

"Uncle Tommy, you there?"

"I'm here."

"You want me to look into anything else? I could use more cash. The new iPhone just came out."

"Maybe. I'll let you know. Kid?"

"Yeah?"

"Good work. You're a smart-ass, but I like you anyway, and you've been a big help."

There was a pause on the other end. I waited for the smart remark. He hung up instead. Well, I guess that was some progress.

I turned and pushed through the glass door into Fido Feed.

"Pete?"

A narrow head with a big jaw and close-cropped yellow hair peered at me from behind some shelves. Pete looked over his round glasses, which were on the end of his beak.

"Mr. Davin! How is you?"

Pete dropped his clipboard on top of a case of cat food. The store was crammed with shelves crammed with every conceivable cat and dog food, wet and dry, all the way to the ceiling. At my size, I really couldn't go more than a few steps inside. The place had the meaty, yeasty smell of kibble.

"I'm fine, Pete, what's what?"

He emerged from where he was doing inventory. He always wore a plaid shirt and vest. Thin white guy, a little too pleasant.

"I can hardly keep all the whatsis in stock. Have to have every conceivable brand of food on hand, don'tcha know. Look at it all." He waved a hand. "Yet not a day goes by that someone doesn't ask me to stock something new. Makes you think. Is it time for your mixed case of Pristine Pet? Or are you out of the Lab 1 Adult Diet Dry? I always keep some on hand for you. Those kitties of yours are stuck on a pretty obscure food, yessiree Bob."

"No, I'm not in the market for food today. I wanted to ask a favor. Anybody else been buying that food?"

Pete cocked his head, tapping a pen on his chin. "You should be out of food. You always buy every other Tuesday, and it's Friday."

"Someone is taking care of the cats for me. I wanted to make sure he's feeding them the right food. I told him to buy it here because he can't get it nowheres else, that I know of."

Pete shook his head. "Nope. I haven't sold any since the last time you were in, Mr. Davin."

"Can you do me a favor? Remember once your shipment of Pristine Pet didn't come in, and you called around to the other pet food places looking for some?"

He nodded deeply.

"Could you call around and find out? I'd really appreciate it. You know how I worry about the cats. I've been out of town a lot and so figured it was best they spend time with my friend Gustav and not be alone too much. I just want to check up on him, you know how it is."

He looked over his glasses at the shelf stocked with Pristine Pet and Lab 1. "Seems dopey since I have all this here."

"You'd be doing me a big favor. I'll even preorder the next batch of food. Just put it on my card as usual, OK?"

He smiled. "Certainly, Mr. Davin. Let me just finish my stock check and—"

"Can I call you later, like in two hours?"

"Swell."

"Thanks a boatload, Pete. Talk to you later."

I stepped outside into the sunshine.

Time to make someone tip.

THIRTY-SIX

STATEN ISLAND. NEW YORK'S FIFTH and southern-most borough. It is separated from Manhattan and Brooklyn by New York Harbor and a passage to the ocean, both loaded with petroleum tankers. I don't know what you've heard about Staten Island, but it is probably true. This is a place that is both as bad as they say and not as bad as they say. It all depends on what you expect of your town. I think Staten Islanders would agree that they have the most individualistic of the boroughs. I hadn't ever heard of any of the other boroughs threatening to break off from New York City. Then again, I'm not sure any of the other boroughs is the target of so much derision by their neighbors. I avoid derision when I can help it. Bad energy.

None of the other boroughs offer such a nice boat ride, I'll say that. The Staten Island Ferry is a free half-hour boat ride across New York Harbor, and on a warm October afternoon, standing in the front of the boat with the fingers of sea breezes combing your hair, it's hard to feel derisive about your destination.

The breeze was helping to calm me. The encounter in the barbershop and realizing I'd had the whole killing thing wrong had me shaken. I felt real bad for Jocko getting killed. I had to wonder how many he may have made vanish with his razor. Maybe his death was as much a result of a damaged karma as anything else. He sure recognized an assassin when he saw one. Jocko was quick as lightning with that razor when he saw Gustav.

Anyway, Gustav would be licking his wounds for at least a little while, what with that slash across his face. So I felt a little safer in the short term. And after all this ruckus and three murders in broad daylight, you would think that the NYPD might have been able to find Gustav in short order, wouldn't you? Anyhow, I felt like I had at least until Saturday before I had to be looking over my shoulder. That would give me breathing room. I inhaled deeply the salt air. I must have done my tantric exercise ten times on the front of that ferry.

I had wanted to pressure Frank Buckley first, but I couldn't locate him. He didn't answer his bell. The owner at Traviata said Frank didn't come on shift until five. I called the museum to set something up with Atkins, and they said he went home at noon on Fridays. So with almost five hours on my hands I decided to take the subway into Manhattan and walk to the ferry. There's a giant new ferry terminal there. Like the old one, it's full of pigeons for some reason. Architects, smart as they are, can't outwit pigeons. I'm just saying.

The abode of Timothy Atkins was a few stops down the Tottenville Line. That's Staten Island's train, and it looks just like a subway anywhere else in the city except it never goes underground much and is a lot more polite and clean, both in appearance and operation. The conductors aren't under pressure to deliver millions of commuters to Manhattan in two hours twice a day, so the pace is a little more relaxed.

From the train station, it is a short walk up a gentle hill through a bedroom community, ranch homes like you'd find almost anywhere in suburbia. That's part of the reason Staten Island gets a bad rap from the other boroughs—no part of it is urban. Sure enough, there's a downtown, but it has the feel of a county seat somewhere in the Midwest. I could be wrong, but I don't think there are any buildings in Staten Island over twenty stories, or even ten. These ranch homes are nicely spaced, too, not crammed a car width apart like you'd find out in Queens.

I knew where Atkins lived because he'd invited me to a barbe-cue back when I was tight with Sheila. I think he wanted to get in good with me to get in good with her. Even then she was on his ass and he seemed desperate to try to secure his job. Somehow he'd held on to it since then. I had his address and phone number tucked into my phone. Thought a surprise visit might be more productive than calling ahead.

Atkins's ranch home was brick painted white, with an aging Volkswagen parked in the driveway and a life-sized deer lawn ornament. There were also some concrete squirrels and rabbits sneaking around the edge of the bushes. I kid you not, it was like Atkins had a Disney thing going on.

The garage door was open, and there was a wiry woman, mid-fifties, inside. She had curly gray hair, work clothes, and a rake. She stepped outside as I approached, shielding her eyes from the sun.

"Can I help you?" She held the rake sort of pointed at me. Like I said, sometimes my size intimidates people.

"Hi. I'm an associate of Tim's, from the museum. My name is Tommy Davin."

She lowered the rake. A little.

"He went out to Home Depot. Should be back soon."

"Maybe I should have called first, but I'm investigating an art theft and needed to speak with him."

"Sure. You with the police?"

"No, ma'am. I work for an insurance company. I try to track down missing paintings and other art. Here's my card."

She took the card, and it seemed to make her relax.

"Ma'am, I know you don't know me, but Tim does. I've seen him twice this week at the museum. That's how I know he works a half day on Friday. He invited me to a barbecue you guys were having a year or more back. I couldn't come to the shindig but had the address in my phone."

"You missed a good barbecue." She was leaning on the rake now. "Timbo makes the best sausage and peppers."

"Looks like you're about to do some lawn work. Sorry to interrupt with business like this."

"That's why Timbo went to the store. Needed lawn bags. I hate to rake leaves."

"Anybody who likes raking leaves needs a life."

"Timbo likes it."

"Oops, sorry. Let's rephrase that. Raking leaves is not my idea of a good time."

"My name is Jan. I'm his wife. You want some coffee?"

"I'm intruding."

"Why should I rake when there are no leaf bags? He's the one who likes to rake, so why am I not at Home Depot?"

"I see your point. Sure, coffee is always good."

I followed the wiry woman through the front door, one in white with three little windows set at a diagonal.

The interior of the home looked pretty much early nineties, lots of reflective surfaces, and more deer, fawn, and rodent statues on shelves above the gray couch. Just much smaller ones. We continued into the kitchen, which was from the seventies, gold and avocado wallpaper, white counters, dark wood cabinets, and white kitchen table. The kitchen window view over the sink was crowded with shrubs.

"Mind if I reheat?" She held up a clear glass pot.

"That's what I normally do."

"Sit." She gestured at the table, and I hunkered down in one of the chairs. Pouring two cups, she put them in an ancient microwave and revved it up by turning knobs.

"So, Tommy, you know art?"

"I have a degree in art history, if that means anything. And I know how much things go for."

"Is your work dangerous? Do you have to chase criminals?"

"As little as possible."

"Timbo sure is glad his museum never gets robbed. Doesn't keep him from worrying about it. Or from worrying about the museum director—you know her?"

"I know McCracken, but it won't shock me if you don't love her." Never robbed?

"Well, she could be nicer, you know what I mean?" The microwave buzzed loudly, and she unlatched the oven door. "Cream and sugar?"

"Just sugar. Four."

"Dark and sweet. That's the way my father took it."

"My pop took it that way, too."

As she prepped the coffee, I looked at my phone for the time, hoping Atkins would get home with the leaf bags soon. I needed to make Brooklyn in time to push a few of Frank's buttons before his shift. The coffee arrived, but Jan remained standing.

"Do you appraise art, like on *Antiques Roadshow*?"

"Only fine art."

"So not Hummels. I have a large collection, you know, a lot of it vintage."

"You could see what they're going for on eBay."

"I wouldn't trust anybody to send me money on the Internet."

"There are appraisers who would value your Hummels. Are you looking to insure them?"

"Sure, maybe, but I watch all those people getting rich on *Roadshow,* you know? You have to wonder if your things, just anything around the house, is worth a couple grand, or even a hundred grand, who knows?"

I could almost hear the seconds ticking by on my phone.

"If you had it appraised, you would know."

"Sure, but you only do fine art. Like paintings and sculpture."

"I'm not an accredited appraiser, but I would know something valuable if I saw it."

She crooked a finger at me. "Let me show you something, then."

In a spare bedroom there was a closet. In the back of the closet were two unframed paintings covered by a sheet. They were fairly large, and she slid them out into the light by the window.

"We picked these up a year ago." Jan slid off the sheet.

No, it wasn't the Hoffman or the Ramirez or the La Marr.

Thick black lines separated squares of white and red and blue and yellow. One was mostly white with only a little yellow, red, and blue and a more irregular grid pattern.

I looked at the back, at the canvas and mounting. Paris, for sure. You can tell by the cloven tacks used to secure the canvas to the frame. There were no marks indicating the tacks had been removed and replaced or that the canvas had been restretched. They were signed on the back, not the front, in block letters MONDRIAN. 1914. Also on the back was a patch. Looked like a small piece of canvas covering a small tear, yellowed glue around the side.

"So, Tommy, do you think these are worth anything? Timbo likes them, and when he came home with them I said, 'Not in my living room!' So he put them here. I keep saying why not sell them, but he says he likes them even if he can't look at them."

My mind was five different places at once. These paintings, though—could only be at one place, not two.

"Jan . . . I'd hold on to them. These will get more valuable in a few years."

"Well, I suppose they don't take up a lot of space."

"Wait. Put them back in the closet and wait."

"Sure."

"You know, Jan, I realize I can't wait any longer for Tim. But I wouldn't mention you showed these to me. You know."

"I know?"

"Men are funny about this sort of thing. He may get angry that you were trying to sell his stuff. I'm just saying."

"You're a smart man, Tommy. Sure, he might get mad. How will I know when to sell them?"

"Here's my card. Don't sell them without calling me, and if I happen to run into a buyer who will pay top dollar—whenever that may be—I'll let you know."

"I'll tell Timbo you stopped by."

"Yeah, I'd appreciate that."

Mondrians. In a closet on Staten Island.

Mondrians. On the wall of the Lee J. Rosenburg wing at the Whitbread Museum.

The same Mondrians both places.

One set was forgeries. The other easily worth a cool couple million.

I wasn't just thinking about the Mondrians, though. I was also thinking about Gloria the locksmith and the missing Henris. About the timing, both around a year ago. Monkey business over there at the Whitbread.

The sea air ran its fingers through my hair. I had a lot to think about on my ferry ride, Manhattan's silver blades flashing in the blue October sky ahead.

THIRTY-SEVEN

FRANK'S ABODE WAS IN FAR west Cobble Hill, near the Gowanus Expressway, which like I said is also known as Interstate 278. A month or so back a truck fire closed I-278. Our quiet streets were turned into a parking lot, Union and Carroll Street bridges stacked with traffic trying to reach Fourth Avenue and a shot at reconnecting with the interstate farther north. There's a boatload of cars on the expressway, especially Friday afternoons. Like a storm on the horizon, the growing rumble of rush hour echoed down Luquer Street.

I'd come to Frank's abode because it was still only four in the afternoon and his shift was at five. Traviata was on Court Street five blocks away.

I leaned on the buzzer awhile but got no answer. When I stepped away from the door, I could look up and see his apartment on the top floor, the window partway open and facing a hundred thousand cars on the elevated highway. Must have been noisy up there. I hoped the bell worked, or that it was loud enough that he could hear it. The foyer door was locked, so there was no way in to go knock on his apartment door. I didn't want to disturb anybody else in the building to try knocking, because if Frank wasn't there I didn't want him to find out I knew where he lived and was looking for him. So I backtracked toward Court Street.

My phone buzzed. Incoming e-mail from Blaise. It was the report on McCracken.

```
MUSEUM REDHEAD
PM:
510     LEAVES MUSEUM
515     SUBWAY
540     EXIT SUBWAY, PACIFIC STREET
550     B BANK
630     EXIT B BANK
640     SUBWAY
700     EXIT SUBWAY, BOROUGH HALL
715     RESTAURANT NATALIE'S ON MONTAGUE
        ALONE AT BAR
815     EXIT NATALIE'S
820     INTO APARTMENT BUILDING 555 MONROE
        STREET
AM:
730     LEAVES APARTMENT BUILDING 555 MON-
        ROE STREET
740     ENTER BOROUGH HALL SUBWAY
800     EXIT SUBWAY TO MUSUEUM
1000    EXIT MUSEUM, SMOKES TWO CIGARETTES
1020    INTO MUSEUM
12PM    IN MUSEUM
2PM     IN MUSEUM
===END===
```

I thought McCracken had quit smoking. As much as any smoker really quits, I guessed.

"Excuse me." A petite strom pushing a double-wide baby carriage was trying to make it past me. I had stopped in the middle of the sidewalk, so I stepped to one side.

TGIF. The truth was finally beginning to rub its whiskers on my chair leg. Everybody was tied to Billy Bank: Huey, French, Molly, Robay, and McCracken. I just had to hope that this pattern meant something. Remember how wrong I was about the killings?

Sure, I was on a roll. I kid you not, though, I was tired. I'd started the day way back at the rooster bar, had the confrontation at Jocko's, and discovered Mondrians in Staten Island all in one screwed-up day. Let's not even review that whole week up to that point. My mind was drifting to more important matters.

Cocktail hour approached. I was more or less hardwired by that stage in my life to expect a libation on Friday promptly at five. Just a little rule I had. That was the carrot that kept me pulling the cart all week. It wasn't like I didn't drink during the week, especially that week, but Friday cocktail hour was the cannon shot signaling that my workweek was over and that I could indulge myself in pursuits other than chasing down the stuff museums and collectors lose. To read up on and savor Sunday's football games. To sit at the bar in the wood-paneled oasis of Monahan's, to have one too many martinis and discuss the Giants with Petey B the bartender and whoever else was there. To sit at the bar and devour a Caesar salad, a giant porterhouse, and a pile of fries. I'd barely eaten that week except for that stack of pancakes the other morning, and my stomach ached from stress. What with witnessing three murders, and all the bullshit trying to track down the paintings, I hadn't exactly been very hungry. Jenny Craig had nothing on this.

I'd earned my Friday cocktail. I'd earned my Friday porterhouse.

My phone buzzed. It was Max.

"Max." I started walking toward Traviata.

"What do you have?"

"A stomachache."

"What do you have?"

"I'm working it."

"This weekend?"

"Yes, I'm still working on it."

"Where are you now."

"In Brooklyn. I was just about to meet one last time with one of the goofballs who jacked the pips, to get him to tip the others, but it's a low percentage play."

"Who?"

"You know I never tell you who."

"We can do seventy-five." Max actually sounded a little anxious. Another twenty-five grand was more in the ballpark. Too bad the paintings were probably gone already.

"I'll see if that helps."

"It better."

"I'll keep working it, see what I can do. Max?"

"Tommy?"

"Any Mondrians missing out there?"

"Why?"

"I stumbled into two of them. Possible forgeries, I don't know."

"You look at the canvas tacks?"

"They're cloven."

"Where?" I heard him clack away at his laptop.

"Max, I never tell you who or where, so stop asking. Are you looking it up in the database?"

"Which paintings?"

"How do I know?"

Mondrians look a lot the same, and they all have similar names like *Composition in Red, White, and Black* or *Composition in White, Red, and Black*. Kind of annoying. Then again, what are you going to call a painting that is a black grid on white with some of the squares colored in? *Coney Island in Bloom*?

"How big?"

"Eighty by seventy, I guess." Typically, paintings are measured by centimeters. Not a fan of the metric system, but there's a European influence on how we do business.

"Don't see it."

"Nothing?"

"None listed as missing. Not since the Antwerp theft."

So Atkins stole the Mondrians, and McCracken never reported them stolen to her insurer, United Southern Assurance, and to Max. Not to the police, either, or we would have heard about that. Lee J. Rosenburg would have hit the roof if his paintings were stolen. McCracken covered it up to dodge Rosenburg's getting extra crisp with her. She went to Dunwoody for forgeries to replace them. Of course, maybe Atkins was storing A-1 forgeries in his closet. Somehow I didn't think so.

The cat was sitting right by my chair.

"I'll let you know about the seventy-five."

"Call when you know, no matter when."

"Later."

I was standing in front of Traviata. I went in and had a seltzer at the bar. Then another. Then a vodka on the rocks. The owner was pissed off—Frank Buckley hadn't shown up for his shift.

I left Traviata and found a working pay phone. I called a 911 on Frank's apartment, told them there was smoke coming from under the door at the fourth floor. I went back to the bar for another vodka. Then another. I walked back to Frank Buckley's place.

There were ambulances. There were cop cars. There were fire engines.

I asked one of the EMS guys what was up.

She told me they found Frank Buckley. He was lying on the bed in front of the open window.

His wrists were duct-taped. His head was wrapped in Saran Wrap. Flat, dead eyes in Frank's purple face watched the traffic creep by on the Gowanus Expressway.

THIRTY-EIGHT

FRANK BUCKLEY GETTING TWEAKED WAS good news, though maybe only for me. Unless his death was unrelated to the Whitbread rip-off, it meant the money or the paintings were probably still around. My intuition told me that Gustav's murder of Jo-Ball and Huey had caused panic in Molly Lee aka Ms. French's string, and now the goofballs needed to be silenced. You didn't have to be Einstein with a chalkboard to figure out that this probably meant Kootie was next. Either way, no time to waste deciding if I wanted to press Kootie about Sunday night, and maybe save his skin.

I know that sounds kind of cold. About Frank. Well, it sucks what happened to him, but more than likely he had it coming somehow. It's what happens to guys who get cute. I didn't cause what happened to him, and I couldn't change what happened to him. He worked in a dangerous profession, with sometimes dangerous people. His chi was compromised.

Wrapping a guy's face in plastic wrap like that is what's commonly known as leftovers. When I say commonly, I mean on the street, and in the mob. Like concrete overshoes, sleeping with the fishes, dirt naps, like that. Gustav hadn't made Frank into leftovers. It was the work of Robay's crew or Coney Island Russians. Or possibly someone who wanted it to look like one of those two.

Friday had already been a very long day, and a couple drinks had stretched it to the limit. I was about out of gas, but there was no time for a nap. I had to find Kootie before it was too late. If it wasn't already too late.

I hailed a town car, and fifteen minutes later I was at Nevins Street and Atlantic Avenue—sort of halfway from my neighborhood to Billy Bank. On the corner there was a dive bar called Hank's. It was kind of like Canal Bar, except more so. I still remembered when it was called Doray Tavern, before hipsters started going there to see low-rent indie bands, three a night. Doray Tavern was lower than a dive, and I'm not sure what you'd call that. Only the most bugged-out aging alcoholics went there, the ones who laced their drinks with lighter fluid.

I didn't have long to enjoy the atmosphere at Hank's. Too early for music, which meant that there were only a few kids in porkpie hats drinking Pabsts. Hipsters. There was a woman behind the bar. A red ponytail sat straight up on top of her head like Pebbles on *The Flintstones*.

I says, "Sweetheart, is Kootie working tonight?"

So she shakes her head and blows a bubble with her gum.

I says, "I thought he worked Friday nights."

So she shrugs.

I says, "Any idea why he's not working tonight?"

So she finally says, "Called sick."

I didn't like the sound of that.

He lived nearby in a basement apartment on State Street, a narrow brick four-story next to a parking lot. It was a shadowy block, the streetlight flickering orange across from the building.

For the second time that day I had a little luck. First piece of luck was the two Mondrians in Atkins's Staten Island closet. This one was catching Kootie leaving his building with a bag over his shoulder.

Like Pop used to say, *Luck is the fruit from the tree of persistence.*

Even in that dim orange light I knew it was Kootie. How? Who else went out at night in October in just a T-shirt? Kootie was making tracks for the subway.

Unless I was mistaken, it looked like our pal Kootie was getting out of town.

There was some movement in an old baby blue Lincoln across the street from Kootie's building.

I followed Kootie, hanging back, but ahead of the Lincoln, which scrunched into the curb behind me as I trotted down the subway steps.

This was going to be tight.

I swiped my MetroCard.

Empty.

In the old days I would have jumped the turnstile. Now the turnstiles have roofs. For a guy my size, jumping the turnstile would have been like getting a moose through a tennis racket.

I went to the fare machine and quickly started pushing buttons.

Footsteps came quickly down the stairs. Two men. Goons?

One says to the other, "You got a token?"

The other says, "They don't take tokens no more."

"No tokens?"

I fed twenty dollars into the machine.

"They take cards."

"Oo. We don't got no cards. I'm going over the turnstile."

"That ain't easy. Look, you better cover the other exit, take the car. I'll get a card from the machine. I'll call if I got him. Or if you should come with the car."

I pushed another button on the vending machine, and a new card hummed from the slot into my hand.

One goon went up the steps; the other was behind me.

He says, " 'Scuze me."

I turned. He was almost as tall as me, older by ten years, and not nearly as muscular or heavy as me. His eyes carried big bags, and his hair was orange, gray on the side. One of Robay's crew, for sure. I hadn't seen him at the funeral, so I didn't figure he knew me.

So I says, "What's what?"

"I dunno how this card machine works, and I'm kind of in a hurry. Could you swipe me in? I'll give you five bucks." He held out a five.

I either needed a lot more drinks or a lot fewer for what was ahead. At the time I was thinking more, now I'm thinking less.

So I says, "Sounds fair."

We went to the turnstile. I had no idea what I was going to do, but I had to stop this goon from making leftovers out of Kootie. If I let Kootie get tweaked, I'd miss out on the valuable information in his head, and to some extent his blood would be on my hands.

So I swiped my card and waved Eye Bags ahead. I swiped again for me and followed through the turnstile.

Eye Bags was ahead, moving up the platform, blocking Kootie's view of me. Like I said, he was about as tall as I was, and Kootie was shorter.

Eye Bags put his hand in his pocket and slowed. I stepped to one side and caught a glimpse of Kootie.

Kootie caught a glimpse of me. His eyes bugged.

There were other people around, too: a few hipsters, an old black lady in a fancy hat, two day laborers with spackle on their shoes. They were standing at the platform edge or leaning on the steel columns.

I says, "Kootie! Hey, it's good to see you. How's the police academy treating you?"

I took two long strides, fast.

Eye Bags stopped and turned.

I was right behind him and twisted my torso. Elbow up. Fast.

I elbowed Eye Bags under the chin. His head snapped back, and his eyes wobbled.

You ever want to knock someone's lights out, you don't punch them in the face. That will only make their nose break, make them bleed, and make them mad. You want someone to konk out, you need to snap their head back, compress their neck nerves or whatever. I'm not a doctor, so I won't try to explain it beyond that. I'm just saying: I clobbered Eye Bags under the chin, his head snapped back, and his knees went. I caught him in my arms. He was too heavy to keep from going all the way to the floor, but not so heavy I couldn't direct his fall away from the tracks and keep his head from smashing the concrete platform.

The hipster couple, the day workers, and the old lady took a step back.

I says, "My God! Kootie, help me. This poor guy almost fell on the tracks."

Kootie at that point was ready to bolt, but the onlookers were now looking at him, expecting him to help. He looked at the nice old hat lady.

She says, "For God's sake, man! Help him!"

It's possible the bystanders actually saw me hit Eye Bags, but you can revise what people see by the way you act. Con men will back me up on that.

Kootie and I dragged Eye Bags to the back of the platform. The two day laborers came over. I motioned for them to hold Eye Bags sitting upright leaning against the wall, and they did, which gave me the opportunity to swipe the knife from the victim's pocket.

I grabbed Kootie by the shoulder. "Let's go get this man some help. Ma'am?"

I looked at the nice old hat lady. Looked like she'd just come from church. "Can you help look after this man?"

So she says, "I most certainly will!"

The hipster couple stood there with their mouths hanging open. We headed back down the platform, toward where we'd come in.

Kootie says, "What is this?"

"The goon with the headache was about to tweak you, Kootie." I showed him the knife and tossed it in a trash can. "I just saved your bacon."

Now the eyes were extra bugged, almost out of his head.

A rush of air punched out of the subway tunnel, and a train rumbled into the station, brakes hissing.

"Let's jump on." I glanced back up the platform. Eye Bags was leaning forward, the onlookers crowded around him. Looked like he was coming to.

The train squeaked to a stop, and we hopped on the last car.

Kootie says, "He was going to tweak me?"

So I says, "You knew someone was coming." I nodded at the bag over his shoulder. "That's why you called in sick at Hank's and were winking out of town."

The train doors seemed to be taking a long time to close.

There were only four other people in the car, a group of Latino lads talking fast and laughing, probably from the projects, looked like they were dressed to party. They weren't paying any attention to us.

The doors weren't closing, so one of the Latino lads stuck his head out the door. He came back to his amigos and told them something. I heard the word *enfermo,* which means sick.

The loudspeaker said, "Watch the closing doors."

*Ding-dong—*doors slid shut. The train jolted and began to move.

I pulled Kootie around the corner of the conductor's booth, out of view of the platform passing by the window.

Kootie says, "I heard Frank got tweaked."

So I says, "Why do you think I'm here?"

"You're not the killer?"

"I think it's pretty obvious I'm not, Kootie. Hold on." I looked around the corner, toward the platform sliding by out the window. The train slid into the dark tunnel. "That sucks."

"What?"

I looked Kootie in the eye. "Nobody on the platform."

"I don't understand."

"That means all the people who were on the platform are now on the train."

The Latino boys were looking at where we were huddled, and seemed to be making smart remarks about our sexual orientation.

"Tommy, you mean that guy you knocked out, he's on the train?"

"I don't know where else he could be."

"But he hasn't got his knife."

"Since when do wiseguys carry just one weapon?"

"What'll we do?"

"This is your mess. I don't have to do anything. I can walk out of here at the next station. That guy may want to follow me for what I just did to him, but he has orders to follow and tweak you."

"What are you saying?"

"Just because I saved you once don't mean I have to save you again."

Now those bugged-out eyes were filling with tears. Funny,

because like I said, Kootie was not a small guy; he should have been able to hold his own with just about anybody. Even if a guy is Mr. Muscles, it doesn't mean he knows how to use them to defend himself.

Most important part of self-defense? Surprise. Like me elbowing Eye Bags. Punch the asshole before he punches you, or before he's even made up his mind to punch you, or before he even knows you're there. Some may think that's chickenshit. Some of the same people are probably taking dirt naps.

Anyway, Kootie had sweat beading up on his forehead. He was trying to express his anxiety about me abandoning him, but couldn't find any words. I filled in the blank.

"Kootie, I'll help you out—but you have to come clean with me. Right now."

"Whatever." He sat down on the seat, drooping with exhaustion, bag on his lap. "I don't know why we let Huey talk us into it."

"Keep it coming."

He winced. "We didn't steal anything."

"Explain."

"We broke in. We taped the kitchen staff. We pried open the door to the museum. Whatever."

The train began to slow, and the announcer came on to tell us the next stop.

"You better hurry, Kootie. Next stop I'm getting out if I don't know what happened."

Kootie boiled over red with frustration, the muscles and veins in his neck rippling. "Are you stupid? I just told you! We just walked out with the frames so it would look to the kitchen staff like we had them. But we didn't!"

"Yeah, I'm real stupid. You'll have to explain it to me so an idiot like me can understand, and in about five seconds."

The train began to roll slowly into the next station, the white tiles and pillars sliding past the windows.

Kootie says, "That was the plan. We were just supposed to go into the museum and pretend to take the paintings. Then feed you the story about being ripped off. We popped them out of the frames and hid them in a janitor's closet. That's what we were supposed to do. That's what we did."

So I says, "An inside job."

"That's the buy back. Someone at the museum wanted it to look like we stole the paintings so they could steal them. They get the insurance money, and then they sell them. They get money two ways, not one. That's how Frank and me figured it, anyway."

"Who is *they*?"

"Whatever. The museum. Or someone at the museum. That's the way Huey explained it. What the fuck do I care as long as I get paid."

"Who told you this?"

"Huey."

"Who told him?"

"Ms. French."

I looked around to make sure nobody was going to kill Kootie before he answered my next question.

"Who is Ms. French?"

"Dunwoody Exports."

"How did she get wind of our gig at the Whitbread?"

"Through Huey, that's all I know. I'd tell you, man, because what the fuck does it matter now? Why would I lie?"

"Open the bag." If he had his share of the money in there, it meant he was lying.

The train jolted to a stop.

"What?"

"The bag. Open it. You just went to see her to get your cut, didn't you?"

The doors opened.

Kootie made a run for it.

I grabbed the strap to the bag and jerked him back into the subway car. Kootie spun and fell to the floor, one hand on the bag strap.

I glanced through the forward car window into the next car. Eye Bags wasn't in sight. Kootie didn't know that. He could have been.

"He's coming." I pointed toward the next car. "I'm giving you to him."

The loudspeaker said, "Stand clear of the closing doors."

Kootie let go of the bag and rolled out the door just as it closed.

I was kind of surprised. Most of these goofballs would sooner die than let go of their take. Maybe he wasn't totally convinced I wasn't the one who tweaked Huey and Frank.

I went to the doors and watched him get to his feet. He grinned at me like he'd won. Then his eyes snapped toward the front of the train. That terrified look was back, and the winner took off down the platform.

A second later Eye Bags flew by after him, shooting me a glance as he passed by.

The train jolted and began moving forward, out of the station.

The Latino boys were smiling. I guess they enjoyed the show.

I hope Kootie kept running and didn't stop until he was out of state. That was the last anybody ever saw of him.

Not a bright guy, but I still like to think he got away.

THIRTY-NINE

I TOOK THE TRAIN ALL the way to Lorimer Street, transferred to the L train into Manhattan, switched to the R train, and came all the way back to Brooklyn the long way in a giant counterclockwise circle. Best to remain a moving target, especially with Robay making a clean sweep of things. It was going on ten before I exited the subway at Union Street and Fourth Avenue. I still hadn't opened the bag. Not that I hadn't wanted to, but I knew it probably contained some serious cash, and it was better not to risk having anybody on the train see I had such a thick wallet.

On the street I checked my phone. I had a message.

"Hello, Mr. Davin! This is Pete at Fido Feed. You never called and seemed in a hurry for the information about your cat sitter. Yes! Chuck's Pet Food Wagon down on Fourth Avenue. They sold the Pristine Pet and Lab 1 Adult Diet Dry to your Russian friend. Anyway, not to worry, they delivered the food two days ago to the Holiday Inn Express. I didn't know they took pets. Thought you'd like to know. We'll deliver that food you ordered first thing Monday. Thanks, and have a nice evening."

I ducked into a deli on Fourth Avenue for a cup of coffee and a refuge from the traffic roar. I rang Detective Doh. He picked up on the fourth ring.

"Yes?"

"It's Davin. I think you'll find Gustav staying at the Holiday Inn Express on Union Street. If you need the gun he lost, I might have a line on that, too. If I do get it, the weapon may turn up on your doorstep anonymously. I don't want any static about how or who had it all this time."

"What makes you think he's at the Holiday Inn?" Doh sounded like he was eating and in no hurry.

"Because Pristine Pet and Lab 1 Adult Diet Dry were delivered there two days ago by Chuck's Pet Food Wagon."

"Huhn?"

"The cats. He took them from me, and he has to feed them, right?"

"Mmm."

"They only eat that specific food. He only took enough food for a day when he swiped the cats. So he needed to find more, and it's not that easy to find. I asked around, and they delivered the food to a Russian staying at the Holiday Inn Express."

"Damn, you sure?"

"Sound like worth checking out?"

"Later."

I felt pretty smart as I walked back across the Gowanus Canal on Union Street. That cute bit of intelligence should have had me in the pink, the killer kid out of my hair.

At the green loft, the lights on the second floor didn't seem to be on, but Bridget could have been entertaining a customer by candlelight. I keyed myself into the first-floor apartment.

Bridget was in the living room reading the *Economist,* glasses perched on her nose. Turner was at the scratching post.

Bridget says, "There you are."

So I says, "Just barely. Any trouble?"

"None here. Did you hear about the barbershop?"

"Not news to me." I unzipped the duffel bag. At the bottom was a black plastic bag. I took it out and dumped ten stacks of Jacksons on the coffee table. Looked like thirty grand—a thousand dollars in twenties is about half an inch thick. Kootie's payoff from Ms. French. Once they had him located, it was just a matter of following him. Robay sent in Eye Bags to tie off the loose ends and take back the money.

Bridget tossed her magazine aside. "That's serious cash!"

"I need you to keep an eye on it for me. I can't exactly deposit that in the bank, and it would strain my wallet."

"Are you OK?" Bridget brushed her hair away from her eyes, which were now on mine, not the money. "What happened to you today?"

"Been a long one. And it's not over. Yet."

"Have you eaten?"

"I had something on the ferry."

"The ferry?"

"Staten Island."

"Don't move, I'll make you some soup, pour you a drink."

"No time for that. No more threats? Nobody hanging around outside? No tall Russian kid?"

"Uhn uhn. But Tommy, you have to rest. Just for a little while, get your strength. I heard you go out early this morning. You've been going all day."

I continued to paw through the duffel bag. Just clothes, toiletries.

"Honey, I've still got the strength of a couple of guys on a bad day, which is enough. Just tuck the money away somewhere for me, OK? That will be doing a lot right there."

The duffel over my shoulder, I made for the door.

Bridget followed. "Tommy, I'm worried about you!"

"Pop used to say, *Don't drop anchor in stormy seas.* I'll just be extra worried if I don't keep at this and see it through."

"What did your father say about knowing when to take a breather?"

"I don't think he covered that. He covered a lot, too."

"Damn you, Tommy." Bridget practically spit she was getting so worked up.

"Look, try that tantric exercise. It will calm you down." I wasn't quite sure why she was experiencing so much anxiety.

"So because your father said . . . what are you, your father? Did he not know when to stop? When to butt out?"

I guessed that was supposed to be some sort of pop-psych button to make me do what she wanted.

"Pop was an optimist, and so am I. But he lost his way and blew his brains out in our living room. I'm not Pop."

Bridget blinked. Hard. "What?"

"I'm not like Pop. He gave up. I keep going."

I opened the door and looked both ways along the street. Just a couple people in the shadows, walking their dogs for the last time that evening.

"Tommy—"

"See you in the morning."

Making tracks for Fourth Avenue, away from Smith Street, I kept a sharp eye out, crossing the street whenever someone was ahead on the sidewalk. Eye Bags would have reported in, and Jimmy Robay would be arranging a hit on me just about then.

If he hadn't already.

FORTY

My Heart, Yvette:

Perhaps you remember the story of Girp, from our childhood. I am now Girp. Injured by Yop the Ogre but undaunted in a quest for the fair Gorta, Girp retreats to his cave to fashion a magic sword to free his lover even if it should cost him his life. It will be worth it if you are there to touch my brow and release me to the starlight. I fear our eternity is to be shared as tragedy. If you do not come, and Girp is vanquished without his Gorta, know in the full moon of your cool night of heartfelt serenity that I am ever passionately yours no matter my ill consequence.

Yop the Ogre is elusive. He is not at the cave. So I will watch the mountain.

Gustav

FORTY-ONE

THE WHITBREAD MUSEUM'S DRIVEWAY WAS a parking lot of limousines, so I guessed the board meeting, dinner, and reception were still under full swing. A special entrance for the invitees was on one side of the flying saucer, with event security in tuxedos. I'd forgotten to bring my invitation, so went to the employees' entrance on the other side.

My pal Unsteady Freddy was at his post. His sad, watery eyes widened when he saw me. "Good evening, Mr. Douglas. Pretty late for a meeting with the boss."

I patted the poor guy on the shoulder. "How are you, Freddy? Get home OK?"

He smiled. "Always do, somehow. Thanks for swinging by this morning."

"Like I said, I was in the neighborhood. Atkins and McCracken here?"

"Both. Only McHitler is at the reception with the board, giving a presentation."

"That so?"

"So she's busy, but I can call up to Atkins, see if he's in his office." He began to fumble with his radio.

"Or I can just go up. He's probably expecting me."

"Sure. Just don't steal anything, Kirk."

I laughed softly at his soft joke. "I promise." Then I noticed the banner for the Lee J. Rosenburg wing. "Actually, could you call Atkins and have him come meet me in the Mondrian collection?"

"You got it, pal."

Buy a drunk a drink, pals for life.

I veered again into the Mondrian wing. Catering staff were folding tables, rolling away a bar, and sweeping up. Looked like they'd had the cocktail reception in Lee J. Rosenburg's wing of the museum. Real political move on Sheila's part. I wondered how long she'd get traction with the board director with such obvious brownnosing. Atkins, I guessed, was there to make an appearance and suck up to Rosenburg himself, try to keep his job cemented in case Sheila was bad-mouthing him.

There they were. I stood in front of the two Mondrians that were also in Atkins's closet. I wandered away and then looked back at them from a distance. I came up close, looked at the brush-work, the cracks in the paint. I wanted to flip one of them over and look at the tacks, see if they were cloven, but Atkins entered the room behind me. I actually heard him gasp and felt his nervous energy.

"Davin, this is not a good time. The board is here." He stayed where he was, I guess trying to draw me away from the two Mondrians.

"Atkins, do you like art?"

"What?"

"Do you like art? Like these two paintings?"

He looked a little unsteady on his feet, sort of swaying a little as all the blood drained out of his head. His mouth made a couple attempts to say something. I helped him out.

I whispered, "Look, if you want to put them back, I think this is the perfect time to do it, don't you?"

He looked like he might faint, and steadied himself on the wall.

"Atkins, I'm willing to be big about this, because I know you're not a bad guy. You could use some stress management. Maybe some aromatherapy candles in your office would help. Raking leaves isn't the answer."

His eyes darted toward the catering people.

"Call your wife, Timbo, and have her bring the paintings right away. We'll switch them out."

His eyeballs were swimming in tears, and they dripped off his careful little mustache onto his jacket. He stepped close to me, one hand still on the wall. "I only did it to save my job. It was just when she was in trouble with Rosenburg last year, and I figured, well, I figured if two of his paintings went missing from storage just before they were to be hung in the new wing, that she lost his paintings, well, McCracken would lose her job, I'd keep mine. A man has a right to his job. I work hard. I know I'm not the best at what I do, I know that, but . . ."

"I understand, Atkins. That's why I'm here to help. Tell me something. What did you think when you saw these two paintings suddenly appear here?"

Atkins sniffed deeply, trying to compose himself. "Forgeries, plain and simple."

"Did she suspect you took the originals? Did you mention this to anybody?"

His head vibrated, shaking his chin "no" very rapidly. "It was my ace in the hole. If she put the screws to me, I'd blow the lid on those two paintings with Rosenburg. Never came to that. A man has a right to his job."

I smiled at the two paintings, then at Atkins. "Don't worry

about it, Timbo. You'll still have your ace in the hole. Just get the paintings here. Only put them in storage. That way you don't have them, the museum does, and the forgeries are still on the wall. How would McCracken explain that?"

Tears clung to his waxed mustache, but a laugh and some drool burst from his lips. "Ha, yes, well . . . ha!"

I let my friendly deportment fade. "I need something in return for helping you."

His eyes widened. In the last sixty seconds he'd gone from weepy to laughing and now to terror. "What?"

"You were here Sunday night when the paintings were stolen. Why did you have a meeting with the guards at the time that you did? Did you steal them?"

Now he looked aghast. Aghast means insulted, but also sort of disgusted.

"Tommy, I did not steal any paintings. I wouldn't have worked that night if McCracken weren't here. Whenever she's here late I get a call and do a spot inspection. Makes me look good. She can't fire me if I'm diligent, can she?"

"Let me get this straight. She stays late, or in this case shows up at three in the morning, and you automatically show up, do a spot inspection, call a meeting of the guards?"

"I'm sure she knew I only did the spot inspections when she was here, but what could she say? I got the call at two in the morning that she had showed up after a dinner party to collect some files to work on at home for tonight's event. So I raced in to do an inspection."

I smiled. McCracken showed up for the very purpose of having Atkins show up and pull the guards. "Call your wife; get those paintings here as soon as possible. Call me when they're here."

Atkins scurried from the room.

I took one of my business cards and wrote on the back:

Please call me about your missing Mondrians.

I went outside and asked around among the limo drivers. I found the one who drove Lee J. Rosenburg and handed him the card for delivery. Now all I had to do was wait for the paintings to arrive, so I crossed the boulevard and found a deli. I walked out with a cup of coffee, and my phone vibrated.

"Bridget?"

"I just got a threatening call." Her tone was flat.

"What did they say?"

"That they knew you were staying here, and that they'd kill you and me."

"That all?"

"Yes . . . Tommy, I need to get out of here, but I don't know how. I'm trapped, and they know where I live."

I wondered how Jimmy Robay found out I was staying with Bridget. Blaise? Not Carol.

"Stay put. I'll come by in a car service. I'll take a look around, and then call you to come down and jump in if it's safe, OK?"

I hailed a town car, and it was a Blue Diamond. I told him to take me to Bond and Union.

"Driver, were you working last Sunday?"

"Yes, boss."

"Did you pick up anybody at Donut House and take them to the Williamsburg Savings Bank?"

His dark eyes met mine in the mirror. "Boss, how you know this?"

I sat forward. "So you did pick up someone from Donut House on Sunday?"

"Yes! How you know this?"

"You drove this person to the Williamsburg Savings Bank Building, early, say nine o'clock or ten?"

"Please, how does boss know this?"

"All I knew was that a Blue Diamond driver picked this person up. I'll give you twenty dollars if you tell me everything that happened, what the person looked like, everything."

"It was a woman, in an orange hat and scarf. Not tall, not big, normal. An American, white."

"Hair?"

"Yes, I think so."

I sighed. "What color? Black?"

"I don't know, boss. The hat is what I saw."

"Did she talk on the phone, make any calls?"

"Yes, she was talking with someone named Jimmy. I remember because my name is Jimi. I am from Pakistan."

"What did they talk about?"

"Hmm. I don't know. I think maybe about paint."

"Paint? Or paintings?"

"I am not sure, boss."

"Would you know her if you saw her?"

"It is maybe yes."

We came to a light, and I showed him the picture of McCracken on my phone.

His head bobbled. "No, boss, I not remember this person."

"Why?"

He made a gesture with his hands indicating big tits.

"The one you drove, not big tits?"

"No, I did not see."

My phone vibrated.

"Davin? It's Detective Doh. This is his place, alright."

"How are the cats?"

"Tearing the place apart."

I smiled. That meant they were healthy.

Doh continued. "The Holiday Inn people aren't happy about the damage."

"You can throw some extra charges onto the indictment. Cat-napping, destruction of property. You arraigning him tonight?"

"No."

"Why?"

"He isn't here."

"Where is he?"

"If I knew I would be there instead of here. Gustav's still on the loose, and there's another love letter."

"Were the others translated?"

"Uh huhn. Love letters to your girlfriend. They mention you, too, Davin. He calls you an oaf."

"An oaf?"

"That's a big fat person."

"I know what oaf means."

"I don't have to read this latest letter to know that he's out to get you. He has a weapon, too. Must have bagged it out in Coney from the Russians. Soviet made. The assembly instructions are here on the table. Not really a gun. Somebody here says it looks like an automatic grenade launcher."

"Are you telling me that I should be careful?"

"I'm telling you not to go anywhere or do anything until we find Gustav. Stay low. I don't care about you, Davin, so much as I worry about Brooklyn and innocent people when this idiot starts firing this missile launcher out in the open. I don't read Russian, so I don't know exactly what this thing can do, but a lot of people could get hurt if he finds you in a public place. We have people on your apartment, all over the Smith Street area. He can't be that hard to find. There's empty boxes of medical tape and gauze all over the place here. He must have white bandages covering most of his face."

"I'll stay as low as I can."

"Make it lower." He hung up.

I instructed the driver to pass the green loft slowly three times before we pulled up in front. I rang Bridget. Just a few people walking their dogs on the street.

"Coast is clear. I'm out front."

I looked at the time and hoped Atkins's wife, Jan, was close to the museum with those paintings. The museum gala for the board wouldn't last all night. Atkins would need that distraction to make good on tucking the Mondrians into storage.

The car door opened, and Bridget climbed in next to me.

Jimmy Robay climbed in after her. "Driver, to the scrap yard."

The car lurched forward, and the driver said, "Boss!"

I looked at Bridget and Robay. "What's what?"

Robay just smiled like he had a seed stuck in his teeth, and Bridget tried to look anywhere but at me.

"Boss! This is the one."

I locked eyes with Bridget, then with the driver in the rearview.

"I tell you, boss. This is the one I pick up on Sunday, the one at the Donut House."

Bridget was in her red beret and scarf.

I looked out the rear window. There was a car following right on our bumper.

"Sit tight, Davin." Robay smirked.

My stomach felt like it was full of gravel.

Bridget was Ms. French.

Bridget was Molly Lee.

"SO LET ME GET THIS straight, Jimmy." The dull night glow of industrial Brooklyn out the window was quiet as a cemetery. The town car passed under the subway trestle. The scrap yard was ahead on the left, the Gowanus Expressway twinkling in the sky beyond it.

"McCracken was in a jam and had read about Dunwoody Exports in the news, knew they reproduced paintings and were shady. She came to Molly Lee here to replace two missing Mondrians with fakes. Molly helps her, but then you put the squeeze on McCracken, the way the mob does, and threaten to expose the fakes on the wall unless she continues to do business with you. Or maybe McCracken isn't so innocent, and it was a business deal for McCracken to make ends meet at the museum. Doesn't matter. Same difference. McCracken was feeding you guys the occasional art from museum storage while trying to hold on to the collection and not dig her own grave. Or in the case of the four Henris that were stolen through the roof hatch, McCracken grabbed three to sell to Molly and said all seven were stolen.

"Molly here is under the radar after last year's publicity over Dunwoody. She's gone back to her previous profession—not too much of a stretch to think anybody who ran massage parlors knew the business from the ground up. She does this to make ends meet until the next scam, or until this one is over, meanwhile speculating on industrial property waiting for zoning changes. Along comes Huey, a customer at the green loft, who spills the beans about his Whitbread heist. So Bridget hijacks the heist to get at some of the Whitbread's main collection, the good stuff on display, not just the art in storage, so you call Sheila. McCracken shows up to make Atkins pull the guards, and she goes into the closet and just brings them to you. A lot safer than letting the goofballs take them. Huey gets the payoff from you at Billy Bank, puts it in storage, but Bridget filches the key when he drops by for some afternoon delight. Then Huey gets killed. It looks like a pattern with Jo-Ball's death, and I'm the common factor, so I must be at the center of it. So you both got close to me to see what I was up to. Kootie and Frank panic and look unreliable, so you paid them off to bring them close and then sent guys to tweak them once you had them tagged. They knew the paintings never left the museum."

They didn't say anything.

They didn't have to. I was really just laying it out for myself, so I could understand it, finally. If I was wrong about any of it, I was sure they wouldn't have told me. Why would they? Didn't matter to them anyway. I was on a ride to a necktie party.

Necktie party? That's dark humor. The necktie is a noose. That's figurative, which means that I didn't think they meant to hang me, just kill me.

"Then realizing I'm a loose cannon, Bridget contacts me and brings me in close to where she can keep an eye on me. Even has me move in with her. Then the fake letter from Ariel, the call about being in danger. Cute."

Bridget kept her eyes down but whispered, "You had to be a good guy, didn't you? Like your dad. Which is how you'll end up."

Neither of them would look at me. Robay seemed tense but confident. Bridget Molly Lee French had her arms folded. Hell with it: I'm going back to calling her Bridget. Bridget didn't want to be there, to be an accessory to murder, but I could see why Jimmy would want her there. If he was going to tweak me, she would have to be there, too, to make it one big happy conspiracy, nobody tells on nobody. Robay was there to make sure Eye Bags didn't let me get away. Like a good businessman, Jimmy was there to oversee the completion of a crucial detail personally. I thought briefly about trying to appeal to his business side, but he was no dummy. Once you take a guy for a ride, there's no letting him go, it's a done deal.

Gab wouldn't get me out of this. I was going to have to find a mousehole to squeeze through. Where I'd find that hole I didn't have any idea; I'd just have to play it by ear. Which sucked.

Ahead the giant grabbers were lit by spotlights, motionless, their giant claws resting on mountains of shredded rusty steel ten stories high.

Monday night I had come down to meditate at the scrap yard, the night I found the cats gone. I had seen Gustav that night for the first time. He could have killed me right there, but he was just tracking me, hoping I would lead him to Yvette.

Monday. The scrap yard was karmic, the circle of life, a whole of parts, destruction and renewal, positive energy.

Friday. The grabbers eyed me from the heaps, executioners, negative energy.

I was probably going to be fed to one of these monsters, my body buried under ten thousand tons of rusty metal for a trip to a smelting plant in China. The flies and maggots would have a leisurely time taking my body apart over that long sea voyage.

My situation was transformative, and I was forcing myself not to experience anxiety that would obstruct the flow of energy. My ace in the hole was my strength and size. Of course, like I said, a gun can trump that card.

"Pull up at the scrap yard gate." Jimmy patted the driver on the shoulder and handed him a hundred-dollar bill. "You never saw me, you never saw her, you never saw him."

"Yes, boss."

"I ever hear or see of you again and you die, but first you watch your family die. Got it?"

The poor little Pakistani driver was trembling so violently that he couldn't even answer.

At the gate, I found Eye Bags was standing at my door, wearing one of those foam neck braces. He flashed a gun, then held it back under his coat.

I got out and stood next to him.

"Sorry about the sucker punch. Better than pushing you on the tracks, am I right?"

Eye Bags wasn't in a talking mood either.

It was that blue Lincoln that had been following our car, and it pulled to the curb.

Just like art theft isn't like you see in the movies, neither is the business of killing. I was finding out firsthand. There was no room for discussion, for bartering. It was common knowledge that the mob would kill people by acting like a friend. Get close, and when the victim's guard is down, make the move from behind. I had been moving around too much for them to surprise me, much less pretend to be my friend. Though maybe that was why Bridget didn't want me going out again. Instead, they had to bait me with Bridget, hook me in the town car, and reel me in to the scrap yard.

The town car zoomed away. From the blue Lincoln, two members of the broken nose squad made for the gate. Jimmy was under a streetlight next to the driveway. Bridget was to the side. There was a loud buzz, and the sheet metal fence began to roll up.

I looked behind me at the gas station a hundred or more feet away. There was a car or two at the pumps, someone inside the mini mart at the register, but they had no reason to look past the shadows to where the scrap yard was. The back of the gas station was in deep shadow.

Eye Bags jabbed me in the ribs with the gun. *Move.*

I stepped forward and stopped at the curb, next to the streetlight.

Eye Bags gave me another jab. *Keep moving.*

The gates rattled and locked into place, the mountains of scrap and the grabbers wide before me.

If I went in those gates, I was dead. I had to previsualize a way out. If I could manage to twist and not take a fatal shot from Eye Bags's gun, the other goons would have a hard time drawing and targeting me from any distance. What little I know about pistols is that people usually can't hit anything with them beyond twenty feet. Unless they practice. Most hoods don't rely on finesse, so they don't need to practice.

There was an orange flash from behind me.

The right side of the gate support exploded in flame. So did the goon standing next to it—shrapnel tore through his trench coat and his scalp. He fell flat, a puff of his hair floating in the smoke where he had just been standing.

I fell flat, too, only I was still in one piece and aimed to stay that way if I could.

Guns ratcheted on all sides.

In front of me was the mob with pistols; behind me was Gustav the lovesick assassin with a grenade launcher. That's what I call a rock and a hard place.

I heard only one gun go off before a bunch of orange flashes boomed back by the gas station and I heard the gate and fence exploding, sparks like fireworks in the air, sheet metal clattering to the ground. I felt a jolt to my calf, like I'd been whipped with a rope, and my leg went numb. That would mean I was hit.

Heart pounding, I listened to see if I was going to hear my pulse stop, and then feel myself fade into whatever is on the other side. I almost hoped so, because so far whatever had happened didn't hurt too bad. Yet.

The explosions had stopped, a wave of spent grenade shrapnel falling onto the pavement all around me. Ringing in my ears drowned out my heartbeat. It was my cell phone ringing. Probably Atkins.

When the phone stopped ringing I heard footsteps.

They approached from the direction of the gas station.

Gustav.

I rolled on my side.

Yup, here came the punk kid from the shadows behind the gas station, with what looked like a giant black revolver cradled in his arms. The weapon was about the size of a sawed-off shotgun, with a bucket-sized ammunition drum on the underside. Smoke from the gun trailed behind him as he limped toward me. White surgical taped crisscrossed the left side of his face and ear, across the chin and right neck. Only one of those rosy cheeks was showing.

I could hear people at the gas station, across Smith Street, saying:

Did you see that?

That dude blew up that fence.

Whoa!

My leg was stinging. I tried to look at it, but the streetlight was out. I looked at the fence, where the grabbers and the mountains of scrap loomed. The gate was in tatters, and nobody was standing. I couldn't make out what was what, but there seemed to be some heaps that were probably Robay, the goons, and Bridget. Sparks were drizzling down from the busted streetlight, which was bent and leaning out over me.

The footsteps stopped.

Gustav was standing over me, his spiked hair silhouetted by the light of the gas station, the roar of the Gowanus Expressway beyond. Sparks from the streetlight flecked his watery eyes with fire.

Man, this really sucked.

Breathe slowly in through the nose; close the eyes.

Breathe slowly out through the lips; stroke back my face where the beard used to be.

Breathe slowly in through the nose; open the eyes.

Breathe slowly out through the lips; focus on the punk kid who was about to shoot me full of fragmenting explosives.

"What is this you do, Yop?" he said, one eye cocked. His voice was unexpectedly deep. I would have thought he'd sound like a teenager, kind of squeaky.

"It's a tantric exercise I do to improve the energy flow from my head to my heart. I'm experiencing some anxiety right now."

A car slowed as it passed us, the driver looking out curiously but not stopping.

He says, "A last time, hm? Tell to me, Yop the Ogre, where is my Yvette?"

So I says, "Miami. She was just arrested there. That's all I know. I tried to send her your messages, but she was kind of hard to reach in jail. Can I ask why you have to call me Yop the Ogre?"

"That is your name now. I am Girp. So Gorta is arrest? Police?"

"Gorta? You mean Yvette?"

"Yes, of course."

"She was staying with friends who were growing grass in the basement."

"Grass?" Another car passed slowly, the occupants wide-eyed at Gustav's gun.

"Pot. You know, marijuana."

His forehead creased. "This sounds like something that would happen to my Gorta."

"It does, doesn't it? I have to tell you, Gustav, that Gorta is no end of trouble."

"You are telling this to me, Yop?" He gestured toward the shredded fence and crumpled bodies. Then he pointed at his bandaged face. "Hm?"

"So you know." I sighed. My leg was aching, and I hoped it wasn't bleeding too much. I didn't want to pass out while I had the kid going. "A little advice, Gustav? She isn't worth it. No woman is worth all this destruction, which, if I do say so, is not doing your karma a lot of good."

"Karma? What is this?"

"Can I ask you a question?"

"Of course."

"Do you think good things happen to good people?"

"My father, he spoke of this." Gustav cocked his head, grimacing philosophically. "Blood washes your enemy into the pit of hell."

"Never mind. How are the cats?"

He rolled his eyes. "Well, you know, the one is not eat, and the other is not go in the box, and the other has the shots. Hm?"

I laughed, weakly. "The Fuzz Face Four are a pain in the neck, aren't they?"

"Yes. The other one is make food from stomach on bed." Gustav smiled. "Are you bad injured?"

"I don't know." I growled as I moved my leg. "I can't tell for sure."

"Should I kill you?"

I had to chuckle at that, longer than maybe I should have.

"What is so fun?" He sounded serious again, not conversational, as he waved another gawking car past us. "In my tradition, it is courtesy to ask."

"I just thought the question was sort of ironic, Girp. Had you asked Yop the Ogre that question a month ago, when Gorta left, he would have said go ahead, sure, do me a favor. Now, I dunno. I just about had Gorta out of my life until you came around. It was a good feeling. Well, do what you have to. I'm exhausted. Careful, though. Better step back if you're going to shoot me with that cannon. You'll hurt yourself."

There was a zap-pop overhead, and a fresh cascade of sparks rained down on me from the streetlight bulb, Gustav and his grenade launcher shimmering before me in a fluttery glow. Real pretty in a way, sort of like how dark clouds sometimes light up red just before sunset.

A shout came from the gas station. "Hey, man, you need the cops over there?"

Gustav looked back toward the gas station.

The streetlight croaked, then whooshed.

Half the streetlight crashed down across the road next to Gustav, and he fell backward into the road. I heard the gun clatter onto the pavement, a car screech and honk.

My leg wasn't too badly injured. How did I know? Because it was under me, taking me past the splayed bodies of Robay and his goons and into the scrap yard. Why into the scrap yard? It was the

only place to go where Gustav wouldn't have a clear shot at me
with his automatic cannon.

Ahead were the mountains of scrap; the monster grabbers eyed
me from above. I veered right, behind a welding truck and next to
a metal shed.

BOOM.

Fire erupted from the mountain of rust, one of the grenades
sending scrap high into the air.

Someone screamed, and it wasn't me.

It was Bridget. In the half-light, I could see her face was bloody
but couldn't tell if it was her blood, Robay's, or one of the goons'.

I grabbed her around the waist and slung her over my shoulder. Bridget was hitting me, but the pounding of her little fists on
my back felt like a massage. I guess she thought I was hostile
toward her. Well, maybe I would be later. No sense in any more
people getting killed.

The scrap was so spread out it was piled up to the side of the
metal shed and up to the top of a wall beyond. At the top of the
heap I stood on the wall. Below me was a sand pit, part of a concrete mixing plant. Beyond that, a conveyor belt up to the gravel
mixer, and cement silos. A few cement trucks were parked on the
other side, and at the canal bulkhead was a Cat excavator for un-
loading barges of gravel.

BOOM.

WHAM.

The sky lit up behind me, and the force of the explosion pushed
me over the wall. I tossed Bridget to one side. We both landed on
our backs on the sand, sliding down the pile.

Flame, debris, and black smoke rolled over the wall where we'd
been standing. I guessed the tanks in the welding trucks had ex-

ploded. Gustav must have heard me climbing the scrap pile and fired in that direction.

I rolled the rest of the way down the sand pile and tried to get Bridget to her feet. She kept collapsing, so I threw her over my shoulder again.

Flames towering behind me, I trotted toward the canal, hoping there was a path along the bulkhead that would take me up to Hamilton Avenue and the drawbridge there. I heard Gustav yelling.

"Yop! Yop!"

I jogged behind the Cat excavator to catch my breath in the shadows. I tested Bridget's neck pulse. She had one.

The bulkhead north was blocked by the scrap heaps. To the south, toward Hamilton Avenue, the path was blocked by razor wire. In front of me two feet from the bulkhead was an empty steel barge big enough to park a dozen cars. Beyond that was eighty feet of open canal, then a bulkhead and a Pathmark parking lot.

"Yop!" Gustav's spiked hair and bandaged head rose above the scrap yard wall, and a second later he and his automatic grenade launcher were framed by the flames from the burning welding truck. He was busy reloading the weapon.

"Yop!"

How many grenades could the thing hold? I had no idea, and wasn't about to bet my life on guessing.

Remember when Gustav had to jump into the canal? And like I said about the slick of spent condoms, fuel oil, and dead birds and shit? Strong as I was, jumping into the cold Gowanus Canal with a hundred-and-thirty-pound woman over my shoulder didn't seem like a good plan for escape. If I had to swim for it, there was no way I was putting my head under that water.

I slid Bridget off my shoulder and put her in the bucket of a small excavator parked to one side of the Cat. I took a plastic tarp from the ground and draped it over her.

There was an orange flash.

BAM!

BOOM!

Debris scattered across the canal. To my left, the conveyor to the gravel silo had been shattered.

Behind Gustav there was still the fire, but also the flashing lights of emergency vehicles, and I hoped the police with their largest weapons. A .38 against an automatic grenade launcher would be like a twig against a battleaxe.

There was another orange flash from the launcher's barrel.

BAM!

A gravel hopper at the base of the conveyor took the next round. The grenade skipped off the top of a gravel pile and landed inside the hopper. No explosion.

BOOM!

For some reason the grenade didn't go off right away. Curious, but not any help to me. It was clear that Gustav was going to shoot left to right, destroying everything in sight until he hit the thing I was hiding behind. I was right of center, and I didn't want him blowing up Bridget. Well, if she got exploded, I at least tried to salvage a life out of that mess. I'm just saying.

Bulkhead to the edge of the barge was a short hop, and I was still out of Gustav's sight lines—but I was behind an obvious target, an obvious hiding place: the excavator.

Orange flash. This grenade missed a rowboat on the bulkhead and landed in the water. The explosion was delayed again.

I trotted along the edge of the barge to the far end and stripped off my overcoat. There was an outer shelf to the barge about four feet wide, outside the rim of the container part of the barge. So I tossed my overcoat down and lay on it on the shelf, out of sight. There were also some tires draped along the back edge of the barge I could use to climb down into that filthy water. I wasn't sure when I had my last tetanus shot, but I'd need a dozen plus one of them if I got into that muck. Throw in a rabies shot just for fun.

Orange flash. The excavator's cab windows blew out. I glanced over the edge of the barge, and smoke was pouring from the excavator.

Screwy: The grenades were now all taking about five long seconds to explode once they found their target. Maybe when he reloaded it was a different kind of ammo? I had no idea, but there was a pattern.

Orange flash, and this one landed in the front shovel part of the excavator. It didn't go off for five whole seconds.

Shrapnel clattered inside the barge and pinged off the steel edge inches from my shoulder.

Gustav had pretty much hit every target where someone could hide, though he couldn't see the small frontloader where Bridget was konked out.

I held my breath.

I listened.

Sure enough, I heard footsteps approach and stop somewhere over by the excavator.

Gustav whispered, "Yop. *Yop,* where is Yop . . ."

Poor lovesick dummy would soon walk along the bulkhead far enough to see me by the light of the Pathmark, lying on the outer edge of the barge.

I should have slipped into the canal right then, but I talked myself out of it, reasoning that I would be a sitting duck out there in the water, an easy target, and no way was I going to try to swim underwater in that canal, much less get wounded by shrapnel and drown, inhaling a lungful of algae-laden oily scuzz water. Who wants that as a last sensation before death? What if I inhaled a spent condom in that last glimmering moment? I decided I would rather be blown up making a run for it. Or maybe do something idiotic like roll into the container with my coat out before me and catch the grenade he fired at me, throw it back.

Footsteps came closer along the bulkhead.

I tensed, my eyes stinging with the futility of having no good choices.

There was a shout, then a struggle.

I lifted my head.

Silhouetted by the flaming welding truck in the next yard, Gustav was struggling with Eye Bags. I recognized him by the neck brace. Obviously he'd been hiding somewhere around the excavator.

I jumped up, holding my overcoat as a shield, and ran for it. New plan: Run and don't look back.

Gustav glared at me, pushed his weapon under his assailant's arm, and fired. At me.

My overcoat walloped me in the chest like a Giants linebacker. A bolt of pain cracked through my chest, spun me backward. I was looking down at the water, light from the Pathmark snaking on the oily surface.

I fell.

There was just air.

I thonked down into the bottom of the barge, on my shoulder. I tried to move that arm, and it didn't want to. I moved the other arm, and the trench coat fell to one side.

So did the live grenade.

It lay there two feet in front of me hissing, like a cobra ready to strike me in the eyes.

Grabbing the grenade, I got a fistful of lava—the damn thing was kind of hot, times two.

I sent it toward the top of the bulkhead.

Clunk.

Splash.

I'd missed. It had gone between the barge and the bulkhead.

There was a shout, and another, bigger splash—one of them had fallen into the river.

BOOM!

The side of the barge jolted me, and water rained down from the explosion.

Gustav or Eye Bags? I didn't really like either one. I just hoped whoever fell in and got blown up had the grenade launcher with him.

I heard heavy breathing from the bulkhead.

Gustav or Eye Bags?

My left hand was in flames of pain from the burning hot grenade. My right shoulder felt dislocated. Ribs definitely cracked—the impact from taking that shot almost point-blank was ferocious.

"Yop!"

Had I really heard that?

"Yop, I see you!"

I gasped and rolled onto my back.

There was that lovesick idiot, pointing the gun at me. It was Eye Bags that was fish bait, not Gustav.

"Good-bye, Yop!"

I closed my eyes this time, but the orange burst of the grenade launcher penetrated my eyelids.

BAM!

THONK-THANK!

I heard Gustav's footsteps retreating. If he stood there the shrapnel would kill him, too.

Where was the cobra? There should have been a cobra. I opened my eyes and searched my surroundings.

No cobra, no hissing grenade—but I had heard the grenade hit bottom near me and then hit the corner.

In the air above me I heard a whirring sound, like a pigeon coming in to land on a statue. Or the wings of the angel of death coming in to land on me.

BOOM!

Blindfolded by my brain for the execution, I passed out.

Hard to say how much time passed until an EMS guy was shining a light in my eyes and talking into a radio. In and out, I remember being lifted from the barge in a plastic litter and strapped in place. Someone said, "Jeez, this guy is heavy!"

Lights were flashing everywhere, and I think I saw Detective Doh before I was suddenly in an ambulance swaying back and forth with tubes hanging down all over the place and the siren wailing. It was then that I managed to focus on the Hispanic EMS guy sitting next to me.

"I guess I made it."

He tried to laugh at what he thought was a joke. "Made what?"

"Anybody else make it? The kid?"

"Kid?" He looked a little anxious. "There was a child?"

"Kid with the weapon?"

He looked confused. Then he did a long blink. "You mean the other fella, with the bandages?"

"He make it?"

"Leg blown off below the knee. He was picked up trying to hail a cab on Hamilton Avenue."

He probably didn't know, and I didn't ask, but I wondered if the car he stopped was a Blue Diamond car.

The EMS guy patted my shoulder. "Hey, keep quiet now. You're on some heavy drugs. You don't want to tell me anything that could get you in trouble. The cops question us."

"He shot it at me three times, but I made it."

The EMS guy was trying to ignore me, but he couldn't help himself and asked, "Three times? I would say that you, my friend, are a cat that just used one or two lives."

"He missed the first time and blew up those gates. The second I caught in my coat."

"Broken ribs."

"Threw it back."

"Second degree burns on your hand. It'll hurt for a while, but it'll be OK."

I didn't say anything, just closed my eyes and replayed the *THONK-THANK* and the flying pigeon sound above the barge.

"Hey." The EMS guy had a hand on my shoulder. "What about the third?"

"Bounce." I tried to smile, but even that hurt. "It bounced." It had hit the floor, then the wall, and sailed high in the air—that was the strange pigeon sound I'd heard just before passing out.

"You are a lucky cat, my friend. Now lay still and shut up."

I closed my eyes, and supposed maybe it was more than luck.

FORTY-THREE

THAT FRACAS ALL HAPPENED SATURDAY, early. If you were to define fracas, the episode with Gustav and his little grenade launcher fit the bill and the rest of the bird, right down to the toes.

By Sunday noon I was home at my abode, the one with the Godzilla door and the Cuban stylings of Bebo Valdés on the stereo. I was on my back deck, overlooking sunny restaurant patios and residential backyards littered with fallen leaves. It was Indian summer; a tropical depression had pushed up from the south, and the temps were in the low sixties. Bebo's piano tinkled and cha-chaed through the screen door. The remains of a Cuban sandwich were on the patio table—there's a fine Cuban café around the corner that I like to order from pre-football on Sundays. I was on the phone.

"Max."

"Tommy?"

"You sound surprised."

"I am."

"Why?"

"Out of the hospital?"

"Out."

"Injured?"

"Aches and pains."

"You actually get shot with an automatic grenade launcher?"

"So where are we with the museum? The Hoffman, Le Marr, and Ramirez. I see from the paper that Atkins got caught trying to put the Mondrians back into the Whitbread's storage."

"I read that. Still not clear."

"Seems like the cops pretty much put all the pieces together. McCracken replaced the Mondrians Atkins stole from storage to get her fired. She went to Dunwoody for forgeries, and from there a shady business relationship began."

I had passed along a few tidbits to the cops through Detective Doh. He didn't know how I came across the information, and didn't ask. I figured after the fracas with Gustav, his superiors might have been as grumpy as he was. A little peace offering from me.

"So the Whitbread's art storage was an art store. McCracken was financing the museum shortfalls."

"That's the jigsaw, almost complete. Now we'll see if McCracken makes bail."

"Where are the Hoffman, Le Marr, and Ramirez?"

"Have you asked McCracken?"

Max cleared his throat. "Cops still haven't let us talk to her."

"Well, I'll tell you, then. The Hoffman, Ramirez, and Le Marr are still in storage at the Whitbread."

"Fact?"

"Fact." I'd had a call from Doh minutes before this call. "They didn't get the chance to move them out to Dunwoody yet, just get them off the walls. What with me snooping around, they were playing their cards close to the vest. The goofballs got anxious when the payoff went missing and with the killings, so when they pressured Molly Lee for the money she swiped from Huey's locker, Robay put the bite on them. So, Max, where's my cut?"

"Your what?"

"Max, don't grudge me this. What I went through for these paintings? I deserve a million dollars. How many other stolen paintings did all this uncover? Dozens, I'll bet."

"That's good how?"

"I stopped a lot more from being stolen."

"We may have to pay off on those dozen that were shipped out of storage through Dunwoody. The museum will submit claims."

I says, "Even though the museum itself stole the paintings?"

So he says, "Not the museum, one of their employees."

"Same thing."

"A court will probably have to decide that." I could hear Max's polite, crooked little smile over the phone.

"So what are you saying?"

"It is United Southern Assurance's position that the Hoffman, Le Marr, and Ramirez were not technically stolen. They never left the museum."

I was beginning to feel hostile. "Max, you asked me to find the paintings. I found them."

"We asked you to recover stolen paintings. They were only in the process of being stolen but had not technically been stolen."

I says, "Looks like I'll be seeing you in court, too."

So he says, "You hear about the Cloisters?"

"No." The Cloisters is a museum that looks like a medieval monastery, in upper Manhattan, perched on a hill, has a lot of monastic art from the 1400s, like you would expect. "I've been kind of busy."

"They had a roof leak, some art got moved to another room for safekeeping."

"Went missing?"

"Can you cover?"

"You have to be kidding me, Max. You stiff me on the Whitbread and now you expect me to go chasing relics and icons for you?"

"Let me know by tomorrow. Pays fifteen."

The bastard hung up. Do I need to express my conflicting emotions at that juncture?

I checked my e-mail. I had one from Blaise.

THX 4 TIP ON HARDWARE. 2 HOT. MADE DEAL WITH
COPS. O U A DRINK, MY FREN.

I took that to mean he passed Gustav's gun to the cops in exchange for some favors.

Another e-mail confirmed my FTD order. I sent flowers to Walter.

My phone hummed.

"Carol, honey, tell me you have good news."

"How are you today? Want me to bring you a heating pad?"

"News?"

"Gustav is still alive, believe it or not. Jumping around out on Hamilton Avenue without a leg, can you imagine? And you'll never guess what car service he stopped."

"Blue Diamond."

"Someone tell you that?"

"What about the thirty thousand?"

"Bridget skipped town. With the money, not that the cops would have let you keep it anyway. They didn't find any cash in that green loft. Just the wig and sunglasses she wore when posing as Molly Lee. Her real name was Holly McGirr."

I think I was beginning to feel worse than when they brought me into the hospital. How Bridget French Molly Lee Holly Mc-Girr slipped out of that concrete plant was anybody's guess. To look at her history you had to figure her for a survivor.

"That sucks, Carol. I needed that money. The pink monkey was expecting his due." My brain started considering chasing down those icons and relics for fifteen. I'd miss this week's payment to the pink monkey, but would at least maybe have something for him next week. Things had come full circle, and I was right back where I was but worse. Except for the homicidal maniac Slavic sniper, of course. I wanted to cry, I kid you not.

"Pink monkey?"

"Vince Scanlon."

"Pink monkey?"

"Never mind. At least tell me I'm straight with the NYPD."

"They won't come knocking, but I think you'd do best to stay under their radar for a while."

That was good news. I was a little worried that maybe McCracken knew my part in the previous Sunday's heist. Then again, why would Bridget have told her? Anyway, McCracken would have fingered me right away and I'd have gone from the hospital to the precinct, do not pass go.

"Not exactly my fault a love puppy with a grenade launcher comes after me."

"I wish I had better news about that money. There was a note."

"A note?"

"From Bridget. To you."

"Great, more notes to me from women who've skipped town." I sighed. Isn't there some sort of limit on how many troublesome double-crossing women a person should have to suffer in a lifetime? There should be. "Read it."

"Tommy: Take good care of Turner. Bridget."

My vision swam. I'd managed to get Pet Food Pete on the phone from the hospital the day before, and he and a bunch of other pet food store owners in the area managed to find homes for the Fuzz Face Four. Otherwise it was the ASPCA gas chambers for them.

Now I was being saddled with another cat? By another trouble woman who skipped out? You had to be shitting me.

"You there, Tommy? Want me to bring the cat around?"

What had I done in a previous life to deserve this? *Blood washes your enemy into the pit of hell.* That about summed it up.

"Tommy?"

"Bring whatever food and cat boxes are there, OK? And please don't forget the scratching post."

"I'm so sorry, Tommy. You want me to talk to Vinny?"

"No."

"You sure?"

"I'll take care of it. My responsibility."

"No, it was Yvette's responsibility. It got stuck on you."

"Nobody stuck me with anything but cats. I stuck myself."

I hung up, stood, and hobbled inside. The shrapnel-wounded leg was stiff.

Poured myself a few fingers of brandy and sat on the couch.

Somehow this must all be my fault. I was a sucker, a rube, an idiot.

The bell rang.

Too soon for Carol.

I peeked out the blinds. It was a short, older gentleman in an expensive suit. Not exactly a pollster or cable TV salesman. So I went out to see what was what. Whatever he had for me could hardly be any worse than the kick in the teeth I'd already had. In fact, if I was to get any more of a beating, I'd just as soon get it all over with that afternoon. Because at four I was limping over to

Monahan's for football, martinis, and steak. I was too sore for Delilah, though maybe I'd go over to cheer myself up after I saw Vinny on Tuesday. I opened the front door.

"What's what?"

He handed me a card. It was mine. On the back in my writing it said:

PLEASE CALL ME ABOUT YOUR MISSING MONDRIANS.

I cocked an eye at him. "Rosenburg?"

"May I come in?"

He followed me through the foyer into my dark apartment. I mean, it was daytime, but I didn't have any lights on. I realized it looked like I was lumbering around in a cave, so I flicked on a few lamps.

Rosenburg smiled weakly at my cheap art prints.

"You want some brandy, Mr. Rosenburg? I wouldn't be having any myself except—"

"Yes."

"It's not the best, but . . ." I felt like my life must be pretty shabby compared to his. My self-esteem has been a lot higher than it was that day.

He didn't respond, he just waited. I splashed some brandy in a snifter and handed it down to him. Like I said, he was a little guy with bushy gray eyebrows that looked like check marks on his forehead. Dignified and small—kind of a common combination among the rich. I'm just saying.

"Have a seat." I waved a hand at the couch, and he perched on the edge, gently swirling the snifter at his knee.

I sat down in the wing chair across from him with a groan. "I'd have offered you the good chair here, Mr. Rosenburg, except if I sit on the couch I can't get up. I had a little accident."

"Accident?" He cocked a gray check mark. "I wouldn't call what you've been through an accident." His nose huffed at the snifter, and he sipped.

"Whatever this week was, it left me a little busted up, temporarily. By the way, I really admire your collection of Mondrians. Top notch. That wing at the museum, just standing there surrounded by them all was kind of magical."

"Magical?" He seemed to like that word. "You are an interesting man, Tommy."

I felt negative energies weighing down on me. "I'm not sure interesting is exactly the right word."

"Let me try again." His silver eyes squinted at the brandy in his snifter and then at me. "You are a crook, and that card was an extortion note. Is there any reason I shouldn't consider you a part of Atkins and McCracken's cabal? You were at the museum Friday night conspiring with Atkins to sneak the paintings back into storage. Why?"

First Max, then another cat, now this. Another kick in the balls for Tommy Davin.

I says, "If I hadn't gone to Staten Island, and if his wife hadn't shown me those paintings, you never would have seen those two pips again. It was my idea to get the paintings back to the museum and then spring the news that there were two too many paintings at the museum. To you. To catch McCracken in a bad spot and stop the looting of the Whitbread's storage. Also to hopefully find the Hoffman, Le Marr, and Ramirez I'd been contracted to find by United Southern Assurance. How's that grab you?"

So he says, "McCracken tried to implicate you and Atkins."

I shrugged. "Why would I leave you a note if I was looting the Whitbread Museum?"

"Exactly. You seem pellucid on your place in this."

"I am." Pellucid? I made a note to look that up in Dee's Scrabble dictionary.

"The police have checked the records and found cash inflow from Dunwoody through a dummy corporation into the Whitbread coffers."

I almost sipped my brandy. "So why are you here?"

He stood and handed me an envelope. "A token of our appreciation."

I opened the envelope. There was a check for fifteen thousand dollars.

Now I drank the brandy, then looked up at him. "So why the third degree?"

He smiled like Father Christmas. "I had to be sure."

"And you're sure?"

"I never liked McCracken. I know character. You've got some." He tugged on his bottom lip. "So what are your plans?"

I struggled to my feet. "I have some medieval icons and relics to locate. Thanks for the check, I really appreciate that. Especially because USA shafted me. Seeing as how the three paintings I was looking for never left the building, they say they were never stolen in the first place. I knock myself out for them for nothing. Cute, huhn? So thanks, this will help toward some expenses." I still had to pay Carol and Blaise.

He responded by turning toward the front door, chuckling the way rich men do: to themselves, and deep in their profit-driven souls. Nice guy, though.

At the top of the stoop I put out a hand. "Please shake it gently—my shoulder was dislocated."

He curled his bottom lip and shook my hand hard. I didn't yelp.

Two steps down Rosenburg stopped. "Mr. Davin?"

He cocked one of those check marks at me, a silver eye turned my direction.

"The Whitbread has an opening for head of security. Interview."

Rosenburg cleared his throat and went on his way. I watched until he reached Smith Street, where he hailed his limo and zoomed north toward Manhattan.

The Giants beat Dallas.

The martinis were dry.

The porterhouse was rare.

I was dancing inside.

MONDAY MORNING, THE CAT FOOD arrived from Pet Food Pete, and I fed some of it to Turner. He looked at the food and then at me, sort of saying, "She's not coming back, is she?"

"I'm not so bad, Turner." I stroked his tail. "Just so you know, though, if you act out and decide to start shitting outside the box, that kind of negativity won't help establish a positive energy flow between us."

I suited up and went to my bank to cash the check from Lee J. Rosenburg.

After that I went to pay Vince. Didn't matter that I was a day early. Not for nothing, but I wanted this little adventure in my life over with and done.

After that I went to see Delilah. She had to work around my dislocated shoulder, and afterward she rebandaged my left hand with comfrey leaf salve, a natural remedy. I filled her in on most of what happened.

We sat at the Scrabble board. I had mostly vowels so I played "cooee" for only seven points—the first "e" was on a double letter space. Cooee is an Australian shout. It was Delilah's turn.

She says, "Ever find out why Yvette left you, Tommy?"

So I says, "She told the Miami cops she left me because she got word Gustav found out where she was."

"That change anything?"

"Can't see why it would. I know it's early, but mind if I have a glass of wine?"

Almond eyes looked up from her tile pew. "It's five o'clock somewhere, Tom."

Dee's smile meant I had permission to go to the pantry and pop a cork.

Delilah was still studying her tiles when I got back with a glass of pinot. "Detective Doh tells me Yvette skipped bail."

"Think she'll come back?"

"Walter tells me she showed up back in Vegas. I think I'll be hitting Atlantic City from now on."

"And what about the other one?"

"Other one?"

"The indie girl in the green loft."

"I told you, I got her cat."

Dee smiled and rolled her eyes. "You see a pattern here, Tom?"

"Women keep taking my money and sticking me with their cats. Except . . ."

"Except?"

"When I went to Vince, a funny thing happened."

Those beautiful brown almond eyes met mine. "Funny how?"

I sipped my wine and leaned back. "So I hand over the envelope with the fifteen thousand I got from Rosenburg to Vince, who was in a blue jumpsuit. The pink monkey wasn't there.

"He says, 'All here?'

"I says, 'Fifteen thou. We're square.'

"He tapped the envelope against his chin, thinking, and then handed it back.

"So I says, 'What's this?'"

"And he says, 'The debt is already paid. Saturday.'"

"So I says, 'I was in the hospital Saturday.'"

"Vinny looked a little annoyed and pointed at the envelope. He says, 'I *could* have taken that money just now.'"

"I says, 'What's what, Vinny? I don't get it.'"

"He says, 'I already told you the debt is paid.'"

"Now I says, 'Not by me. You're going to have to explain this to me, Vinny. I'm a clever guy, but I'm not too smart sometimes.'"

"'A young lady paid it,' he says. I'm thinking Carol or you was the only lady who would have put that kind of cash up for me.

"I ask, 'Who?'"

"He says, 'Red beret and red scarf. She paid me, you can pay her. I may be a strict lender, but I'm not a crook. I won't steal money. Even yours.'"

Delilah began laying out some tiles. "She paid your debt with half the thirty thousand you got from Kootie?"

"Looks that way. Bridget used that cash to pay my debt on Yvette before skipping town and sticking me with her cat. Guess she felt saving her bacon out there in the scrap yard was worth something. So I can pay you for the last couple sessions, Dee. And my lawyer. And my locksmith. And Blaise for the snoops. I should have a little left over for my rent and groceries."

Across the word "spine" she had laid out the word "sublime."

Like Pop used to say, *What goes around, comes around.*

FIC   Wiprud, Brian M.
Wiprud
           Buy back.

$24.99

DATE			